Something New by P G Wodehouse

Pelham Grenville Wodehouse on born on 15th October, 1881 in Guildford, England to distinguished parents who were visiting the UK from Hong Kong where his father was a magistrate.

After two years in Hong Kong Wodehouse and his two brothers were sent back to England to live and be schooled.

Failing family finances meant that Wodehouse did not go on to University but began work straight away. He wrote in the evenings and during a two-year stint as a bank clerk managed to have over 80 pieces published. With the publication of his first book 'The Pothunters' in 1902 he devoted himself full time to writing.

His career was both prolific and commercially successful. Whether it was novels, short stories or plays everything seemed to be a hit.

His wonderful characterisation of the English upper classes combined with his mastery of prose left a lasting legacy most notably in his series of the humorous, and sometimes hilarious, Jeeves and Wooster stories that are at the pinnacle of comic writing and continue to be widely read and enjoyed.

Despite controversy over his broadcasts for the Germans during World War Two, which stemmed more from naivety than any possible Nazi sympathies, but which left a lingering stain against his name, he continued to write although with diminishing success.

P G Wodehouse died on 14th February 1975 in the United States.

Index of Contents
Chapter I
Chapter II
Chapter III
Chapter IV
Chapter V
Chapter VI
Chapter VII
Chapter VIII
Chapter IX
Chapter X
Chapter XI
Chapter XII
P G Wodehouse – A Short Biography
P G Wodehouse – A Concise Bibliography

CHAPTER I

The sunshine of a fair Spring morning fell graciously on London town. Out in Piccadilly its heartening warmth seemed to infuse into traffic and pedestrians alike a novel jauntiness, so that bus drivers jested and even the lips of chauffeurs uncurled into not unkindly smiles. Policemen whistled at their posts—clerks, on their way to work; beggars approached the task of trying to persuade perfect strangers to bear the burden of their maintenance with that optimistic vim which makes all the difference. It was one of those happy mornings.

At nine o'clock precisely the door of Number Seven Arundell Street, Leicester Square, opened and a young man stepped out.

Of all the spots in London which may fairly be described as backwaters there is none that answers so completely to the description as Arundell Street, Leicester Square. Passing along the north sidewalk of the square, just where it joins Piccadilly, you hardly notice the bottleneck opening of the tiny cul-de-sac. Day and night the human flood roars past, ignoring it. Arundell Street is less than forty yards in length; and, though there are two hotels in it, they are not fashionable hotels. It is just a backwater.

In shape Arundell Street is exactly like one of those flat stone jars in which Italian wine of the cheaper sort is stored. The narrow neck that leads off Leicester Square opens abruptly into a small court. Hotels occupy two sides of this; the third is at present given up to rooming houses for the impecunious. These are always just going to be pulled down in the name of progress to make room for another hotel, but they never do meet with that fate; and as they stand now so will they in all probability stand for generations to come.

They provide single rooms of moderate size, the bed modestly hidden during the day behind a battered screen. The rooms contain a table, an easy-chair, a hard chair, a bureau, and a round tin bath, which, like the bed, goes into hiding after its useful work is performed. And you may rent one of these rooms, with breakfast thrown in, for five dollars a week.

Ashe Marson had done so. He had rented the second-floor front of Number Seven.

Twenty-six years before this story opens there had been born to Joseph Marson, minister, and Sarah his wife, of Hayling, Massachusetts, in the United States of America, a son. This son, christened Ashe after a wealthy uncle who subsequently double-crossed them by leaving his money to charities, in due course proceeded to Harvard to study for the ministry. So far as can be ascertained from contemporary records, he did not study a great deal for the ministry; but he did succeed in running the mile in four minutes and a half and the half mile at a correspondingly rapid speed, and his researches in the art of long jumping won him the respect of all.

That he should be awarded, at the conclusion of his Harvard career, one of those scholarships at Oxford University instituted by the late Cecil Rhodes for the encouragement of the liberal arts, was a natural sequence of events.

That was how Ashe came to be in England.

The rest of Ashe's history follows almost automatically. He won his blue for athletics at Oxford, and gladdened thousands by winning the mile and the half mile two years in succession against Cambridge at Queen's Club. But owing to the pressure of other engagements he unfortunately omitted to do any studying, and when the hour of parting arrived he was peculiarly unfitted for any of the learned professions. Having, however, managed to obtain a sort of degree, enough to enable him to call himself a Bachelor of Arts, and realizing that you can fool some of the people some of the time, he applied for and secured a series of private tutorships.

A private tutor is a sort of blend of poor relation and nursemaid, and few of the stately homes of England are without one. He is supposed to instill learning and deportment into the small son of the house; but what he is really there for is to prevent the latter from being a nuisance to his parents when he is home from school on his vacation.

Having saved a little money at this dreadful trade, Ashe came to London and tried newspaper work. After two years of moderate success he got in touch with the Mammoth Publishing Company.

The Mammoth Publishing Company, which controls several important newspapers, a few weekly journals, and a number of other things, does not disdain the pennies of the office boy and the junior clerk. One of its many profitable ventures is a series of paper-covered tales of crime and adventure. It was here that Ashe found his niche. Those adventures of Gridley Quayle, Investigator, which are so popular with a certain section of the reading public, were his work.

Until the advent of Ashe and Mr. Quayle, the British Pluck Library had been written by many hands and had included the adventures of many heroes: but in Gridley Quayle the proprietors held that the ideal had been reached, and Ashe received a commission to conduct the entire British Pluck Library—monthly—himself. On the meager salary paid him for these labors he had been supporting himself ever since.

That was how Ashe came to be in Arundell Street, Leicester Square, on this May morning.

He was a tall, well-built, fit-looking young man, with a clear eye and a strong chin; and he was dressed, as he closed the front door behind him, in a sweater, flannel trousers, and rubber-soled gymnasium shoes. In one hand he bore a pair of Indian clubs, in the other a skipping rope.

Having drawn in and expelled the morning air in a measured and solemn fashion, which the initiated observer would have recognized as that scientific deep breathing so popular nowadays, he laid down his clubs, adjusted his rope and began to skip.

When he had taken the second-floor front of Number Seven, three months before, Ashe Marson had realized that he must forego those morning exercises which had become a second nature to him, or else defy London's unwritten law and brave London's mockery. He had not hesitated long. Physical fitness was his gospel. On the subject of exercise he was confessedly a crank. He decided to defy London.

The first time he appeared in Arundell Street in his sweater and flannels he had barely whirled his Indian clubs once around his head before he had attracted the following audience:

a) Two cabmen—one intoxicated; b) Four waiters from the Hotel Mathis; c) Six waiters from the Hotel Previtali; d) Six chambermaids from the Hotel Mathis; e) Five chambermaids from the Hotel Previtali; f) The proprietor of the Hotel Mathis; g) The proprietor of the Hotel Previtali; h) A street cleaner; i) Eleven nondescript loafers; j) Twenty-seven children; k) A cat.

They all laughed—even the cat—and kept on laughing. The intoxicated cabman called Ashe "Sunny Jim." And Ashe kept on swinging his clubs.

A month later, such is the magic of perseverance, his audience had narrowed down to the twenty-seven children. They still laughed, but without that ringing conviction which the sympathetic support of their elders had lent them.

And now, after three months, the neighborhood, having accepted Ashe and his morning exercises as a natural phenomenon, paid him no further attention.

On this particular morning Ashe Marson skipped with even more than his usual vigor. This was because he wished to expel by means of physical fatigue a small devil of discontent, of whose presence within him he had been aware ever since getting out of bed. It is in the Spring that the ache for the larger life comes on us, and this was a particularly mellow Spring morning. It was the sort of morning when the air gives us a feeling of anticipation—a feeling that, on a day like this, things surely cannot go jogging along in the same dull old groove; a premonition that something romantic and exciting is about to happen to us.

But the southwest wind of Spring brings also remorse. We catch the vague spirit of unrest in the air and we regret our misspent youth.

Ashe was doing this. Even as he skipped, he was conscious of a wish that he had studied harder at college and was now in a position to be doing something better than hack work for a soulless publishing company. Never before had he been so completely certain that he was sick to death of the rut into which he had fallen.

Skipping brought no balm. He threw down his rope and took up the Indian clubs. Indian clubs left him still unsatisfied. The thought came to him that it was a long time since he had done his Larsen Exercises. Perhaps they would heal him.

The Larsen Exercises, invented by a certain Lieutenant Larsen, of the Swedish Army, have almost every sort of merit. They make a man strong, supple, and slender. But they are not dignified. Indeed, to one seeing them suddenly and without warning for the first time, they are markedly humorous. The only reason why King Henry, of England, whose son sank with the White Ship, never smiled again, was because Lieutenant Larsen had not then invented his admirable exercises.

So complacent, so insolently unselfconscious had Ashe become in the course of three months, owing to his success in inducing the populace to look on anything he did with the indulgent eye of understanding, that it simply did not occur to him, when he abruptly twisted his body into the shape of a corkscrew, in accordance with the directions in the lieutenant's book for the consummation of Exercise One, that he was doing anything funny.

And the behavior of those present seemed to justify his confidence. The proprietor of the Hotel Mathis regarded him without a smile. The proprietor of the Hotel Previtali might have been in a trance, for all the interest he displayed. The hotel employees continued their tasks impassively. The children were blind and dumb. The cat across the way stropped its backbone against the railings unheeding.

But, even as he unscrambled himself and resumed a normal posture, from his immediate rear there rent the quiet morning air a clear and musical laugh. It floated out on the breeze and hit him like a bullet.

Three months ago Ashe would have accepted the laugh as inevitable, and would have refused to allow it to embarrass him; but long immunity from ridicule had sapped his resolution. He spun round with a jump, flushed and self-conscious.

From the window of the first-floor front of Number Seven a girl was leaning. The Spring sunshine played on her golden hair and lit up her bright blue eyes, fixed on his flanneled and sweatered person with a fascinated amusement. Even as he turned, the laugh smote him afresh.

For the space of perhaps two seconds they stared at each other, eye to eye. Then she vanished into the room.

Ashe was beaten. Three months ago a million girls could have laughed at his morning exercises without turning him from his purpose. Today this one scoffer, alone and unaided, was sufficient for his undoing. The depression which exercise had begun to dispel surged back on him. He had no heart to continue. Sadly gathering up his belongings, he returned to his room, and found a cold bath tame and uninspiring.

The breakfasts—included in the rent—provided by Mrs. Bell, the landlady of Number Seven, were held by some authorities to be specially designed to quell the spirits of their victims, should they tend to soar excessively. By the time Ashe had done his best with the disheveled fried egg, the chicory blasphemously called coffee, and the charred bacon, misery had him firmly in its grip. And when he forced himself to the table, and began to try to concoct the latest of the adventures of Gridley Quayle, Investigator, his spirit groaned within him.

This morning, as he sat and chewed his pen, his loathing for Gridley seemed to have reached its climax. It was his habit, in writing these stories, to think of a good title first, and then fit an adventure to it. And overnight, in a moment of inspiration, he had jotted down on an envelope the words: "The Adventure of the Wand of Death."

It was with the sullen repulsion of a vegetarian who finds a caterpillar in his salad that he now sat glaring at them.

The title had seemed so promising overnight—so full of strenuous possibilities. It was still speciously attractive; but now that the moment had arrived for writing the story its flaws became manifest.

What was a wand of death? It sounded good; but, coming down to hard facts, what was it? You cannot write a story about a wand of death without knowing what a wand of death is; and, conversely, if you have thought of such a splendid title you cannot jettison it offhand. Ashe rumpled his hair and gnawed his pen.

There came a knock at the door.

Ashe spun round in his chair. This was the last straw! If he had told Mrs. Ball once that he was never to be disturbed in the morning on any pretext whatsoever, he had told her twenty times. It was simply too infernal to be endured if his work time was to be cut into like this. Ashe ran over in his mind a few opening remarks.

"Come in!" he shouted, and braced himself for battle.

A girl walked in—the girl of the first-floor front; the girl with the blue eyes, who had laughed at his Larsen Exercises.

Various circumstances contributed to the poorness of the figure Ashe cut in the opening moments of this interview. In the first place, he was expecting to see his landlady, whose height was about four feet six, and the sudden entry of somebody who was about five feet seven threw the universe temporarily out of focus. In the second place, in anticipation of Mrs. Bell's entry, he had twisted his face into a forbidding scowl, and it was no slight matter to change this on the spur of the moment into a pleasant smile. Finally, a man who has been sitting for half an hour in front of a sheet of paper bearing the words: "The Adventure of the Wand of Death," and trying to decide what a wand of death might be, has not his mind under proper control.

The net result of these things was that, for perhaps half a minute, Ashe behaved absurdly. He goggled and he yammered. An alienist, had one been present, would have made up his mind about him without further investigation. For an appreciable time he did not think of rising from his seat. When he did, the combined leap and twist he executed practically amounted to a Larsen Exercise.

Nor was the girl unembarrassed. If Ashe had been calmer he would have observed on her cheek the flush which told that she, too, was finding the situation trying. But, woman being ever better equipped with poise than man, it was she who spoke first.

"I'm afraid I'm disturbing you."

"No, no!" said Ashe. "Oh, no; not at all—not at all! No. Oh, no—not at all—no!" And would have continued to play on the theme indefinitely had not the girl spoken again.

"I wanted to apologize," she said, "for my abominable rudeness in laughing at you just now. It was idiotic of me and I don't know why I did it. I'm sorry."

Science, with a thousand triumphs to her credit, has not yet succeeded in discovering the correct reply for a young man to make who finds himself in the appalling position of being apologized to by a pretty girl. If he says nothing he seems sullen and unforgiving. If he says anything he makes a fool of himself. Ashe, hesitating between these two courses, suddenly caught sight of the sheet of paper over which he had been poring so long.

"What is a wand of death?" he asked.

"I beg your pardon?"

"A wand of death?"

"I don't understand."

The delirium of the conversation was too much for Ashe. He burst out laughing. A moment later the girl did the same. And simultaneously embarrassment ceased to be.

"I suppose you think I'm mad?" said Ashe.

"Certainly," said the girl.

"Well, I should have been if you hadn't come in."

"Why was that?"

"I was trying to write a detective story."

"I was wondering whether you were a writer."

"Do you write?"

"Yes. Do you ever read Home Gossip?"

"Never!"

"You are quite right to speak in that thankful tone. It's a horrid little paper—all brown-paper patterns and advice to the lovelorn and puzzles. I do a short story for it every week, under various names. A duke or an earl goes with each story. I loathe it intensely."

"I am sorry for your troubles," said Ashe firmly; "but we are wandering from the point. What is a wand of death?"

"A wand of death?"

"A wand of death."

The girl frowned reflectively.

"Why, of course; it's the sacred ebony stick stolen from the Indian temple, which is supposed to bring death to whoever possesses it. The hero gets hold of it, and the priests dog him and send him threatening messages. What else could it be?"

Ashe could not restrain his admiration.

"This is genius!"

"Oh, no!"

"Absolute genius. I see it all. The hero calls in Gridley Quayle, and that patronizing ass, by the aid of a series of wicked coincidences, solves the mystery; and there am I, with another month's work done."

She looked at him with interest.

"Are you the author of Gridley Quayle?"

"Don't tell me you read him!"

"I do not read him! But he is published by the same firm that publishes Home Gossip, and I can't help seeing his cover sometimes while I am waiting in the waiting room to see the editress."

Ashe felt like one who meets a boyhood's chum on a desert island. Here was a real bond between them.

"Does the Mammoth publish you, too? Why, we are comrades in misfortune—fellow serfs! We should be friends. Shall we be friends?"

"I should be delighted."

"Shall we shake hands, sit down, and talk about ourselves a little?"

"But I am keeping you from your work."

"An errand of mercy."

She sat down. It is a simple act, this of sitting down; but, like everything else, it may be an index to character. There was something wholly satisfactory to Ashe in the manner in which this girl did it. She neither seated herself on the extreme edge of the easy-chair, as one braced for instant flight; nor did she wallow in the easy-chair, as one come to stay for the week-end. She carried herself in an unconventional situation with an unstudied self-confidence that he could not sufficiently admire.

Etiquette is not rigid in Arundell Street; but, nevertheless, a girl in a first-floor front may be excused for showing surprise and hesitation when invited to a confidential chat with a second-floor front young man whom she has known only five minutes. But there is a freemasonry among those who live in large cities on small earnings.

"Shall we introduce ourselves?" said Ashe. "Or did Mrs. Bell tell you my name? By the way, you have not been here long, have you?"

"I took my room day before yesterday. But your name, if you are the author of Gridley Quayle, is Felix Clovelly, isn't it?"

"Good heavens, no! Surely you don't think anyone's name could really be Felix Clovelly? That is only the cloak under which I hide my shame. My real name is Marson—Ashe Marson. And yours?"

"Valentine—Joan Valentine."

"Will you tell me the story of your life, or shall I tell mine first?"

"I don't know that I have any particular story. I am an American."

"Not American!"

"Why not?"

"Because it is too extraordinary, too much like a Gridley Quayle coincidence. I am an American!"

"Well, so are a good many other people."

"You miss the point. We are not only fellow serfs—we are fellow exiles. You can't round the thing off by telling me you were born in Hayling, Massachusetts, I suppose?"

"I was born in New York."

"Surely not! I didn't know anybody was."

"Why Hayling, Massachusetts?"

"That was where I was born."

"I'm afraid I never heard of it."

"Strange. I know your home town quite well. But I have not yet made my birthplace famous; in fact, I doubt whether I ever shall. I am beginning to realize that I am one of the failures."

"How old are you?"

"Twenty-six."

"You are only twenty-six and you call yourself a failure? I think that is a shameful thing to say."

"What would you call a man of twenty-six whose only means of making a living was the writing of Gridley Quayle stories—an empire builder?"

"How do you know it's your only means of making a living? Why don't you try something new?"

"Such as?"

"How should I know? Anything that comes along. Good gracious, Mr. Marson; here you are in the biggest city in the world, with chances for adventure simply shrieking to you on every side."

"I must be deaf. The only thing I have heard shrieking to me on every side has been Mrs. Bell—for the week's rent."

"Read the papers. Read the advertisement columns. I'm sure you will find something sooner or later. Don't get into a groove. Be an adventurer. Snatch at the next chance, whatever it is."

Ashe nodded.

"Continue," he said. "Proceed. You are stimulating me."

"But why should you want a girl like me to stimulate you? Surely London is enough to do it without my help? You can always find something new, surely? Listen, Mr. Marson. I was thrown on my own resources about five years ago—never mind how. Since then I have worked in a shop, done typewriting, been on the stage, had a position as governess, been a lady's maid—"

"A what! A lady's maid?"

"Why not? It was all experience; and I can assure you I would much rather be a lady's maid than a governess."

"I think I know what you mean. I was a private tutor once. I suppose a governess is the female equivalent. I have often wondered what General Sherman would have said about private tutoring if he expressed himself so breezily about mere war. Was it fun being a lady's maid?"

"It was pretty good fun; and it gave me an opportunity of studying the aristocracy in its native haunts, which has made me the Gossip's established authority on dukes and earls."

Ashe drew a deep breath—not a scientific deep breath, but one of admiration.

"You are perfectly splendid!"

"Splendid?"

"I mean, you have such pluck."

"Oh, well; I keep on trying. I'm twenty-three and I haven't achieved anything much yet; but I certainly don't feel like sitting back and calling myself a failure."

Ashe made a grimace.

"All right," he said. "I've got it."

"I meant you to," said Joan placidly. "I hope I haven't bored you with my autobiography, Mr. Marson. I'm not setting myself up as a shining example; but I do like action and hate stagnation."

"You are absolutely wonderful!" said Ashe. "You are a human correspondence course in efficiency, one of the ones you see advertised in the back pages of the magazines, beginning, 'Young man, are you earning enough?' with a picture showing the dead beat gazing wistfully at the boss' chair. You would galvanize a jellyfish."

"If I have really stimulated you—"

"I think that was another slam," said Ashe pensively. "Well, I deserve it. Yes, you have stimulated me. I feel like a new man. It's queer that you should have come to me right on top of everything else. I don't remember when I have felt so restless and discontented as this morning."

"It's the Spring."

"I suppose it is. I feel like doing something big and adventurous."

"Well, do it then. You have a Morning Post on the table. Have you read it yet?"

"I glanced at it."

"But you haven't read the advertisement pages? Read them. They may contain just the opening you want."

"Well, I'll do it; but my experience of advertisement pages is that they are monopolized by philanthropists who want to lend you any sum from ten to a hundred thousand pounds on your note of hand only. However, I will scan them."

Joan rose and held out her hand.

"Good-by, Mr. Marson. You've got your detective story to write, and I have to think out something with a duke in it by to-night; so I must be going." She smiled. "We have traveled a good way from the point where we started, but I may as well go back to it before I leave you. I'm sorry I laughed at you this morning."

Ashe clasped her hand in a fervent grip.

"I'm not. Come and laugh at me whenever you feel like it. I like being laughed at. Why, when I started my morning exercises, half of London used to come and roll about the sidewalks in convulsions. I'm not an attraction any longer and it makes me feel lonesome. There are twenty-nine of those Larsen Exercises and you saw only part of the first. You have done so much for me that if I can be of any use to you, in helping you to greet the day with a smile, I shall be only too proud. Exercise Six is a sure-fire mirth-provoker; I'll start with it to-morrow morning. I can also recommend Exercise Eleven—a scream! Don't miss it."

"Very well. Well, good-by for the present."

"Good-by."

She was gone; and Ashe, thrilling with new emotions, stared at the door which had closed behind her. He felt as though he had been wakened from sleep by a powerful electric shock.

Close beside the sheet of paper on which he had inscribed the now luminous and suggestive title of his new Gridley Quayle story lay the Morning Post, the advertisement columns of which he had promised her to explore. The least he could do was to begin at once.

His spirits sank as he did so. It was the same old game. A Mr. Brian MacNeill, though doing no business with minors, was willing—even anxious—to part with his vast fortune to anyone over the age of twenty-one whose means happened to be a trifle straitened. This good man required no security whatever; nor did his rivals in generosity, the Messrs. Angus Bruce, Duncan Macfarlane, Wallace Mackintosh and Donald MacNab. They, too, showed a curious distaste for dealing with minors; but anyone of maturer years could simply come round to the office and help himself.

Ashe threw the paper down wearily. He had known all along that it was no good. Romance was dead and the unexpected no longer happened. He picked up his pen and began to write "The Adventure of the Wand of Death."

CHAPTER II

In a bedroom on the fourth floor of the Hotel Guelph in Piccadilly, the Honorable Frederick Threepwood sat in bed, with his knees drawn up to his chin, and glared at the day with the glare of mental anguish. He had very little mind, but what he had was suffering.

He had just remembered. It is like that in this life. You wake up, feeling as fit as a fiddle; you look at the window and see the sun, and thank Heaven for a fine day; you begin to plan a perfectly corking luncheon party with some of the chappies you met last night at the National Sporting Club; and then—you remember.

"Oh, dash it!" said the Honorable Freddie. And after a moment's pause: "And I was feeling so dashed happy!"

For the space of some minutes he remained plunged in sad meditation; then, picking up the telephone from the table at his side, he asked for a number.

"Hello!"

"Hello!" responded a rich voice at the other end of the wire.

"Oh, I say! Is that you, Dickie?"

"Who is that?"

"This is Freddie Threepwood. I say, Dickie, old top, I want to see you about something devilish important. Will you be in at twelve?"

"Certainly. What's the trouble?"

"I can't explain over the wire; but it's deuced serious."

"Very well. By the way, Freddie, congratulations on the engagement."

"Thanks, old man. Thanks very much, and so on—but you won't forget to be in at twelve, will you? Good-by."

He replaced the receiver quickly and sprang out of bed, for he had heard the door handle turn. When the door opened he was giving a correct representation of a young man wasting no time in beginning his toilet for the day.

An elderly, thin-faced, bald-headed, amiably vacant man entered. He regarded the Honorable Freddie with a certain disfavor.

"Are you only just getting up, Frederick?"

"Hello, gov'nor. Good morning. I shan't be two ticks now."

"You should have been out and about two hours ago. The day is glorious."

"Shan't be more than a minute, gov'nor, now. Just got to have a tub and then chuck on a few clothes."

He disappeared into the bathroom. His father, taking a chair, placed the tips of his fingers together and in this attitude remained motionless, a figure of disapproval and suppressed annoyance.

Like many fathers in his rank of life, the Earl of Emsworth had suffered much through that problem which, with the exception of Mr. Lloyd-George, is practically the only fly in the British aristocratic amber—the problem of what to do with the younger sons.

It is useless to try to gloss over the fact—in the aristocratic families of Great Britain the younger son is not required.

Apart, however, from the fact that he was a younger son, and, as such, a nuisance in any case, the honorable Freddie had always annoyed his father in a variety of ways. The Earl of Emsworth was so constituted that no man or thing really had the power to trouble him deeply; but Freddie had come nearer to doing it than anybody else in the world. There had been a consistency, a perseverance, about his irritating performances that had acted on the placid peer as dripping water on a stone. Isolated acts of annoyance would have been powerless to ruffle his calm; but Freddie had been exploding bombs under his nose since he went to Eton.

He had been expelled from Eton for breaking out at night and roaming the streets of Windsor in a false mustache. He had been sent down from Oxford for pouring ink from a second-story window on the junior dean of his college. He had spent two years at an expensive London crammer's and failed to pass into the army. He had also accumulated an almost record series of racing debts, besides as shady a gang of friends—for the most part vaguely connected with the turf—as any young man of his age ever contrived to collect.

These things try the most placid of parents; and finally Lord Emsworth had put his foot down. It was the only occasion in his life when he had acted with decision, and he did it with the accumulated energy of years. He stopped his son's allowance, haled him home to Blandings Castle, and kept him there so relentlessly that until the previous night, when they had come up together by an afternoon train, Freddie had not seen London for nearly a year.

Possibly it was the reflection that, whatever his secret troubles, he was at any rate once more in his beloved metropolis that caused Freddie at this point to burst into discordant song. He splashed and warbled simultaneously.

Lord Emsworth's frown deepened and he began to tap his fingers together irritably. Then his brow cleared and a pleased smile flickered over his face. He, too, had remembered.

What Lord Emsworth remembered was this: Late in the previous autumn the next estate to Blandings had been rented by an American, a Mr. Peters—a man with many millions, chronic dyspepsia, and one fair daughter—Aline. The two families had met. Freddie and Aline had been thrown together; and, only a few days before, the engagement had been announced. And for Lord Emsworth the only flaw in this best of all possible worlds had been removed.

Yes, he was glad Freddie was engaged to be married to Aline Peters. He liked Aline. He liked Mr. Peters. Such was the relief he experienced that he found himself feeling almost affectionate toward Freddie, who emerged from the bathroom at this moment, clad in a pink bathrobe, to find the paternal wrath evaporated, and all, so to speak, right with the world.

Nevertheless, he wasted no time about his dressing. He was always ill at ease in his father's presence and he wished to be elsewhere with all possible speed. He sprang into his trousers with such energy that he nearly tripped himself up. As he disentangled himself he recollected something that had slipped his memory.

"By the way, gov'nor, I met an old pal of mine last night and asked him down to Blandings this week. That's all right, isn't it? He's a man named Emerson, an American. He knows Aline quite well, he says—has known her since she was a kid."

"I do not remember any friend of yours named Emerson."

"Well, as a matter of fact, I met him last night for the first time. But it's all right. He's a good chap, don't you know! —and all that sort of rot."

Lord Emsworth was feeling too benevolent to raise the objections he certainly would have raised had his mood been less sunny.

"Certainly; let him come if he wishes."

"Thanks, gov'nor."

Freddie completed his toilet.

"Doing anything special this morning, gov'nor? I rather thought of getting a bit of breakfast and then strolling round a bit. Have you had breakfast?"

"Two hours ago. I trust that in the course of your strolling you will find time to call at Mr. Peters' and see Aline. I shall be going there directly after lunch. Mr. Peters wishes to show me his collection of—I think scarabs was the word he used."

"Oh, I'll look in all right! Don't you worry! Or if I don't I'll call the old boy up on the phone and pass the time of day. Well, I rather think I'll be popping off and getting that bit of breakfast—what?"

Several comments on this speech suggested themselves to Lord Emsworth. In the first place, he did not approve of Freddie's allusion to one of America's merchant princes as "the old boy." Second, his son's attitude did not strike him as the ideal attitude of a young man toward his betrothed. There seemed to be a lack of warmth. But, he reflected, possibly this was simply another manifestation of the modern spirit; and in any case it was not worth bothering about; so he offered no criticism.

Presently, Freddie having given his shoes a flick with a silk handkerchief and thrust the latter carefully up his sleeve, they passed out and down into the main lobby of the hotel, where they parted—Freddie to his bit of breakfast; his father to potter about the streets and kill time until luncheon. London was always a trial to the Earl of Emsworth. His heart was in the country and the city held no fascinations for him.

On one of the floors in one of the buildings in one of the streets that slope precipitously from the Strand to the Thames Embankment, there is a door that would be all the better for a lick of paint, which bears what is perhaps the most modest and unostentatious announcement of its kind in London. The grimy ground-glass displays the words:

R. JONES

Simply that and nothing more. It is rugged in its simplicity. You wonder, as you look at it—if you have time to look at and wonder about these things—who this Jones may be; and what is the business he conducts with such coy reticence.

As a matter of fact, these speculations had passed through suspicious minds at Scotland Yard, which had for some time taken not a little interest in R. Jones. But beyond ascertaining that he bought and sold curios, did a certain amount of bookmaking during the flat-racing season, and had been known to lend money, Scotland Yard did not find out much about Mr. Jones and presently dismissed him from its thoughts.

On the theory, given to the world by William Shakespeare, that it is the lean and hungry-looking men who are dangerous, and that the "fat, sleek-headed men, and such as sleep o' nights," are harmless, R. Jones should have been above suspicion. He was infinitely the fattest man in the west-central postal district of London. He was a round ball of a man, who wheezed when he walked upstairs, which was seldom, and shook like jelly if some tactless friend, wishing to attract his attention, tapped him unexpectedly on the shoulder. But this occurred still less frequently than his walking upstairs; for in R. Jones' circle it was recognized that nothing is a greater breach of etiquette and worse form than to tap people unexpectedly on the shoulder. That, it was felt, should be left to those who are paid by the government to do it.

R. Jones was about fifty years old, gray-haired, of a mauve complexion, jovial among his friends, and perhaps even more jovial with chance acquaintances. It was estimated by envious intimates that his joviality with chance acquaintances, specially with young men of the upper classes, with large purses and small foreheads—was worth hundreds of pounds a year to him. There was something about his comfortable appearance and his jolly manner that irresistibly attracted a certain type of young man. It was his good fortune that this type of young man should be the type financially most worth attracting.

Freddie Threepwood had fallen under his spell during his short but crowded life in London. They had met for the first time at the Derby; and ever since then R. Jones had held in Freddie's estimation that position of guide, philosopher and friend which he held in the estimation of so many young men of Freddie's stamp.

That was why, at twelve o'clock punctually on this Spring day, he tapped with his cane on R. Jones' ground glass, and showed such satisfaction and relief when the door was opened by the proprietor in person.

"Well, well, well!" said R. Jones rollickingly. "Whom have we here? The dashing bridegroom-to-be, and no other!"

R. Jones, like Lord Emsworth, was delighted that Freddie was about to marry a nice girl with plenty of money. The sudden turning off of the tap from which Freddie's allowance had flowed had hit him hard. He had other sources of income, of course; but few so easy and unfailing as Freddie had been in the days of his prosperity.

"The prodigal son, by George! Creeping back into the fold after all this weary time! It seems years since I saw you, Freddie. The old gov'nor put his foot down—didn't he?—and stopped the funds. Damned shame! I take it that things have loosened up a bit since the engagement was announced—eh?"

Freddie sat down and chewed the knob of his cane unhappily.

"Well, as a matter of fact, Dickie, old top," he said, "not so that you could notice it, don't you know! Things are still pretty much the same. I managed to get away from Blandings for a night, because the gov'nor had to come to London; but I've got to go back with him on the three-o'clock train. And, as for money, I can't get a quid out of him. As a matter of fact, I'm in the deuce of a hole; and that's why I've come to you."

Even fat, jovial men have their moments of depression. R. Jones' face clouded, and jerky remarks about hardness of times and losses on the Stock Exchange began to proceed from him. As Scotland Yard had discovered, he lent money on occasion; but he did not lend it to youths in Freddie's unfortunate position.

"Oh, I don't want to make a touch, you know," Freddie hastened to explain. "It isn't that. As a matter of fact, I managed to raise five hundred of the best this morning. That ought to be enough."

"Depends on what you want it for," said R. Jones, magically genial once more.

The thought entered his mind, as it had so often, that the world was full of easy marks. He wished he could meet the money-lender who had been rash enough to advance the Honorable Freddie five hundred pounds. Those philanthropists cross our path too seldom.

Freddie felt in his pocket, produced a cigarette case, and from it extracted a newspaper clipping.

"Did you read about poor old Percy in the papers? The case, you know?"

"Percy?"

"Lord Stockheath, you know."

"Oh, the Stockheath breach-of-promise case? I did more than that. I was in court all three days." R. Jones emitted a cozy chuckle. "Is he a pal of yours? A cousin, eh? I wish you had seen him in the witness box, with Jellicoe-Smith cross-examining him! The funniest thing I ever heard! And his letters to the girl! They read them out in court; and of all—"

"Don't, old man! Dickie, old top—please! I know all about it. I read the reports. They made poor old Percy look like an absolute ass."

"Well, Nature had done that already; but I'm bound to say they improved on Nature's work. I should think your Cousin Percy must have felt like a plucked chicken."

A spasm of pain passed over the Honorable Freddie's vacant face. He wriggled in his chair.

"Dickie, old man, I wish you wouldn't talk like that. It makes me feel ill."

"Why, is he such a pal of yours as all that?"

"It's not that. It's—the fact is, Dickie, old top, I'm in exactly the same bally hole as poor old Percy was, myself!"

"What! You have been sued for breach of promise?"

"Not absolutely that—yet. Look here; I'll tell you the whole thing. Do you remember a show at the Piccadilly about a year ago called "The Baby Doll"? There was a girl in the chorus."

"Several—I remember noticing."

"No; I mean one particular girl—a girl called Joan Valentine. The rotten part is that I never met her."

"Pull yourself together, Freddie. What exactly is the trouble?"

"Well—don't you see?—I used to go to the show every other night, and I fell frightfully in love with this girl—"

"Without having met her?"

"Yes. You see, I was rather an ass in those days."

"No, no!" said R. Jones handsomely.

"I must have been or I shouldn't have been such an ass, don't you know! Well, as I was saying, I used to write this girl letters, saying how much I was in love with her; and—and—"

"Specifically proposing marriage?"

"I can't remember. I expect I did. I was awfully in love."

"How was that if you never met her?"

"She wouldn't meet me. She wouldn't even come out to luncheon. She didn't even answer my letters—just sent word down by the Johnny at the stage door. And then—"

Freddie's voice died away. He thrust the knob of his cane into his mouth in a sort of frenzy.

"What then?" inquired R. Jones.

A scarlet blush manifested itself on Freddie's young face. His eyes wandered sidewise. After a long pause a single word escaped him, almost inaudible:

"Poetry!"

R. Jones trembled as though an electric current had been passed through his plump frame. His little eyes sparkled with merriment.

"You wrote her poetry!"

"Yards of it, old boy—yards of it!" groaned Freddie. Panic filled him with speech. "You see the frightful hole I'm in? This girl is bound to have kept the letters. I don't remember whether I actually proposed to her or not; but anyway she's got enough material to make it worth while to have a dash at an action—especially after poor old Percy has just got soaked for such a pile of money and made breach-of-promise cases the fashion, so to speak.

"And now that the announcement of my engagement is out she's certain to get busy. Probably she has been waiting for something of the sort. Don't you see that all the cards are in her hands? We couldn't afford to let the thing come into court. That poetry would dish my marriage for a certainty. I'd have to emigrate or something! Goodness knows what would happen at home! My old gov'nor would murder me! So you see what a frightful hole I'm in, don't you, Dickie, old man?"

"And what do you want me to do?"

"Why, to get hold of this girl and get back the letters—don't you see? I can't do it myself, cooped up miles away in the country. And besides, I shouldn't know how to handle a thing like that. It needs a chappie with a lot of sense and a persuasive sort of way with him."

"Thanks for the compliment, Freddie; but I should imagine that something a little more solid than a persuasive way would be required in a case like this. You said something a while ago about five hundred pounds?"

"Here it is, old man—in notes. I brought it on purpose. Will you really take the thing on? Do you think you can work it for five hundred?"

"I can have a try."

Freddie rose, with an expression approximating to happiness on his face. Some men have the power of inspiring confidence in some of their fellows, though they fill others with distrust. Scotland Yard might look askance at R. Jones, but to Freddie he was all that was helpful and reliable. He shook R. Jones' hand several times in his emotion.

"That's absolutely topping of you, old man!" he said. "Then I'll leave the whole thing to you. Write me the moment you have done anything, won't you? Good-by, old top, and thanks ever so much!"

The door closed. R. Jones remained where he sat, his fingers straying luxuriously among the crackling paper. A feeling of complete happiness warmed R. Jones' bosom. He was uncertain whether or not his mission would be successful; and to be truthful he was not letting that worry him much. What he was certain of was the fact that the heavens had opened unexpectedly and dropped five hundred pounds into his lap.

CHAPTER III

The Earl of Emsworth stood in the doorway of the Senior Conservative Club's vast diningroom, and beamed with a vague sweetness on the two hundred or so Senior Conservatives who, with much clattering of knives and forks, were keeping body and soul together by means of the coffee-room luncheon. He might have been posing for a statue of Amiability. His pale blue eyes shone with a friendly light through their protecting glasses; the smile of a man at peace with all men curved his weak mouth; his bald head, reflecting the sunlight, seemed almost to wear a halo.

Nobody appeared to notice him. He so seldom came to London these days that he was practically a stranger in the club; and in any case your Senior Conservative, when at lunch, has little leisure for observing anything not immediately on the table in front of him. To attract attention in the dining-room of the Senior Conservative Club between the hours of one and two-thirty, you have to be a mutton chop—not an earl.

It is possible that, lacking the initiative to make his way down the long aisle and find a table for himself, he might have stood there indefinitely, but for the restless activity of Adams, the head steward. It was Adams' mission in life to flit to and fro, hauling would-be lunchers to their destinations, as a St. Bernard dog hauls travelers out of Alpine snowdrifts. He sighted Lord Emsworth and secured him with a genteel pounce.

"A table, your lordship? This way, your lordship." Adams remembered him, of course. Adams remembered everybody.

Lord Emsworth followed him beamingly and presently came to anchor at a table in the farther end of the room. Adams handed him the bill of fare and stood brooding over him like a providence.

"Don't often see your lordship in the club," he opened chattily.

It was business to know the tastes and dispositions of all the five thousand or so members of the Senior Conservative Club and to suit his demeanor to them. To some he would hand the bill of fare swiftly, silently, almost brusquely, as one who realizes that there are moments in life too serious for talk. Others, he knew, liked conversation; and to those he introduced the subject of food almost as a sub-motive.

Lord Emsworth, having examined the bill of fare with a mild curiosity, laid it down and became conversational.

"No, Adams; I seldom visit London nowadays. London does not attract me. The country—the fields—the woods—the birds—"

Something across the room seemed to attract his attention and his voice trailed off. He inspected this for some time with bland interest, then turned to Adams once more.

"What was I saying, Adams?"

"The birds, your lordship."

"Birds! What birds? What about birds?"

"You were speaking of the attractions of life in the country, your lordship. You included the birds in your remarks."

"Oh, yes, yes, yes! Oh, yes, yes! Oh, yes—to be sure. Do you ever go to the country, Adams?"

"Generally to the seashore, your lordship—when I take my annual vacation."

Whatever was the attraction across the room once more exercised its spell. His lordship concentrated himself on it to the exclusion of all other mundane matters. Presently he came out of his trance again.

"What were you saying, Adams?"

"I said that I generally went to the seashore, your lordship."

"Eh? When?"

"For my annual vacation, your lordship."

"Your what?"

"My annual vacation, your lordship."

"What about it?"

Adams never smiled during business hours—unless professionally, as it were, when a member made a joke; but he was storing up in the recesses of his highly respectable body a large laugh, to be shared with his wife when he reached home that night. Mrs. Adams never wearied of hearing of the eccentricities of the members of the club. It occurred to Adams that he was in luck to-day. He was expecting a little party of friends to supper that night, and he was a man who loved an audience.

You would never have thought it, to look at him when engaged in his professional duties, but Adams had built up a substantial reputation as a humorist in his circle by his imitations of certain members of the club; and it was a matter of regret to him that he got so few opportunities nowadays of studying the absent-minded Lord Emsworth. It was rare luck—his lordship coming in to-day, evidently in his best form.

"Adams, who is the gentleman over by the window—the gentleman in the brown suit?"

"That is Mr. Simmonds, your lordship. He joined us last year."

"I never saw a man take such large mouthfuls. Did you ever see a man take such large mouthfuls, Adams?"

Adams refrained from expressing an opinion, but inwardly he was thrilling with artistic fervor. Mr. Simmonds eating, was one of his best imitations, though Mrs. Adams was inclined to object to it on the score that it was a bad example for the children. To be privileged to witness Lord Emsworth watching and criticizing Mr. Simmonds was to collect material for a double-barreled character study that would assuredly make the hit of the evening.

"That man," went on Lord Emsworth, "is digging his grave with his teeth. Digging his grave with his teeth, Adams! Do you take large mouthfuls, Adams?"

"No, your lordship."

"Quite right. Very sensible of you, Adams—very sensible of you. Very sen—What was I saying, Adams?"

"About my not taking large mouthfuls, your lordship."

"Quite right—quite right! Never take large mouthfuls, Adams. Never gobble. Have you any children, Adams?"

"Two, your lordship."

"I hope you teach them not to gobble. They pay for it in later life. Americans gobble when young and ruin their digestions. My American friend, Mr. Peters, suffers terribly from indigestion."

Adams lowered his voice to a confidential murmur: "If you will pardon the liberty, your lordship—I saw it in the paper—"

"About Mr. Peters' indigestion?"

"About Miss Peters, your lordship, and the Honorable Frederick. May I be permitted to offer my congratulations?"
"Eh, Oh, yes—the engagement. Yes, yes, yes! Yes—to be sure. Yes; very satisfactory in every respect. High time he settled down and got a little sense. I put it to him straight. I cut off his allowance and made him stay at home. That made him think—lazy young devil!"

Lord Emsworth had his lucid moments; and in the one that occurred now it came home to him that he was not talking to himself, as he had imagined, but confiding intimate family secrets to the head steward of his club's dining-room. He checked himself abruptly, and with a slight decrease of amiability fixed his gaze on the bill of fare and ordered cold beef. For an instant he felt resentful against Adams for luring him on to soliloquize; but the next moment his whole mind was gripped by the fascinating spectacle of Mr. Simmonds dealing with a wedge of Stilton cheese, and Adams was forgotten.

The cold beef had the effect of restoring his lordship to complete amiability, and when Adams in the course of his wanderings again found himself at the table he was once more disposed for light conversation.

"So you saw the news of the engagement in the paper, did you, Adams?"

"Yes, your lordship, in the Mail. It had quite a long piece about it. And the Honorable Frederick's photograph and the young lady's were in the Mirror. Mrs. Adams clipped them out and put them in an album, knowing that your lordship was a member of ours. If I may say so, your lordship—a beautiful young lady."

"Devilish attractive, Adams—and devilish rich. Mr. Peters is a millionaire, Adams."

"So I read in the paper, your lordship."

"Damme! They all seem to be millionaires in America. Wish I knew how they managed it. Honestly, I hope. Mr. Peters is an honest man, but his digestion is bad. He used to bolt his food. You don't bolt your food, I hope, Adams?"

"No, your lordship; I am most careful."

"The late Mr. Gladstone used to chew each mouthful thirty-three times. Deuced good notion if you aren't in a hurry. What cheese would you recommend, Adams?"

"The gentlemen are speaking well of the Gorgonzola."

"All right, bring me some. You know, Adams, what I admire about Americans is their resource. Mr. Peters tells me that as a boy of eleven he earned twenty dollars a week selling mint to saloon keepers, as they call publicans over there. Why they wanted mint I cannot recollect. Mr. Peters explained the reason to me and it seemed highly plausible at the time; but I have forgotten it. Possibly for mint sauce. It impressed me, Adams. Twenty dollars is four pounds. I never earned four pounds a week when I was a boy of eleven; in fact, I don't think I ever earned four pounds a week. His story impressed me, Adams. Every man ought to have an earning capacity. I was so struck with what he told me that I began to paint."

"Landscapes, your lordship?"

"Furniture. It is unlikely that I shall ever be compelled to paint furniture for a living, but it is a consolation to me to feel that I could do so if called on. There is a fascination about painting furniture, Adams. I have painted the whole of my bedroom at Blandings and am now engaged on the museum. You would be surprised at the fascination of it. It suddenly came back to me the other day that I had been inwardly longing to mess about with paints and things since I was a boy. They stopped me when I was a boy. I recollect my old father beating me with a walking stick—Tell me, Adams, have I eaten my cheese?"

"Not yet, your lordship. I was about to send the waiter for it."

"Never mind. Tell him to bring the bill instead. I remember that I have an appointment. I must not be late."

"Shall I take the fork, your lordship?"

"The fork?"

"Your lordship has inadvertently put a fork in your coat pocket."

Lord Emsworth felt in the pocket indicated, and with the air of an inexpert conjurer whose trick has succeeded contrary to his expectations produced a silver-plated fork. He regarded it with surprise; then he looked wonderingly at Adams.

"Adams, I'm getting absent-minded. Have you ever noticed any traces of absent-mindedness in me before?"

"Oh, no, your lordship."

"Well, it's deuced peculiar! I have no recollection whatsoever of placing that fork in my pocket . . . Adams, I want a taxicab." He glanced round the room, as though expecting to locate one by the fireplace.

"The hall porter will whistle one for you, your lordship."

"So he will, by George!—so he will! Good day, Adams."

"Good day, your lordship."

The Earl of Emsworth ambled benevolently to the door, leaving Adams with the feeling that his day had been well-spent. He gazed almost with reverence after the slow-moving figure.

"What a nut!" said Adams to his immortal soul.

Wafted through the sunlit streets in his taxicab, the Earl of Emsworth smiled benevolently on London's teeming millions. He was as completely happy as only a fluffy-minded old man with excellent health and a large income can be. Other people worried about all sorts of things—strikes, wars, suffragettes, the diminishing birth rate, the growing materialism of the age, a score of similar subjects.

Worrying, indeed, seemed to be the twentieth-century specialty. Lord Emsworth never worried. Nature had equipped him with a mind so admirably constructed for withstanding the disagreeableness of life that if an unpleasant thought entered it, it passed out again a moment later. Except for a few of life's fundamental facts, such as that his check book was in the right-hand top drawer of his desk; that the Honorable Freddie Threepwood was a young idiot who required perpetual restraint; and that when in doubt about anything he had merely to apply to his secretary, Rupert Baxter—except for these basic things, he never remembered anything for more than a few minutes.

At Eton, in the sixties, they had called him Fathead.

His was a life that lacked, perhaps, the sublimer emotions which raise man to the level of the gods; but undeniably it was an extremely happy one. He never experienced the thrill of ambition fulfilled; but, on the other hand, he never knew the agony of ambition frustrated. His name, when he died, would not live forever in England's annals; he was spared the pain of worrying about this by the fact that he had no desire to live forever in England's annals. He was possibly as nearly contented as a human being could be in this century of alarms and excursions.

Indeed, as he bowled along in his cab and reflected that a really charming girl, not in the chorus of any West End theater, a girl with plenty of money and excellent breeding, had—in a moment, doubtless, of mental aberration—become engaged to be married to the Honorable Freddie, he told himself that life at last was absolutely without a crumpled rose leaf.

The cab drew up before a house gay with flowered window boxes. Lord Emsworth paid the driver and stood on the sidewalk looking up at this cheerful house, trying to remember why on earth he had told the man to drive there.

A few moments' steady thought gave him the answer to the riddle. This was Mr. Peters' town house, and he had come to it by invitation to look at Mr. Peters' collection of scarabs. To be sure! He remembered now—his collection of scarabs. Or was it Arabs?

Lord Emsworth smiled. Scarabs, of course. You couldn't collect Arabs. He wondered idly, as he rang the bell, what scarabs might be; but he was interested in a fluffy kind of way in all forms of collecting, and he was very pleased to have the opportunity of examining these objects; whatever they were. He rather thought they were a kind of fish.

There are men in this world who cannot rest; who are so constituted that they can only take their leisure in the shape of a change of work. To this fairly numerous class belonged Mr. J. Preston Peters, father of Freddie's Aline. And to this merit—or defect—is to be attributed his almost maniacal devotion to that rather unattractive species of curio, the Egyptian scarab.

Five years before, a nervous breakdown had sent Mr. Peters to a New York specialist. The specialist had grown rich on similar cases and his advice was always the same. He insisted on Mr. Peters taking up a hobby.

"What sort of a hobby?" inquired Mr. Peters irritably. His digestion had just begun to trouble him at the time, and his temper now was not of the best.

"Now my hobby," said the specialist, "is the collecting of scarabs. Why should you not collect scarabs?"

"Because," said Mr. Peters, "I shouldn't know one if you brought it to me on a plate. What are scarabs?"

"Scarabs," said the specialist, warming to his subject, "the Egyptian hieroglyphs."

"And what," inquired Mr. Peters, "are Egyptian hieroglyphs?"

The specialist began to wonder whether it would not have been better to advise Mr. Peters to collect postage stamps.

"A scarab," he said—"derived from the Latin scarabeus—is literally a beetle."

"I will not collect beetles!" said Mr. Peters definitely. "They give me the Willies."

"Scarabs are Egyptian symbols in the form of beetles," the specialist hurried on. "The most common form of scarab is in the shape of a ring. Scarabs were used for seals. They were also employed as beads or ornaments. Some scarabaei bear inscriptions having reference to places; as, for instance: 'Memphis is mighty forever.'"

Mr. Peters' scorn changed to active interest.

"Have you got one like that?"

"Like what?"

"A scarab boosting Memphis. It's my home town."

"I think it possible that some other Memphis was alluded to."

"There isn't any other except the one in Tennessee," said Mr. Peters patriotically.

The specialist owed the fact that he was a nerve doctor instead of a nerve patient to his habit of never arguing with his visitors.

"Perhaps," he said, "you would care to glance at my collection. It is in the next room."

That was the beginning of Mr. Peters' devotion to scarabs. At first he did his collecting without any love of it, partly because he had to collect something or suffer, but principally because of a remark the specialist made as he was leaving the room.

"How long would it take me to get together that number of the things?" Mr. Peters inquired, when, having looked his fill on the dullest assortment of objects he remembered ever to have seen, he was preparing to take his leave.

The specialist was proud of his collection. "How long? To make a collection as large as mine? Years, Mr. Peters. Oh, many, many years."

"I'll bet you a hundred dollars I'll do it in six months!"

From that moment Mr. Peters brought to the collecting of scarabs the same furious energy which had given him so many dollars and so much indigestion. He went after scarabs like a dog after rats. He scooped in scarabs from the four corners of the earth, until at the end of a year he found himself possessed of what, purely as regarded quantity, was a record collection.

This marked the end of the first phase of—so to speak—the scarabaean side of his life. Collecting had become a habit with him, but he was not yet a real enthusiast. It occurred to him that the time had arrived for a certain amount of pruning and elimination. He called in an expert and bade him go through the collection and weed out what he felicitously termed the "dead ones." The expert did his job thoroughly. When he had finished, the collection was reduced to a mere dozen specimens.

"The rest," he explained, "are practically valueless. If you are thinking of making a collection that will have any value in the eyes of archeologists I should advise you to throw them away. The remaining twelve are good."

"How do you mean—good? Why is one of these things valuable and another so much punk? They all look alike to me."

And then the expert talked to Mr. Peters for nearly two hours about the New Kingdom, the Middle Kingdom, Osiris, Ammon, Mut, Bubastis, dynasties, Cheops, the Hyksos kings, cylinders, bezels, Amenophis III, Queen Taia, the Princess Gilukhipa of Mitanni, the lake of Zarukhe, Naucratis, and the Book of the Dead. He did it with a relish. He liked to do it.

When he had finished, Mr. Peters thanked him and went to the bathroom, where he bathed his temples with eau de Cologne.

That talk changed J. Preston Peters from a supercilious scooper-up of random scarabs to what might be called a genuine scarab fan. It does not matter what a man collects; if Nature has given him the collector's mind he will become a fanatic on the subject of whatever collection he sets out to make. Mr. Peters had collected dollars; he began to collect scarabs with precisely the same enthusiasm. He would have become just as enthusiastic about butterflies or old china if he had turned his thoughts to them; but it chanced that what he had taken up was the collecting of the scarab, and it gripped him more and more as the years went on.

Gradually he came to love his scarabs with that love, surpassing the love of women, which only collectors know. He became an expert on those curious relics of a dead civilization. For a time they ran neck and neck in his thoughts with business. When he retired from business he was free to make them the master passion of his life. He treasured each individual scarab in his collection as a miser treasures gold.

Collecting, as Mr. Peters did it, resembles the drink habit. It begins as an amusement and ends as an obsession. He was gloating over his treasures when the maid announced Lord Emsworth.

A curious species of mutual toleration—it could hardly be dignified by the title of friendship—had sprung up between these two men, so opposite in practically every respect. Each regarded the other with that feeling of perpetual amazement with which we encounter those whose whole viewpoint and mode of life is foreign to our own.

The American's force and nervous energy fascinated Lord Emsworth. As for Mr. Peters, nothing like the earl had ever happened to him before in a long and varied life. Each, in fact, was to the other a perpetual freak show, with no charge for admission. And if anything had been needed to cement the alliance it would have been supplied by the fact that they were both collectors.

They differed in collecting as they did in everything else. Mr. Peters' collecting, as has been shown, was keen, furious, concentrated; Lord Emsworth's had the amiable dodderingness that marked every branch of his life. In the museum at Blandings Castle you could find every manner of valuable and valueless curio. There was no central motive; the place was simply an amateur junk shop. Side by side with a Gutenberg Bible for which rival collectors would have bidden without a limit, you would come on a bullet from the field of Waterloo, one of a consignment of ten thousand shipped there for the use of tourists by a Birmingham firm. Each was equally attractive to its owner.

"My dear Mr. Peters," said Lord Emsworth sunnily, advancing into the room, "I trust I am not unpunctual. I have been lunching at my club."

"I'd have asked you to lunch here," said Mr. Peters, "but you know how it is with me . . . I've promised the doctor I'll give those nuts and grasses of his a fair trial, and I can do it pretty well when I'm alone with Aline; but to have to sit by and see somebody else eating real food would be trying me too high."

Lord Emsworth murmured sympathetically. The other's digestive tribulations touched a ready chord. An excellent trencherman himself, he understood what Mr. Peters must suffer.

"Too bad!" he said.

Mr. Peters turned the conversation into other channels.

"These are my scarabs," he said.

Lord Emsworth adjusted his glasses, and the mild smile disappeared from his face, to be succeeded by a set look. A stage director of a moving-picture firm would have recognized the look. Lord Emsworth was registering interest—interest which he perceived from the first instant would have to be completely simulated; for instinct told him, as Mr. Peters began to talk, that he was about to be bored as he had seldom been bored in his life.

Mr. Peters, in his character of showman, threw himself into his work with even more than his customary energy. His flow of speech never faltered. He spoke of the New Kingdom, the Middle Kingdom, Osiris and Ammon; waxed eloquent concerning Mut, Bubastis, Cheops, the Hyksos kings, cylinders, bezels and Amenophis III; and became at times almost lyrical when touching on Queen Taia, the Princess Gilukhipa of Mitanni, the lake of Zarukhe, Naucratis and the Book of the Dead. Time slid by.

"Take a look at this, Lord Emsworth."

As one who, brooding on love or running over business projects in his mind, walks briskly into a lamppost and comes back to the realities of life with a sense of jarring shock, Lord Emsworth started, blinked and returned to consciousness. Far away his mind had been—seventy miles away—in the pleasant hothouses and shady garden walks of Blandings Castle. He came back to London to find that his host, with a mingled air of pride and reverence, was extending toward him a small, dingy-looking something.

He took it and looked at it. That, apparently, was what he was meant to do. So far, all was well.

"Ah!" he said—that blessed word; covering everything! He repeated it, pleased at his ready resource.

"A Cheops of the Fourth Dynasty," said Mr. Peters fervently.

"I beg your pardon?"

"A Cheops—of the Fourth Dynasty."

Lord Emsworth began to feel like a hunted stag. He could not go on saying "Ah!" indefinitely; yet what else was there to say to this curious little beastly sort of a beetle kind of thing?

"Dear me! A Cheops!"

"Of the Fourth Dynasty!"

"Bless my soul! The Fourth Dynasty!"

"What do you think of that—eh?"

Strictly speaking, Lord Emsworth thought nothing of it; and he was wondering how to veil this opinion in diplomatic words, when the providence that looks after all good men saved him by causing a knock at the door to occur. In response to Mr. Peters' irritated cry a maid entered.

"If you please, sir, Mr. Threepwood wishes to speak with you on the telephone."

Mr. Peters turned to his guest. "Excuse me for one moment."

"Certainly," said Lord Emsworth gratefully. "Certainly, certainly, certainly! By all means."

The door closed behind Mr. Peters. Lord Emsworth was alone. For some moments he stood where he had been left, a figure with small signs of alertness about it. But Mr. Peters did not return immediately. The booming of his voice came faintly from some distant region. Lord Emsworth strolled to the window and looked out.

The sun still shone brightly on the quiet street. Across the road were trees. Lord Emsworth was fond of trees; he looked at these approvingly. Then round the corner came a vagrom man, wheeling flowers in a barrow.

Flowers! Lord Emsworth's mind shot back to Blandings like a homing pigeon. Flowers! Had he or had he not given Head Gardener Thorne adequate instructions as to what to do with those hydrangeas? Assuming that he had not, was Thorne to be depended on to do the right thing by them by the light of his own intelligence? Lord Emsworth began to brood on Head Gardener Thorne.

He was aware of some curious little object in his hand. He accorded it a momentary inspection. It had no message for him. It was probably something; but he could not remember what. He put it in his pocket and returned to his meditations.

At about the hour when the Earl of Emsworth was driving to keep his appointment with Mr. Peters, a party of two sat at a corner table at Simpson's Restaurant, in the Strand. One of the two was a small, pretty, good-natured-looking girl of about twenty; the other, a thick-set young man, with a wiry crop of red-brown hair and an expression of mingled devotion and determination. The girl was Aline Peters; the young man's name was George Emerson. He, also, was an American, a rising member in a New York law firm. He had a strong, square face, with a dogged and persevering chin.

There are all sorts of restaurants in London, from the restaurant which makes you fancy you are in Paris to the restaurant which makes you wish you were. There are palaces in Piccadilly, quaint lethal chambers in Soho, and strange food factories in Oxford Street and Tottenham Court Road. There are restaurants which specialize in ptomaine and restaurants which specialize in sinister vegetable messes. But there is only one Simpson's.

Simpson's, in the Strand, is unique. Here, if he wishes, the Briton may for the small sum of half a dollar stupefy himself with food. The god of fatted plenty has the place under his protection. Its keynote is solid comfort.

It is a pleasant, soothing, hearty place—a restful temple of food. No strident orchestra forces the diner to bolt beef in ragtime. No long central aisle distracts his attention with its stream of new arrivals. There he sits, alone with his food, while white-robed priests, wheeling their smoking trucks, move to and fro, ever ready with fresh supplies.

All round the room—some at small tables, some at large tables—the worshipers sit, in their eyes that resolute, concentrated look which is the peculiar property of the British luncher, ex-President Roosevelt's man-eating fish, and the American army worm.

Conversation does not flourish at Simpson's. Only two of all those present on this occasion showed any disposition toward chattiness. They were Aline Peters and her escort.

"The girl you ought to marry," Aline was saying, "is Joan Valentine."

"The girl I am going to marry," said George Emerson, "is Aline Peters."

For answer, Aline picked up from the floor beside her an illustrated paper and, having opened it at a page toward the end, handed it across the table.

George Emerson glanced at it disdainfully. There were two photographs on the page. One was of Aline; the other of a heavy, loutish-looking youth, who wore that expression of pained glassiness which Young England always adopts in the face of a camera.

Under one photograph were printed the words: "Miss Aline Peters, who is to marry the Honorable Frederick Threepwood in June"; under the other: "The Honorable Frederick Threepwood, who is to marry Miss Aline Peters in June." Above the photographs was the legend: "Forthcoming International Wedding. Son of the Earl of Emsworth to marry American heiress." In one corner of the picture a Cupid, draped in the Stars and Stripes, aimed his bow at the gentleman; in the other another Cupid, clad in a natty Union Jack, was drawing a bead on the lady.

The subeditor had done his work well. He had not been ambiguous. What he intended to convey to the reader was that Miss Aline Peters, of America, was going to marry the Honorable Frederick Threepwood, son of the Earl of Emsworth; and that was exactly the impression the average reader got.

George Emerson, however, was not an average reader. The subeditor's work did not impress him.

"You mustn't believe everything you see in the papers," he said. "What are the stout children in the one-piece bathing suits supposed to be doing?"

"Those are Cupids, George, aiming at us with their little bow— a pretty and original idea."

"Why Cupids?"

"Cupid is the god of love."

"What has the god of love got to do with it?"

Aline placidly devoured a fried potato. "You're simply trying to make me angry," she said; "and I call it very mean of you. You know perfectly well how fatal it is to get angry at meals. It was eating while he was in a bad temper that ruined father's digestion. George, that nice, fat carver is wheeling his truck this way. Flag him and make him give me some more of that mutton."

George looked round him morosely.

"This," he said, "is England—this restaurant, I mean. You don't need to go any farther. Just take a good look at this place and you have seen the whole country and can go home again. You may judge a country by its meals. A people with imagination will eat with imagination. Look at the French; look at ourselves. The Englishman loathes imagination. He goes to a place like this and says: 'Don't bother me to think. Here's half a dollar. Give me food—any sort of food—until I tell you to stop.' And that's the principle on which he lives his life. 'Give me anything, and don't bother me!' That's his motto."

"If that was meant to apply to Freddie and me, I think you're very rude. Do you mean that any girl would have done for him, so long as it was a girl?"

George Emerson showed a trace of confusion. Being honest with himself, he had to admit that he did not exactly know what he did mean—if he meant anything. That, he felt rather bitterly, was the worst of Aline. She would never let a fellow's good things go purely as good things; she probed and questioned and spoiled the whole effect. He was quite sure that when he began to speak he had meant something, but what it was escaped him for the moment. He had been urged to the homily by the fact that at a neighboring table he had caught sight of a stout young Briton, with a red face, who reminded him of the Honorable Frederick Threepwood. He mentioned this to Aline.

"Do you see that fellow in the gray suit—I think he has been sleeping in it—at the table on your right? Look at the stodgy face. See the glassy eye. If that man sandbagged your Freddie and tied him up somewhere, and turned up at the church instead of him, can you honestly tell me you would know the difference? Come, now, wouldn't you simply say, 'Why, Freddie, how natural you look!' and go through the ceremony without a suspicion?"

"He isn't a bit like Freddie."

"My dear girl, there isn't a man in this restaurant under the age of thirty who isn't just like Freddie. All Englishmen look exactly alike, talk exactly alike, and think exactly alike."

"And you oughtn't to speak of him as Freddie. You don't know him."

"Yes, I do. And, what is more, he expressly asked me to call him Freddie. 'Oh, dash it, old top, don't keep on calling me Threepwood! Freddie to pals!' Those were his very words."

"George, you're making this up."

"Not at all. We met last night at the National Sporting Club. Porky Jones was going twenty rounds with Eddie Flynn. I offered to give three to one on Eddie. Freddie, who was sitting next to me, took me in fivers. And if you want any further proof of your young man's pin-headedness; mark that! A child could have seen that Eddie had him going. Eddie comes from Pittsburgh—God bless it! My own home town!"

"Did your Eddie win?"

"You don't listen—I told you he was from Pittsburgh. And afterward Threepwood chummed up with me and told me that to real pals like me he was Freddie. I was a real pal, as I understood it, because I would have to wait for my money. The fact was, he explained, his old governor had cut off his bally allowance."

"You're simply trying to poison my mind against him; and I don't think it's very nice of you, George."

"What do you mean—poison your mind? I'm not poisoning your mind; I'm simply telling you a few things about him. You know perfectly well that you don't love him, and that you aren't going to marry him—and that you are going to marry me."

"How do you know I don't love my Freddie?"

"If you can look me straight in the eyes and tell me you do, I will drop the whole thing and put on a little page's dress and carry your train up the aisle. Now, then!"

"And all the while you're talking you're letting my carver get away," said Aline.

George called to the willing priest, who steered his truck toward them. Aline directed his dissection of the shoulder of mutton by word and gesture.

"Enjoy yourself!" said Emerson coldly.

"So I do, George; so I do. What excellent meat they have in England!"

"It all comes from America," said George patriotically. "And, anyway, can't you be a bit more spiritual? I don't want to sit here discussing food products."

"If you were in my position, George, you wouldn't want to talk about anything else. It's doing him a world of good, poor dear; but there are times when I'm sorry Father ever started this food-reform thing. You don't know what it means for a healthy young girl to try and support life on nuts and grasses."

"And why should you?" broke out Emerson. "I'll tell you what it is, Aline—you are perfectly absurd about your father. I don't want to say anything against him to you, naturally; but—"

"Go ahead, George. Why this diffidence? Say what you like."

"Very well, then, I will. I'll give it to you straight. You know quite well that you have let your father bully you since you were in short frocks. I don't say it is your fault or his fault, or anybody's fault; I just state it as a fact. It's temperament, I suppose. You are yielding and he is aggressive; and he has taken advantage of it.

"We now come to this idiotic Freddie-marriage business. Your father has forced you into that. It's all very well to say that you are a free agent and that fathers don't coerce their daughters nowadays. The trouble is that your father does. You let him do what he likes with you. He has got you hypnotized; and you won't break away from this Freddie foolishness because you can't find the nerve. I'm going to help you find the nerve. I'm coming down to Blandings Castle when you go there on Friday."

"Coming to Blandings!"

"Freddie invited me last night. I think it was done by way of interest on the money he owed me; but he did it and I accepted."

"But, George, my dear boy, do you never read the etiquette books and the hints in the Sunday papers on how to be the perfect gentleman? Don't you know you can't be a man's guest and take advantage of his hospitality to try to steal his fiancee away from him?"

"Watch me."

A dreamy look came into Aline's eyes. "I wonder what it feels like, being a countess," she said.

"You will never know." George looked at her pityingly. "My poor girl," he said, "have you been lured into this engagement in the belief that pop-eyed Frederick, the Idiot Child, is going to be an earl some day? You have been stung! Freddie is not the heir. His older brother, Lord Bosham, is as fit as a prize-fighter and has three healthy sons. Freddie has about as much chance of getting the title as I have."

"George, your education has been sadly neglected. Don't you know that the heir to the title always goes on a yachting cruise, with his whole family, and gets drowned—and the children too? It happens in every English novel you read."

"Listen, Aline! Let us get this thing straight: I have been in love with you since I wore knickerbockers. I proposed to you at your first dance—"

"Very clumsily."

"But sincerely. Last year, when I found that you had gone to England, I came on after you as soon as the firm could spare me. And I found you engaged to this Freddie excrescence."

"I like the way you stand up for Freddie. So many men in your position might say horrid things about him."

"Oh, I've nothing against Freddie. He is practically an imbecile and I don't like his face; outside of that he's all right. But you will be glad later that you did not marry him. You are much too real a person. What a wife you will make for a hard-working man!"

"What does Freddie work hard at?"

"I am alluding at the moment not to Freddie but to myself. I shall come home tired out. Maybe things will have gone wrong downtown. I shall be fagged, disheartened. And then you will come with your cool, white hands and, placing them gently on my forehead—"

Aline shook her head. "It's no good, George. Really, you had better realize it. I'm very fond of you, but we are not suited!"

"Why not?"

"You are too overwhelming—too much like a bomb. I think you must be one of the supermen one reads about. You would want your own way and nothing but your own way. Now, Freddie will roll through hoops and sham dead, and we shall be the happiest pair in the world. I am much too placid and mild to make you happy. You want somebody who would stand up to you—somebody like Joan Valentine."

"That's the second time you have mentioned this Joan Valentine. Who is she?"

"She is a girl who was at school with me. We were the greatest chums—at least, I worshiped her and would have done anything for her; and I think she liked me. Then we lost touch with one another and didn't meet for years. I met her on the street yesterday, and she is just the same. She has been through the most awful times. Her father was quite rich; he died suddenly while he and Joan were in Paris, and she found that he hadn't left a cent. He had been living right up to his income all the time. His life wasn't even insured. She came to London; and, so far as I could make out from the short talk we had, she has done pretty nearly everything since we last met. She worked in a shop and went on the stage, and all sorts of things. Isn't it awful, George!"

"Pretty tough," said Emerson. He was but faintly interested in Miss Valentine.

"She is so plucky and full of life. She would stand up to you."

"Thanks! My idea of marriage is not a perpetual scrap. My notion of a wife is something cozy and sympathetic and soothing. That is why I love you. We shall be the happiest—"

Aline laughed.

"Dear old George! Now pay the check and get me a taxi. I've endless things to do at home. If Freddie is in town I suppose he will be calling to see me. Who is Freddie, do you ask? Freddie is my fiance, George. My betrothed. My steady. The young man I'm going to marry."

Emerson shook his head resignedly. "Curious how you cling to that Freddie idea. Never mind! I'll come down to Blandings on Friday and we shall see what happens. Bear in mind the broad fact that you and I are going to be married, and that nothing on earth is going to stop us."

It was Aline Peters who had to bear the brunt of her father's mental agony when he discovered, shortly after Lord Emsworth had left him, that the gem of his collection of scarabs had done the same. It is always the innocent bystander who suffers.

"The darned old sneak thief!" said Mr. Peters.

"Father!"

"Don't sit there saying 'Father!' What's the use of saying 'Father!'? Do you think it is going to help—your saying 'Father!'? I'd rather the old pirate had taken the house and lot than that scarab. He knows what's what! Trust him to walk off with the pick of the whole bunch! I did think I could leave the father of the man who's going to marry my daughter for a second alone with the things. There's no morality among collectors—none! I'd trust a syndicate of Jesse James, Captain Kidd and Dick Turpin sooner than I would a collector. My Cheops of the Fourth Dynasty! I wouldn't have lost it for five thousand dollars!"

"But, father, couldn't you write him a letter, asking for it back? He's such a nice old man! I'm sure he didn't mean to steal the scarab."

Mr. Peters' overwrought soul blew off steam in the shape of a passionate snort.

"Didn't mean to steal it! What do you think he meant to do—take it away and keep it safe for me for fear I should lose it? Didn't mean to steal it! Bet you he's well-known in society as a kleptomaniac. Bet you that when his name is announced his friends pick up their spoons and send in a hurry call to police headquarters for a squad to come and see that he doesn't sneak the front door. Of course he meant to steal it! He has a museum of his own down in the country. My Cheops is going to lend tone to that. I'd give five thousand dollars to get it back. If there's a man in this country with the spirit to break into that castle and steal that scarab and hand it back to me, there's five thousand waiting for him right here; and if he wants to he can knock that old safe blower on the head with a jimmy into the bargain."

"But, father, why can't you simply go to him and say it's yours and that you must have it back?"

"And have him come back at me by calling off this engagement of yours? Not if I know it! You can't go about the place charging a man with theft and ask him to go on being willing to have his son marry your daughter, can you? The slightest suggestion that I thought he had stolen this scarab and he would do the Proud Old English Aristocrat and end everything. He's in the strongest position a thief has ever been in. You can't get at him."

"I didn't think of that."

"You don't think at all. That's the trouble with you," said Mr. Peters.

Years of indigestion had made Mr. Peters' temper, even when in a normal mood, perfectly impossible; in a crisis like this it ran amuck. He vented it on Aline because he had always vented his irritabilities on Aline; because the fact of her sweet, gentle disposition, combined with the fact of their relationship, made her the ideal person to receive the overflow of his black moods. While his wife had lived he had bullied her. On her death Aline had stepped into the vacant position.

Aline did not cry, because she was not a girl who was given to tears; but, for all her placid good temper, she was wounded. She was a girl who liked everything in the world to run smoothly and easily, and these scenes with her father always depressed her. She took advantage of a lull in Mr. Peters' flow of words and slipped from the room.

Her cheerfulness had received a shock. She wanted sympathy. She wanted comforting. For a moment she considered George Emerson in the role of comforter; but there were objections to George in this character. Aline was accustomed to tease and chat with George, but at heart she was a little afraid of him; and instinct told her that, as comforter, he would be too volcanic and supermanly for a girl who was engaged to marry another man in June. George, as comforter, would be far too prone to trust to action rather than to the soothing power of the spoken word. George's idea of healing the wound, she felt, would be to push her into a cab and drive to the nearest registrar's.

No; she would not go to George. To whom, then? The vision of Joan Valentine came to her—of Joan as she had seen her yesterday, strong, cheerful, self-reliant, bearing herself, in spite of adversity, with a valiant jauntiness. Yes; she would go and see Joan. She put on her hat and stole from the house.

Curiously enough, only a quarter of an hour before, R. Jones had set out with exactly the same object in view.

At almost exactly the hour when Aline Peters set off to visit her friend, Miss Valentine, three men sat in the cozy smoking-room of Blandings Castle.

They were variously occupied. In the big chair nearest the door the Honorable Frederick Threepwood— Freddie to pals—was reading. Next to him sat a young man whose eyes, glittering through rimless spectacles, were concentrated on the upturned faces of several neat rows of playing cards—Rupert Baxter, Lord Emsworth's invaluable secretary, had no vices, but he sometimes relaxed his busy brain with a game of solitaire. Beyond Baxter, a cigar in his mouth and a weak highball at his side, the Earl of Emsworth took his ease.

The book the Honorable Freddie was reading was a small paper-covered book. Its cover was decorated with a color scheme in red, black and yellow, depicting a tense moment in the lives of a man with a black beard, a man with a yellow beard, a man without any beard at all, and a young woman who, at first sight, appeared to be all eyes and hair. The man with the black beard, to gain some private end, had tied this young woman with ropes to a complicated system of machinery, mostly wheels and pulleys. The man with the yellow beard was in the act of pushing or pulling a lever. The beardless man, protruding through a trapdoor in the floor, was pointing a large revolver at the parties of the second part.

Beneath this picture were the words: "Hands up, you scoundrels!"

Above it, in a meandering scroll across the page, was: "Gridley Quayle, Investigator. The Adventure of the Secret Six. By Felix Clovelly."

The Honorable Freddie did not so much read as gulp the adventure of the Secret Six. His face was crimson with excitement; his hair was rumpled; his eyes bulged. He was absorbed.

This is peculiarly an age in which each of us may, if we do but search diligently, find the literature suited to his mental powers. Grave and earnest men, at Eton and elsewhere, had tried Freddie Threepwood with Greek, with Latin and with English; and the sheeplike stolidity with which he declined to be interested in the masterpieces of all three tongues had left them with the conviction that he would never read anything.

And then, years afterward, he had suddenly blossomed out as a student—only, it is true, a student of the Adventures of Gridley Quayle; but still a student. His was a dull life and Gridley Quayle was the only person who brought romance into it. Existence for the Honorable Freddie was simply a sort of desert, punctuated with monthly oases in the shape of new Quayle adventures. It was his ambition to meet the man who wrote them.

Lord Emsworth sat and smoked, and sipped and smoked again, at peace with all the world. His mind was as nearly a blank as it is possible for the human mind to be. The hand that had not the task of holding the cigar was at rest in his trousers pocket. The fingers of it fumbled idly with a small, hard object.

Gradually it filtered into his lordship's mind that this small, hard object was not familiar. It was something new—something that was neither his keys nor his pencil; nor was it his small change. He yielded to a growing curiosity and drew it out. He examined it. It was a little something, rather like a fossilized beetle. It touched no chord in him. He looked at it with amiable distaste.

"Now how in the world did that get there?" he said.

The Honorable Freddie paid no attention to the remark. He was now at the very crest of his story, when every line intensified the thrill. Incident was succeeding incident. The Secret Six were here, there and everywhere, like so many malignant June bugs.

Annabel, the heroine, was having a perfectly rotten time—kidnapped, and imprisoned every few minutes. Gridley Quayle, hot on the scent, was covering somebody or other with his revolver almost continuously. Freddie Threepwood had no time for chatting with his father. Not so Rupert Baxter. Chatting with Lord Emsworth was one of the things for which he received his salary. He looked up from his cards.

"Lord Emsworth?"

"I have found a curious object in my pocket, Baxter. I was wondering how it got there."

He handed the thing to his secretary. Rupert Baxter's eyes lit up with sudden enthusiasm. He gasped.

"Magnificent!" he cried. "Superb!"

Lord Emsworth looked at him inquiringly.

"It is a scarab, Lord Emsworth; and unless I am mistaken—and I think I may claim to be something of an expert—a Cheops of the Fourth Dynasty. A wonderful addition to your museum!"

"Is it? By Gad! You don't say so, Baxter!"

"It is, indeed. If it is not a rude question, how much did you give for it, Lord Emsworth? It must have been the gem of somebody's collection. Was there a sale at Christie's this afternoon?"

Lord Emsworth shook his head. "I did not get it at Christie's, for I recollect that I had an important engagement which prevented my going to Christie's. To be sure; yes—I had promised to call on Mr. Peters and examine his collection of—Now I wonder what it was that Mr. Peters said he collected!"

"Mr. Peters is one of the best-known living collectors of scarabs."

"Scarabs! You are quite right, Baxter. Now that I recall the episode, this is a scarab; and Mr. Peters gave it to me."

"Gave it to you, Lord Emsworth?"

"Yes. The whole scene comes back to me. Mr. Peters, after telling me a great many exceedingly interesting things about scarabs, which I regret to say I cannot remember, gave me this. And you say it is really valuable, Baxter?"

"It is, from a collector's point of view, of extraordinary value."

"Bless my soul!" Lord Emsworth beamed. "This is extremely interesting, Baxter. One has heard so much of the princely hospitality of Americans. How exceedingly kind of Mr. Peters! I shall certainly treasure it, though I must confess that from a purely spectacular standpoint it leaves me a little cold. However, I must not look a gift horse in the mouth—eh, Baxter?"

From afar came the silver booming of a gong. Lord Emsworth rose.

"Time to dress for dinner? I had no idea it was so late. Baxter, you will be going past the museum door. Will you be a good fellow and place this among the exhibits? You will know what to do with it better than I. I always think of you as the curator of my little collection, Baxter—ha-ha! Mind how you step when you are in the museum. I was painting a chair there yesterday and I think I left the paint pot on the floor."

He cast a less amiable glance at his studious son.

"Get up, Frederick, and go and dress for dinner. What is that trash you are reading?"

The Honorable Freddie came out of his book much as a sleepwalker wakes—with a sense of having been violently assaulted. He looked up with a kind of stunned plaintiveness.

"Eh, gov'nor?"

"Make haste! Beach rang the gong five minutes ago. What is that you are reading?"

"Oh, nothing, gov'nor—just a book."

"I wonder you can waste your time on such trash. Make haste!"

He turned to the door, and the benevolent expression once more wandered athwart his face.

"Extremely kind of Mr. Peters!" he said. "Really, there is something almost Oriental in the lavish generosity of our American cousins."

It had taken R. Jones just six hours to discover Joan Valentine's address. That it had not taken him longer is a proof of his energy and of the excellence of his system of obtaining information; but R. Jones, when he considered it worth his while, could be extremely energetic, and he was a past master at the art of finding out things.

He poured himself out of his cab and rang the bell of Number Seven. A disheveled maid answered the ring.

"Miss Valentine in?"

"Yes, sir."

R. Jones produced his card.

"On important business, tell her. Half a minute—I'll write it."

He wrote the words on the card and devoted the brief period of waiting to a careful scrutiny of his surroundings. He looked out into the court and he looked as far as he could down the dingy passage; and the conclusions he drew from what he saw were complimentary to Miss Valentine.

"If this girl is the sort of girl who would hold up Freddie's letters," he mused, "she wouldn't be living in a place like this. If she were on the make she would have more money than she evidently possesses. Therefore, she is not on the make; and I am prepared to bet that she destroyed the letters as fast as she got them."

Those were, roughly, the thoughts of R. Jones as he stood in the doorway of Number Seven; and they were important thoughts inasmuch as they determined his attitude toward Joan in the approaching interview. He perceived that this matter must be handled delicately—that he must be very much the gentleman. It would be a strain, but he must do it.

The maid returned and directed him to Joan's room with a brief word and a sweeping gesture.

"Eh?" said R. Jones. "First floor?"

"Front," said the maid.

R. Jones trudged laboriously up the short flight of stairs. It was very dark on the stairs and he stumbled. Eventually, however, light came to him through an open door. Looking in, he saw a girl standing at the table. She had an air of expectation; so he deduced that he had reached his journey's end.

"Miss Valentine?"

"Please come in."

R. Jones waddled in.

"Not much light on your stairs."

"No. Will you take a seat?"

"Thanks."

One glance at the girl convinced R. Jones that he had been right. Circumstances had made him a rapid judge of character, for in the profession of living by one's wits in a large city the first principle of offense and defense is to sum people up at first sight. This girl was not on the make.

Joan Valentine was a tall girl with wheat-gold hair and eyes as brightly blue as a November sky when the sun is shining on a frosty world. There was in them a little of November's cold glitter, too, for Joan had been through much in the last few years; and experience, even though it does not harden, erects a defensive barrier between its children and the world.

Her eyes were eyes that looked straight and challenged. They could thaw to the satin blue of the Mediterranean Sea, where it purrs about the little villages of Southern France; but they did not thaw for everybody. She looked what she was—a girl of action; a girl whom life had made both reckless and wary—wary of friendly advances, reckless when there was a venture afoot.

Her eyes, as they met R. Jones' now, were cold and challenging. She, too, had learned the trick of swift diagnosis of character, and what she saw of R. Jones in that first glance did not impress her favorably.

"You wished to see me on business?"

"Yes," said R. Jones. "Yes. . . . Miss Valentine, may I begin by begging you to realize that I have no intention of insulting you?"

Joan's eyebrows rose. For an instant she did her visitor the injustice of suspecting that he had been dining too well.

"I don't understand."

"Let me explain: I have come here," R. Jones went on, getting more gentlemanly every moment, "on a very distasteful errand, to oblige a friend. Will you bear in mind that whatever I say is said entirely on his behalf?"

By this time Joan had abandoned the idea that this stout person was a life-insurance tout, and was inclining to the view that he was collecting funds for a charity.

"I came here at the request of the Honorable Frederick Threepwood."

"I don't quite understand."

"You never met him, Miss Valentine; but when you were in the chorus at the Piccadilly Theatre, I believe, he wrote you some very foolish letters. Possibly you have forgotten them?"

"I certainly have."

"You have probably destroyed them—eh?"

"Certainly! I never keep letters. Why do you ask?"

"Well, you see, Miss Valentine, the Honorable Frederick Threepwood is about to be married; and he thought that possibly, on the whole, it would be better that the letters—and poetry—which he wrote you were nonexistent."

Not all R. Jones' gentlemanliness—and during this speech he diffused it like a powerful scent in waves about him—could hide the unpleasant meaning of the words.

"He was afraid I might try to blackmail him?" said Joan, with formidable calm.

R. Jones raised and waved a fat hand deprecatingly.

"My dear Miss Valentine!"

Joan rose and R. Jones followed her example. The interview was plainly at an end.

"Please tell Mr. Threepwood to make his mind quite easy. He is in no danger."

"Exactly—exactly; precisely! I assured Threepwood that my visit here would be a mere formality. I was quite sure you had no intention whatever of worrying him. I may tell him definitely, then, that you have destroyed the letters?"

"Yes. Good-evening."

"Good-evening, Miss Valentine."

The closing of the door behind him left him in total darkness, but he hardly liked to return and ask Joan to reopen it in order to light him on his way. He was glad to be out of her presence. He was used to being looked at in an unfriendly way by his fellows, but there had been something in Joan's eyes that had curiously discomfited him.

R. Jones groped his way down, relieved that all was over and had ended well. He believed what she had told him, and he could conscientiously assure Freddie that the prospect of his sharing the fate of poor old Percy was nonexistent. It is true that he proposed to add in his report that the destruction of the letters had been purchased with difficulty, at a cost of just five hundred pounds; but that was a mere business formality.

He had almost reached the last step when there was a ring at the front door. With what he was afterward wont to call an inspiration, he retreated with unusual nimbleness until he had almost reached Joan's door again. Then he leaned over the banister and listened.

The disheveled maid opened the door. A girl's voice spoke:

"Is Miss Valentine in?"

"She's in; but she's engaged."

"I wish you would go up and tell her that I want to see her. Say it's Miss Peters—Miss Aline Peters."

The banister shook beneath R. Jones' sudden clutch. For a moment he felt almost faint. Then he began to think swiftly. A great light had dawned on him, and the thought outstanding in his mind was that never again would he trust a man or woman on the evidence of his senses. He could have sworn that this Valentine girl was on the level. He had been perfectly satisfied with her statement that she had destroyed the letters. And all the while she had been playing as deep a game as he had come across in the whole course of his professional career! He almost admired her. How she had taken him in!

It was obvious now what her game was. Previous to his visit she had arranged a meeting with Freddie's fiancee, with the view of opening negotiations for the sale of the letters. She had held him, Jones, at arm's length because she was going to sell the letters to whoever would pay the best price. But for the accident of his happening to be here when Miss Peters arrived, Freddie and his fiancee would have been bidding against each other and raising each other's price. He had worked the same game himself a dozen times, and he resented the entry of female competition into what he regarded as essentially a male field of enterprise.

As the maid stumped up the stairs he continued his retreat. He heard Joan's door open, and the stream of light showed him the disheveled maid standing in the doorway.

"Ow, I thought there was a gentleman with you, miss."

"He left a moment ago. Why?"

"There's a lady wants to see you. Miss Peters, her name is."

"Will you ask her to come up?"

The disheveled maid was no polished mistress of ceremonies. She leaned down into the void and hailed Aline.

"She says will you come up?"

Aline's feet became audible on the staircase. There were greetings.

"Whatever brings you here, Aline?"

"Am I interrupting you, Joan, dear?"

"No. Do come in! I was only surprised to see you so late. I didn't know you paid calls at this hour. Is anything wrong? Come in."

The door closed, the maid retired to the depths, and R. Jones stole cautiously down again. He was feeling absolutely bewildered. Apparently his deductions, his second thoughts, had been all wrong, and

Joan was, after all, the honest person he had imagined at first sight. Those two girls had talked to each other as though they were old friends; as though they had known each other all their lives. That was the thing which perplexed R. Jones.

With the tread of a red Indian, he approached the door and put his ear to it. He found he could hear quite comfortably.

Aline, meantime, inside the room, had begun to draw comfort from Joan's very appearance, she looked so capable.

Joan's eyes had changed the expression they had contained during the recent interview. They were soft now, with a softness that was half compassionate, half contemptuous. It is the compensation which life gives to those whom it has handled roughly in order that they shall be able to regard with a certain contempt the small troubles of the sheltered. Joan remembered Aline of old, and knew her for a perennial victim of small troubles. Even in their schooldays she had always needed to be looked after and comforted. Her sweet temper had seemed to invite the minor slings and arrows of fortune. Aline was a girl who inspired protectiveness in a certain type of her fellow human beings. It was this quality in her that kept George Emerson awake at nights; and it appealed to Joan now.

Joan, for whom life was a constant struggle to keep the wolf within a reasonable distance from the door, and who counted that day happy on which she saw her way clear to paying her weekly rent and possibly having a trifle over for some coveted hat or pair of shoes, could not help feeling, as she looked at Aline, that her own troubles were as nothing, and that the immediate need of the moment was to pet and comfort her friend. Her knowledge of Aline told her the probable tragedy was that she had lost a brooch or had been spoken to crossly by somebody; but it also told her that such tragedies bulked very large on Aline's horizon.

Trouble, after all, like beauty, is in the eye of the beholder; and Aline was far less able to endure with fortitude the loss of a brooch than she herself to bear the loss of a position the emoluments of which meant the difference between having just enough to eat and starving.

"You're worried about something," she said. "Sit down and tell me all about it."

Aline sat down and looked about her at the shabby room. By that curious process of the human mind which makes the spectacle of another's misfortune a palliative for one's own, she was feeling oddly comforted already. Her thoughts were not definite and she could not analyze them; but what they amounted to was that, though it was an unpleasant thing to be bullied by a dyspeptic father, the world manifestly held worse tribulations, which her father's other outstanding quality, besides dyspepsia—wealth, to wit—enabled her to avoid.

It was at this point that the dim beginnings of philosophy began to invade her mind. The thing resolved itself almost into an equation. If father had not had indigestion he would not have bullied her. But, if father had not made a fortune he would not have had indigestion. Therefore, if father had not made a fortune he would not have bullied her. Practically, in fact, if father did not bully her he would not be rich. And if he were not rich—

She took in the faded carpet, the stained wall paper and the soiled curtains with a comprehensive glance. It certainly cut both ways. She began to be a little ashamed of her misery.

"It's nothing at all; really," she said. "I think I've been making rather a fuss about very little."

Joan was relieved. The struggling life breeds moods of depression, and such a mood had come to her just before Aline's arrival. Life, at that moment, had seemed to stretch before her like a dusty, weary road, without hope. She was sick of fighting. She wanted money and ease, and a surcease from this perpetual race with the weekly bills. The mood had been the outcome partly of R. Jones' gentlemanly-veiled insinuations, but still more, though she did not realize it, of her yesterday's meeting with Aline.

Mr. Peters might be unguarded in his speech when conversing with his daughter—he might play the tyrant toward her in many ways; but he did not stint her in the matter of dress allowance, and, on the occasion when she met Joan, Aline had been wearing so Parisian a hat and a tailor-made suit of such obviously expensive simplicity that green-eyed envy had almost spoiled Joan's pleasure at meeting this friend of her opulent days.

She had suppressed the envy, and it had revenged itself by assaulting her afresh in the form of the worst fit of the blues she had had in two years.

She had been loyally ready to sink her depression in order to alleviate Aline's, but it was a distinct relief to find that the feat would not be necessary.

"Never mind," she said. "Tell me what the very little thing was."

"It was only father," said Aline simply.

Joan cast her mind back to the days of school and placed father as a rather irritable person, vaguely reputed to be something of an ogre in his home circle.

"Was he angry with you about something?" she asked.

"Not exactly angry with me; but—well, I was there."

Joan's depression lifted slightly. She had forgotten, in the stunning anguish of the sudden spectacle of that hat and that tailor-made suit, that Paris hats and hundred-and-twenty-dollar suits not infrequently had what the vulgar term a string attached to them. After all, she was independent. She might have to murder her beauty with hats and frocks that had never been nearer Paris than the Tottenham Court Road; but at least no one bullied her because she happened to be at hand when tempers were short.

"What a shame!" she said. "Tell me all about it."

With a prefatory remark that it was all so ridiculous, really, Aline embarked on the narrative of the afternoon's events.

Joan heard her out, checking a strong disposition to giggle. Her viewpoint was that of the average person, and the average person cannot see the importance of the scarab in the scheme of things. The opinion she formed of Mr. Peters was of his being an eccentric old gentleman, making a great to-do about nothing at all. Losses had to have a concrete value before they could impress Joan. It was beyond her to grasp that Mr. Peters would sooner have lost a diamond necklace, if he had happened to possess one, than his Cheops of the Fourth Dynasty.

It was not until Aline, having concluded her tale, added one more strand to it that she found herself treating the matter seriously.

"Father says he would give five thousand dollars to anyone who would get it back for him."

"What!"

The whole story took on a different complexion for Joan. Money talks. Mr. Peters' words might have been merely the rhetorical outburst of a heated moment; but, even discounting them, there seemed to remain a certain exciting substratum. A man who shouts that he will give five thousand dollars for a thing may very well mean he will give five hundred, and Joan's finances were perpetually in a condition which makes five hundred dollars a sum to be gasped at.

"He wasn't serious, surely!"

"I think he was," said Aline.

"But five thousand dollars!"

"It isn't really very much to father, you know. He gave away a hundred thousand a year ago to a university."

"But for a grubby little scarab!"

"You don't understand how father loves his scarabs. Since he retired from business, he has been simply wrapped up in them. You know collectors are like that. You read in the papers about men giving all sorts of money for funny things."

Outside the door R. Jones, his ear close to the panel, drank in all these things greedily. He would have been willing to remain in that attitude indefinitely in return for this kind of special information; but just as Aline said these words a door opened on the floor above, and somebody came out, whistling, and began to descend the stairs.

R. Jones stood not on the order of his going. He was down in the hall and fumbling with the handle of the front door with an agility of which few casual observers of his dimensions would have deemed him capable. The next moment he was out in the street, walking calmly toward Leicester Square, pondering over what he had heard.

Much of R. Jones' substantial annual income was derived from pondering over what he had heard.

In the room Joan was looking at Aline with the distended eyes of one who sees visions or has inspirations. She got up. There are occasions when one must speak standing.

"Then you mean to say that your father would really give five thousand dollars to anyone who got this thing back for him?"

"I am sure he would. But who could do it?"

"I could," said Joan. "And what is more, I'm going to!"

Aline stared at her helplessly. In their schooldays, Joan had always swept her off her feet. Then, she had always had the feeling that with Joan nothing was impossible. Heroine worship, like hero worship, dies hard. She looked at Joan now with the stricken sensation of one who has inadvertently set powerful machinery in motion.

"But, Joan!" It was all she could say.

"My dear child, it's perfectly simple. This earl of yours has taken the thing off to his castle, like a brigand. You say you are going down there on Friday for a visit. All you have to do is to take me along with you, and sit back and watch me get busy."

"But, Joan!"

"Where's the difficulty?"

"I don't see how I could take you down very well."

"Why not?"

"Oh, I don't know."

"But what is your objection?"

"Well—don't you see?—if you went down there as a friend of mine and were caught stealing the scarab, there would be just the trouble father wants to avoid—about my engagement, you see, and so on."

It was an aspect of the matter that had escaped Joan. She frowned thoughtfully.

"I see. Yes, there is that; but there must be a way."

"You mustn't, Joan—really! don't think any more about it."

"Not think any more about it! My child, do you even faintly realize what five thousand dollars—or a quarter of five thousand dollars—means to me? I would do anything for it—anything! And there's the fun of it. I don't suppose you can realize that, either. I want a change. I've been grubbing away here on nothing a week for years, and it's time I had a vacation. There must be a way by which you could get me down—Why, of course! Why didn't I think of it before! You shall take me on Friday as your lady's maid!"

"But, Joan, I couldn't!"

"Why not?"

"I—I couldn't."

"Why not?"

"Oh, well!"

Joan advanced on her where she sat and grasped her firmly by the shoulders. Her face was inflexible.

"Aline, my pet, it's no good arguing. You might just as well argue with a wolf on the trail of a fat Russian peasant. I need that money. I need it in my business. I need it worse than anybody has ever needed anything. And I'm going to have it! From now on, until further notice, I am your lady's maid. You can give your present one a holiday."

Aline met her eyes waveringly. The spirit of the old schooldays, when nothing was impossible where Joan was concerned, had her in its grip. Moreover, the excitement of the scheme began to attract her.

"But, Joan," she said, "you know it's simply ridiculous. You could never pass as a lady's maid. The other servants would find you out. I expect there are all sorts of things a lady's maid has got to do and not do."

"My dear Aline, I know them all. You can't stump me on below-stairs etiquette. I've been a lady's maid!"

"Joan!"

"It's quite true—three years ago, when I was more than usually impecunious. The wolf was glued to the door like a postage stamp; so I answered an advertisement and became a lady's maid."

"You seem to have done everything."

"I have—pretty nearly. It's all right for you idle rich, Aline—you can sit still and contemplate life; but we poor working girls have got to hustle."

Aline laughed.

"You know, you always could make me do anything you wanted in the old days, Joan. I suppose I have got to look on this as quite settled now?"

"Absolutely settled! Oh, Aline, there's one thing you must remember: Don't call me Joan when I'm down at the castle. You must call me Valentine."

She paused. The recollection of the Honorable Freddie had come to her. No; Valentine would not do!

"No; not Valentine," she went on—"it's too jaunty. I used it once years ago, but it never sounded just right. I want something more respectable, more suited to my position. Can't you suggest something?"

Aline pondered.

"Simpson?"

"Simpson! It's exactly right. You must practice it. Simpson! Say it kindly and yet distantly, as though I were a worm, but a worm for whom you felt a mild liking. Roll it round your tongue."

"Simpson."

"Splendid! Now once again—a little more haughtily."

"Simpson—Simpson—Simpson."

Joan regarded her with affectionate approval.

"It's wonderful!" she said. "You might have been doing it all your life."

"What are you laughing at?" asked Aline.

"Nothing," said Joan. "I was just thinking of something. There's a young man who lives on the floor above this, and I was lecturing him yesterday on enterprise. I told him to go and find something exciting to do. I wonder what he would say if he knew how thoroughly I am going to practice what I preach!"

CHAPTER IV

In the morning following Aline's visit to Joan Valentine, Ashe sat in his room, the Morning Post on the table before him. The heady influence of Joan had not yet ceased to work within him; and he proposed, in pursuance of his promise to her, to go carefully through the columns of advertisements, however pessimistic he might feel concerning the utility of that action.

His first glance assured him that the vast fortunes of the philanthropists, whose acquaintance he had already made in print, were not yet exhausted. Brian MacNeill still dangled his gold before the public; so did Angus Bruce; so did Duncan Macfarlane and Wallace Mackintosh and Donald MacNab. They still had the money and they still wanted to give it away.

Ashe was reading listlessly down the column when, from the mass of advertisements, one of an unusual sort detached itself.

WANTED: Young Man of good appearance, who is poor and reckless, to undertake a delicate and dangerous enterprise. Good pay for the right man. Apply between the hours of ten and twelve at offices of Mainprice, Mainprice & Boole, 3, Denvers Street, Strand.

And as he read it, half past ten struck on the little clock on his mantelpiece. It was probably this fact that decided Ashe. If he had been compelled to postpone his visit to the offices of Messrs. Mainprice, Mainprice & Boole until the afternoon, it is possible that barriers of laziness might have reared themselves in the path of adventure; for Ashe, an adventurer at heart, was also uncommonly lazy. As it was, however, he could make an immediate start.

Pausing but to put on his shoes, and having satisfied himself by a glance in the mirror that his appearance was reasonably good, he seized his hat, shot out of the narrow mouth of Arundell Street like a shell, and scrambled into a taxicab, with the feeling that—short of murder—they could not make it too delicate and dangerous for him.

He was conscious of strange thrills. This, he told himself, was the only possible mode of life with spring in the air. He had always been partial to those historical novels in which the characters are perpetually vaulting on chargers and riding across country on perilous errands. This leaping into taxicabs to answer stimulating advertisements in the Morning Post was very much the same sort of thing. It was with fine fervor animating him that he entered the gloomy offices of Mainprice, Mainprice & Boole. His brain was afire and he felt ready for anything.

"I have come in ans—" he began, to the diminutive office boy, who seemed to be the nearest thing visible to a Mainprice or a Boole.

"Siddown. Gottatakeyerturn," said the office boy; and for the first time Ashe perceived that the anteroom in which he stood was crowded to overflowing.

This, in the circumstances, was something of a damper. He had pictured himself, during his ride in the cab, striding into the office and saying. "The delicate and dangerous enterprise. Lead me to it!" He had not realized until now that he was not the only man in London who read the advertisement columns of the Morning Post, and for an instant his heart sank at the sight of all this competition. A second and more comprehensive glance at his rivals gave him confidence.

The Wanted column of the morning paper is a sort of dredger, which churns up strange creatures from the mud of London's underworld. Only in response to the dredger's operations do they come to the surface in such numbers as to be noticeable, for as a rule they are of a solitary habit and shun company; but when they do come they bring with them something of the horror of the depths.

It is the saddest spectacle in the world—that of the crowd collected by a Wanted advertisement. They are so palpably not wanted by anyone for any purpose whatsoever; yet every time they gather together with a sort of hopeful hopelessness. What they were originally—the units of these collections—Heaven knows. Fate has battered out of them every trace of individuality. Each now is exactly like his neighbor—no worse; no better.

Ashe, as he sat and watched them, was filled with conflicting emotions. One-half of him, thrilled with the glamour of adventure, was chafing at the delay, and resentful of these poor creatures as of so many obstacles to the beginning of all the brisk and exciting things that lay behind the mysterious brevity of the advertisement; the other, pitifully alive to the tragedy of the occasion, was grateful for the delay.

On the whole, he was glad to feel that if one of these derelicts did not secure the "good pay for the right man," it would not be his fault. He had been the last to arrive, and he would be the last to pass through that door, which was the gateway of adventure—the door with Mr. Boole inscribed on its ground glass, behind which sat the author of the mysterious request for assistance, interviewing applicants. It would be through their own shortcomings—not because of his superior attractions—if they failed to please that unseen arbiter.

That they were so failing was plain. Scarcely had one scarred victim of London's unkindness passed through before the bell would ring; the office boy, who, in the intervals of frowning sternly on the throng, as much as to say that he would stand no nonsense, would cry, "Next!" and another dull-eyed wreck would drift through, to be followed a moment later by yet another. The one fact at present ascertainable concerning the unknown searcher for reckless young men of good appearance was that he appeared to be possessed of considerable decision of character, a man who did not take long to make up his mind. He was rejecting applicants now at the rate of two a minute.

Expeditious though he was, he kept Ashe waiting for a considerable time. It was not until the hands of the fat clock over the door pointed to twenty minutes past eleven that the office boy's "Next!" found him the only survivor. He gave his clothes a hasty smack with the palm of his hand and his hair a fleeting dab to accentuate his good appearance, and turned the handle of the door of fate.

The room assigned by the firm to their Mr. Boole for his personal use was a small and dingy compartment, redolent of that atmosphere of desolation which lawyers alone know how to achieve. It gave the impression of not having been swept since the foundation of the firm, in the year 1786. There was one small window, covered with grime. It was one of those windows you see only in lawyers' offices. Possibly some reckless Mainprice or harebrained Boole had opened it in a fit of mad excitement induced by the news of the Battle of Waterloo, in 1815, and had been instantly expelled from the firm. Since then, no one had dared to tamper with it.

Gazing through this window—or, rather, gazing at it, for X-rays could hardly have succeeded in actually penetrating the alluvial deposits on the glass—was a little man. As Ashe entered, he turned and looked at him as though he hurt him rather badly in some tender spot.

Ashe was obliged to own to himself that he felt a little nervous. It is not every day that a young man of good appearance, who has led a quiet life, meets face to face one who is prepared to pay him well for doing something delicate and dangerous. To Ashe the sensation was entirely novel. The most delicate and dangerous act he had performed to date had been the daily mastication of Mrs. Bell's breakfast—included in the rent. Yes, he had to admit it—he was nervous: and the fact that he was nervous made him hot and uncomfortable.

To judge him by his appearance, the man at the window was also hot and uncomfortable. He was a little, truculent-looking man, and his face at present was red with a flush that sat unnaturally on a normally lead-colored face. His eyes looked out from under thick gray eyebrows with an almost tortured expression. This was partly owing to the strain of interviewing Ashe's preposterous predecessors, but principally to the fact that the little man had suddenly been seized with acute indigestion, a malady to which he was peculiarly subject.

He removed from his mouth the black cigar he was smoking, inserted a digestive tabloid, and replaced the cigar. Then he concentrated his attention on Ashe. As he did so the hostile expression of his face became modified. He looked surprised and—grudgingly—pleased.

"Well, what do you want?" he said.

"I came in answer to—"

"In answer to my advertisement? I had given up hope of seeing anything part human. I thought you must be one of the clerks. You're certainly more like what I advertised for. Of all the seedy bunches of dead beats I ever struck, the aggregation I've just been interviewing was the seediest! When I spend good money in advertising for a young man of good appearance, I want a young man of good appearance—not a tramp of fifty-five."

Ashe was sorry for his predecessors, but he was bound to admit that they certainly had corresponded somewhat faithfully to the description just given. The comparative cordiality of his own reception removed the slight nervousness that had been troubling him. He began to feel confident—almost jaunty.

"I'm through," said the little man wearily. "I've had enough of interviewing applicants. You're the last one I'll see. Are there any more hobos outside?"

"Not when I came in."

"Then we'll get down to business. I'll tell you what I want done, and if you are willing you can do it; if you are not willing you can leave it—and go to the devil! Sit down."

Ashe sat down. He resented the little man's tone, but this was not the moment for saying so. His companion scrutinized him narrowly.

"So far as appearance goes," he said, "you are what I want." Ashe felt inclined to bow. "Whoever takes on this job has got to act as my valet, and you look like a valet." Ashe felt less inclined to bow.

"You're tall and thin and ordinary-looking. Yes; so far as appearance goes, you fill the bill."

It seemed to Ashe that it was time to correct an impression the little man appeared to have formed.

"I am afraid," he said, "if all you want is a valet, you will have to look elsewhere. I got the idea from your advertisement that something rather more exciting was in the air. I can recommend you to several good employment agencies if you wish." He rose. "Good-morning!" he said.

He would have liked to fling the massive pewter inkwell at this little creature who had so keenly disappointed him.

"Sit down!" snapped the other.

Ashe resumed his seat. The hope of adventure dies hard on a Spring morning when one is twenty-six, and he had the feeling that there was more to come.

"Don't be a damned fool!" said the little man. "Of course I'm not asking you to be a valet and nothing else."

"You would want me to do some cooking and plain sewing on the side, perhaps?"

Their eyes met in a hostile glare. The flush on the little man's face deepened.

"Are you trying to get fresh with me?" he demanded dangerously.

"Yes," said Ashe.

The answer seemed to disconcert his adversary. He was silent for a moment.

"Well," he said at last, "maybe it's all for the best. If you weren't full of gall probably you wouldn't have come here at all; and whoever takes on this job of mine has got to have gall if he has nothing else. I think we shall suit each other."

"What is the job?"

The little man's face showed doubt and perplexity.

"It's awkward. If I'm to make the thing clear to you I've got to trust you. And I don't know a thing about you. I wish I had thought of that before I inserted the advertisement."

Ashe appreciated the difficulty.

"Couldn't you make an A—B case out of it?"

"Maybe I could if I knew what an A—B case was."

"Call the people mixed up in it A and B."

"And forget, halfway through, who was which! No; I guess I'll have to trust you."

"I'll play square."

The little man fastened his eyes on Ashe's in a piercing stare. Ashe met them smilingly. His spirits, always fairly cheerful, had risen high by now. There was something about the little man, in spite of his brusqueness and ill temper, which made him feel flippant.

"Pure white!" said Ashe.

"Eh?"

"My soul! And this"—he thumped the left section of his waistcoat—"solid gold. You may fire when ready, Gridley. Proceed, professor."

"I don't know where to begin."

"Without presuming to dictate, why not at the beginning?"

"It's all so darned complicated that I don't rightly know which is the beginning. Well, see here . . . I collect scarabs. I'm crazy about scarabs. Ever since I quit business, you might say that I have practically lived for scarabs."

"Though it sounds like an unkind thing to say of anyone," said Ashe. "Incidentally, what are scarabs?" He held up his hand. "Wait! It all comes back to me. Expensive classical education, now bearing belated fruit. Scarabaeus—Latin; noun, nominative—a beetle. Scarabaee—vocative—O you beetle!

Scarabaeum— accusative—the beetle. Scarabaei—of the beetle. Scarabaeo—to or for the beetle. I remember now. Egypt—Rameses—pyramids— sacred scarabs! Right!"

"Well, I guess I've gotten together the best collection of scarabs outside the British Museum, and some of them are worth what you like to me. I don't reckon money when it comes to a question of my scarabs. Do you understand?"

"Sure, Mike!"

Displeasure clouded the little man's face.

"My name is not Mike."

"I used the word figuratively, as it were."

"Well, don't do it again. My name is J. Preston Peters, and Mr. Peters will do as well as anything else when you want to attract my attention."

"Mine is Marson. You were saying, Mr. Peters—?"

"Well, it's this way," said the little man.

Shakespeare and Pope have both emphasized the tediousness of a twice-told tale; the Episode Of the Stolen Scarab need not be repeated at this point, though it must be admitted that Mr. Peters' version of it differed considerably from the calm, dispassionate description the author, in his capacity of official historian, has given earlier in the story.

In Mr. Peters' version the Earl of Emsworth appeared as a smooth and purposeful robber, a sort of elderly Raffles, worming his way into the homes of the innocent, and only sparing that portion of their property which was too heavy for him to carry away. Mr. Peters, indeed, specifically described the Earl of Emsworth as an oily old second-story man.

It took Ashe some little time to get a thorough grasp of the tangled situation; but he did it at last.

Only one point perplexed him.

"You want to hire somebody to go to this castle and get this scarab back for you. I follow that. But why must he go as your valet?"

"That's simple enough. You don't think I'm asking him to buy a black mask and break in, do you? I'm making it as easy for him as possible. I can't take a secretary down to the castle, for everybody knows that, now I've retired, I haven't got a secretary; and if I engaged a new one and he was caught trying to steal my scarab from the earl's collection, it would look suspicious. But a valet is different. Anyone can get fooled by a crook valet with bogus references."

"I see. There's just one other point: Suppose your accomplice does get caught—what then?"

"That," said Mr. Peters, "is the catch; and it's just because of that I am offering good pay to my man. We'll suppose, for the sake of argument, that you accept the contract and get caught. Well, if that happens you've got to look after yourself. I couldn't say a word. If I did it would all come out, and so far as the breaking off of my daughter's engagement to young Threepwood is concerned, it would be just as bad as though I had tried to get the thing back myself.

"You've got to bear that in mind. You've got to remember it if you forget everything else. I don't appear in this business in any way whatsoever. If you get caught you take what's coming to you without a word. You can't turn round and say: 'I am innocent. Mr. Peters will explain all'—because Mr. Peters certainly won't. Mr. Peters won't utter a syllable of protest if they want to hang you.

"No; if you go into this, young man, you go into it with your eyes open. You go into it with a full understanding of the risks—because you think the reward, if you are successful, makes the taking of those risks worth while. You and I know that what you are doing isn't really stealing; it's simply a tactful way of getting back my own property. But the judge and jury will have different views."

"I am beginning to understand," said Ashe thoughtfully, "why you called the job delicate and dangerous."

Certainly it had been no overstatement. As a writer of detective stories for the British office boy, he had imagined in his time many undertakings that might be so described, but few to which the description was more admirably suited.

"It is," said Mr. Peters; "and that is why I'm offering good pay. Whoever carries this job through gets one thousand pounds." Ashe started.

"One thousand pounds—five thousand dollars!"

"Five thousand."

"When do I begin?"

"You'll do it?"

"For five thousand dollars I certainly will."

"With your eyes open?"

"Wide open!"

A look of positive geniality illuminated Mr. Peters' pinched features. He even went so far as to pat Ashe on the shoulder.

"Good boy!" he said. "Meet me at Paddington Station at four o'clock on Friday. And if there's anything more you want to know come round to this address."

There remained the telling of Joan Valentine; for it was obviously impossible not to tell her. When you have revolutionized your life at the bidding of another you cannot well conceal the fact, as though nothing had happened. Ashe had not the slightest desire to conceal the fact. On the contrary, he was glad to have such a capital excuse for renewing the acquaintance.

He could not tell her, of course, the secret details of the thing. Naturally those must remain hidden. No, he would just go airily in and say:

"You know what you told me about doing something new? Well, I've just got a job as a valet."

So he went airily in and said it.

"To whom?" said Joan.

"To a man named Peters—an American."

Women are trained from infancy up to conceal their feelings. Joan did not start or otherwise express emotion.

"Not Mr. J. Preston Peters?"

"Yes. Do you know him? What a remarkable thing."

"His daughter," said Joan, "has just engaged me as a lady's maid."

"What!"

"It will not be quite the same thing as three years ago," Joan explained. "It is just a cheap way of getting a holiday. I used to know Miss Peters very well, you see. It will be more like traveling as her guest."

"But—but—" Ashe had not yet overcome his amazement.

"Yes?"

"But what an extraordinary coincidence!"

"Yes. By the way, how did you get the situation? And what put it into your head to be a valet at all? It seems such a curious thing for you to think of doing."

Ashe was embarrassed.

"I—I—well, you see, the experience will be useful to me, of course, in my writing."

"Oh! Are you thinking of taking up my line of work? Dukes?"

"No, no—not exactly that."

"It seems so odd. How did you happen to get in touch with Mr. Peters?"

"Oh, I answered an advertisement."

"I see."

Ashe was becoming conscious of an undercurrent of something not altogether agreeable in the conversation. It lacked the gay ease of their first interview. He was not apprehensive lest she might have guessed his secret. There was, he felt, no possible means by which she could have done that. Yet the fact remained that those keen blue eyes of hers were looking at him in a peculiar and penetrating manner. He felt damped.

"It will be nice, being together," he said feebly.

"Very!" said Joan.

There was a pause.

"I thought I would come and tell you."

"Quite so."

There was another pause.

"It seems so funny that you should be going out as a lady's maid."

"Yes?"

"But, of course, you have done it before."

"Yes."

"The really extraordinary thing is that we should be going to the same people."

"Yes."

"It—it's remarkable, isn't it?"

"Yes."

Ashe reflected. No; he did not appear to have any further remarks to make.

"Good-by for the present," he said.

"Good-by."

Ashe drifted out. He was conscious of a wish that he understood girls. Girls, in his opinion, were odd.

When he had gone Joan Valentine hurried to the door and, having opened it an inch, stood listening. When the sound of his door closing came to her she ran down the stairs and out into Arundell Street. She went to the Hotel Mathis.

"I wonder," she said to the sad-eyed waiter, "if you have a copy of the Morning Post?"

The waiter, a child of romantic Italy, was only too anxious to oblige youth and beauty. He disappeared and presently returned with a crumpled copy. Joan thanked him with a bright smile.

Back in her room, she turned to the advertisement pages. She knew that life was full of what the unthinking call coincidences; but the miracle of Ashe having selected by chance the father of Aline Peters as an employer was too much of a coincidence for her. Suspicion furrowed her brow.

It did not take her long to discover the advertisement that had sent Ashe hurrying in a taxicab to the offices of Messrs. Mainprice, Mainprice & Boole. She had been looking for something of the kind.

She read it through twice and smiled. Everything was very clear to her. She looked at the ceiling above her and shook her head.

"You are quite a nice young man, Mr. Marson," she said softly; "but you mustn't try to jump my claim. I dare say you need that money too; but I'm afraid you must go without. I am going to have it—and nobody else!"

CHAPTER V

The four-fifteen express slid softly out of Paddington Station and Ashe Marson settled himself in the corner seat of his second-class compartment. Opposite him Joan Valentine had begun to read a magazine. Along the corridor, in a first-class smoking compartment, Mr. Peters was lighting a big black cigar. Still farther along the corridor, in a first-class non-smoking compartment, Aline Peters looked through the window and thought of many things.

In English trains the tipping classes travel first; valets, lady's maids, footmen, nurses, and head stillroom maids, second; and housemaids, grooms, and minor and inferior stillroom maids, third. But for these social distinctions, the whole fabric of society would collapse and anarchy stalk naked through the land—as in the United States.

Ashe was feeling remarkably light-hearted. He wished he had not bought Joan that magazine and thus deprived himself temporarily of the pleasure of her conversation; but that was the only flaw in his happiness. With the starting of the train, which might be considered the formal and official beginning of the delicate and dangerous enterprise on which he had embarked, he had definitely come to the conclusion that the life adventurous was the life for him. He had frequently suspected this to be the case, but it had required the actual experiment to bring certainty.

Almost more than physical courage, the ideal adventurer needs a certain lively inquisitiveness, the quality of not being content to mind his own affairs; and in Ashe this quality was highly developed. From boyhood up he had always been interested in things that were none of his business. And it is just that attribute which the modern young man, as a rule, so sadly lacks.

The modern young man may do adventurous things if they are thrust on him; but left to himself he will edge away uncomfortably and look in the other direction when the goddess of adventure smiles at him. Training and tradition alike pluck at his sleeve and urge him not to risk making himself ridiculous. And from sheer horror of laying himself open to the charge of not minding his own business he falls into a stolid disregard of all that is out of the ordinary and exciting. He tells himself that the shriek from the lonely house he passed just now was only the high note of some amateur songstress, and that the maiden in distress whom he saw pursued by the ruffian with a knife was merely earning the salary paid her by some motion-picture firm. And he proceeds on his way, looking neither to left nor right.

Ashe had none of this degenerate coyness toward adventure. Though born within easy distance of Boston and deposited by circumstances in London, he possessed, nevertheless, to a remarkable degree, that quality so essentially the property of the New Yorker—the quality known, for want of a more polished word, as rubber. It is true that it had needed the eloquence of Joan Valentine to stir him from his groove; but that was because he was also lazy. He loved new sights and new experiences. Yes; he was happy. The rattle of the train shaped itself into a lively march. He told himself that he had found the right occupation for a young man in the Spring.

Joan, meantime, intrenched behind her magazine, was also busy with her thoughts. She was not reading the magazine; she held it before her as a protection, knowing that if she laid it down Ashe would begin to talk. And just at present she had no desire for conversation. She, like Ashe, was contemplating the immediate future, but, unlike him, was not doing so with much pleasure. She was regretting heartily that she had not resisted the temptation to uplift this young man and wishing that she had left him to wallow in the slothful peace in which she had found him.

It is curious how frequently in this world our attempts to stimulate and uplift swoop back on us and smite us like boomerangs. Ashe's presence was the direct outcome of her lecture on enterprise, and it added a complication to an already complicated venture.

She did her best to be fair to Ashe. It was not his fault that he was about to try to deprive her of five thousand dollars, which she looked on as her personal property; but illogically she found herself feeling a little hostile.

She glanced furtively at him over the magazine, choosing by ill chance a moment when he had just directed his gaze at her. Their eyes met and there was nothing for it but to talk; so she tucked away her hostility in a corner of her mind, where she could find it again when she wanted it, and prepared for the time being to be friendly. After all, except for the fact that he was her rival, this was a pleasant and amusing young man, and one for whom, until he made the announcement that had changed her whole attitude toward him, she had entertained a distinct feeling of friendship—nothing warmer.

There was something about him that made her feel that she would have liked to stroke his hair in a motherly way and straighten his tie, and have cozy chats with him in darkened rooms by the light of open fires, and make him tell her his inmost thoughts, and stimulate him to do something really worth while with his life; but this, she held, was merely the instinct of a generous nature to be kind and helpful even to a comparative stranger.

"Well, Mr. Marson," she said, "Here we are!"

"Exactly what I was thinking," said Ashe.

He was conscious of a marked increase in the exhilaration the starting of the expedition had brought to him. At the back of his mind he realized there had been all along a kind of wistful resentment at the change in this girl's manner toward him. During the brief conversation when he had told her of his having secured his present situation, and later, only a few minutes back, on the platform of Paddington Station, he had sensed a coldness, a certain hostility—so different from her pleasant friendliness at their first meeting.

She had returned now to her earlier manner and he was surprised at the difference it made. He felt somehow younger, more alive. The lilt of the train's rattle changed to a gay ragtime. This was curious, because Joan was nothing more than a friend. He was not in love with her. One does not fall in love with a girl whom one has met only three times. One is attracted—yes; but one does not fall in love.

A moment's reflection enabled him to diagnose his sensations correctly. This odd impulse to leap across the compartment and kiss Joan was not love. It was merely the natural desire of a good-hearted young man to be decently chummy with his species.

"Well, what do you think of it all, Mr. Marson?" said Joan. "Are you sorry or glad that you let me persuade you to do this perfectly mad thing? I feel responsible for you, you know. If it had not been for me you would have been comfortably in Arundell Street, writing your Wand of Death."

"I'm glad."

"You don't feel any misgivings now that you are actually committed to domestic service?"

"Not one."

Joan, against her will, smiled approval on this uncompromising attitude. This young man might be her rival, but his demeanor on the eve of perilous times appealed to her. That was the spirit she liked and admired—that reckless acceptance of whatever might come. It was the spirit in which she herself had gone into the affair and she was pleased to find that it animated Ashe also—though, to be sure, it had its drawbacks. It made his rivalry the more dangerous. This reflection injected a touch of the old hostility into her manner.

"I wonder whether you will continue to feel so brave."

"What do you mean?"

Joan perceived that she was in danger of going too far. She had no wish to unmask Ashe at the expense of revealing her own secret. She must resist the temptation to hint that she had discovered his.

"I meant," she said quickly, "that from what I have seen of him Mr. Peters seems likely to be a rather trying man to work for."

Ashe's face cleared. For a moment he had almost suspected that she had guessed his errand.

"Yes. I imagine he will be. He is what you might call quick-tempered. He has dyspepsia, you know."

"I know."

"What he wants is plenty of fresh air and no cigars, and a regular course of those Larsen Exercises that amused you so much."

Joan laughed.

"Are you going to try and persuade Mr. Peters to twist himself about like that? Do let me see it if you do."

"I wish I could."

"Do suggest it to him."

"Don't you think he would resent it from a valet?"

"I keep forgetting that you are a valet. You look so unlike one."

"Old Peters didn't think so. He rather complimented me on my appearance. He said I was ordinary-looking."

"I shouldn't have called you that. You look so very strong and fit."

"Surely there are muscular valets?"

"Well, yes; I suppose there are."

Ashe looked at her. He was thinking that never in his life had he seen a girl so amazingly pretty. What it was that she had done to herself was beyond him; but something, some trick of dress, had given her a touch of the demure that made her irresistible. She was dressed in sober black, the ideal background for her fairness.

"While on the subject," he said, "I suppose you know you don't look in the least like a lady's maid? You look like a disguised princess."

She laughed.

"That's very nice of you, Mr. Marson, but you're quite wrong. Anyone could tell I was a lady's maid, a mile away. You aren't criticizing the dress, surely?"

"The dress is all right. It's the general effect. I don't think your expression is right. It's—it's—there's too much attack in it. You aren't meek enough."

Joan's eyes opened wide.

"Meek! Have you ever seen an English lady's maid, Mr. Marson?"

"Why, no; now that I come to think of it, I don't believe I have."

"Well, let me tell you that meekness is her last quality. Why should she be meek? Doesn't she go in after the groom of the chambers?"

"Go in? Go in where?"

"In to dinner." She smiled at the sight of his bewildered face. "I'm afraid you don't know much about the etiquette of the new world you have entered so rashly. Didn't you know that the rules of precedence among the servants of a big house in England are more rigid and complicated than in English society?"

"You're joking!"

"I'm not joking. You try going in to dinner out of your proper place when we get to Blandings and see what happens. A public rebuke from the butler is the least you could expect."

A bead of perspiration appeared on Ashe's forehead.

"Heavens!" he whispered. "If a butler publicly rebuked me I think I should commit suicide. I couldn't survive it."

He stared, with fallen jaw, into the abyss of horror into which he had leaped so light-heartedly. The servant problem, on this large scale, had been nonexistent for him until now. In the days of his youth, at Mayling, Massachusetts, his needs had been ministered to by a muscular Swede. Later, at Oxford, there had been his "scout" and his bed maker, harmless persons both, provided you locked up your whisky. And in London, his last phase, a succession of servitors of the type of the disheveled maid at Number Seven had tended him.

That, dotted about the land of his adoption, there were houses in which larger staffs of domestics were maintained, he had been vaguely aware. Indeed, in "Gridley Quayle, Investigator; the Adventure of the Missing Marquis"—number four of the series—he had drawn a picture of the home life of a duke, in which a butler and two powdered footmen had played their parts; but he had had no idea that rigid and complicated rules of etiquette swayed the private lives of these individuals. If he had given the matter a thought he had supposed that when the dinner hour arrived the butler and the two footmen would troop into the kitchen and squash in at the table wherever they found room.

"Tell me," he said. "Tell me all you know. I feel as though I had escaped a frightful disaster."

"You probably have. I don't suppose there is anything so terrible as a snub from a butler."

"If there is I can't think of it. When I was at Oxford I used to go and stay with a friend of mine who had a butler that looked like a Roman emperor in swallowtails. He terrified me. I used to grovel to the man. Please give me all the pointers you can."

"Well, as Mr. Peters' valet, I suppose you will be rather a big man."

"I shan't feel it."

"However large the house party is, Mr. Peters is sure to be the principal guest; so your standing will be correspondingly magnificent. You come after the butler, the housekeeper, the groom of the chambers, Lord Emsworth's valet, Lady Ann Warblington's lady's maid—"

"Who is she?"

"Lady Ann? Lord Emsworth's sister. She has lived with him since his wife died. What was I saying? Oh, yes! After them come the honorable Frederick Threepwood's valet and myself—and then you."

"I'm not so high up then, after all?"

"Yes, you are. There's a whole crowd who come after you. It all depends on how many other guests there are besides Mr. Peters."

"I suppose I charge in at the head of a drove of housemaids and scullery maids?"

"My dear Mr. Marson, if a housemaid or a scullery maid tried to get into the steward's room and have her meals with us, she would be—"

"Rebuked by the butler?"

"Lynched, I should think. Kitchen maids and scullery maids eat in the kitchen. Chauffeurs, footmen, under-butler, pantry boys, hall boy, odd man and steward's-room footman take their meals in the servants' hall, waited on by the hall boy. The stillroom maids have breakfast and tea in the stillroom, and dinner and supper in the hall. The housemaids and nursery maids have breakfast and tea in the housemaid's sitting-room, and dinner and supper in the hall. The head housemaid ranks next to the head stillroom maid. The laundry maids have a place of their own near the laundry, and the head laundry maid ranks above the head housemaid. The chef has his meals in a room of his own near the kitchen. Is there anything else I can tell you, Mr. Marson?"

Ashe was staring at her with vacant eyes. He shook his head dumbly.

"We stop at Swindon in half an hour," said Joan softly. "Don't you think you would be wise to get out there and go straight back to London, Mr. Marson? Think of all you would avoid!"

Ashe found speech.

"It's a nightmare!"

"You would be far happier in Arundell Street. Why don't you get out at Swindon and go back?"

Ashe shook his head.

"I can't. There's—there's a reason."

Joan picked up her magazine again. Hostility had come out from the corner into which she had tucked it away and was once more filling her mind. She knew it was illogical, but she could not help it. For a moment, during her revelations of servants' etiquette, she had allowed herself to hope that she had frightened her rival out of the field, and the disappointment made her feel irritable. She buried herself in a short story, and countered Ashe's attempts at renewing the conversation with cold monosyllables, until he ceased his efforts and fell into a moody silence.

He was feeling hurt and angry. Her sudden coldness, following on the friendliness with which she had talked so long, puzzled and infuriated him. He felt as though he had been snubbed, and for no reason.

He resented the defensive magazine, though he had bought it for her himself. He resented her attitude of having ceased to recognize his existence. A sadness, a filmy melancholy, crept over him. He brooded on the unutterable silliness of humanity, especially the female portion of it, in erecting artificial barriers to friendship. It was so unreasonable.

At their first meeting, when she might have been excused for showing defensiveness, she had treated him with unaffected ease. When that meeting had ended there was a tacit understanding between them that all the preliminary awkwardnesses of the first stages of acquaintanceship were to be considered as having been passed; and that when they met again, if they ever did, it would be as friends. And here she was, luring him on with apparent friendliness, and then withdrawing into herself as though he had presumed.

A rebellious spirit took possession of him. He didn't care! Let her be cold and distant. He would show her that she had no monopoly of those qualities. He would not speak to her until she spoke to him; and when she spoke to him he would freeze her with his courteous but bleakly aloof indifference.

The train rattled on. Joan read her magazine. Silence reigned in the second-class compartment. Swindon was reached and passed. Darkness fell on the land. The journey began to seem interminable to Ashe; but presently there came a creaking of brakes and the train jerked itself to another stop. A voice on the platform made itself heard, calling:

"Market Blandings! Market Blandings Station!"

The village of Market Blandings is one of those sleepy English hamlets that modern progress has failed to touch; except by the addition of a railroad station and a room over the grocer's shop where moving pictures are on view on Tuesdays and Fridays. The church is Norman and the intelligence of the majority of the natives Paleozoic. To alight at Market Blandings Station in the dusk of a rather chilly Spring day, when the southwest wind has shifted to due east and the thrifty inhabitants have not yet lit their windows, is to be smitten with the feeling that one is at the edge of the world with no friends near.

Ashe, as he stood beside Mr. Peters' baggage and raked the unsympathetic darkness with a dreary eye, gave himself up to melancholy. Above him an oil lamp shed a meager light. Along the platform a small but sturdy porter was juggling with a milk can. The east wind explored Ashe's system with chilly fingers.

Somewhere out in the darkness into which Mr. Peters and Aline had already vanished in a large automobile, lay the castle, with its butler and its fearful code of etiquette. Soon the cart that was to convey him and the trunks thither would be arriving. He shivered.

Out of the gloom and into the feeble rays of the oil lamp came Joan Valentine. She had been away, tucking Aline into the car. She looked warm and cheerful. She was smiling in the old friendly way.

If girls realized their responsibilities they would be so careful when they smiled that they would probably abandon the practice altogether. There are moments in a man's life when a girl's smile can have as important results as an explosion of dynamite.

In the course of their brief acquaintance Joan had smiled at Ashe many times, but the conditions governing those occasions had not been such as to permit him to be seriously affected. He had been pleased on such occasions; he had admired her smile in a detached and critical spirit; but he had not been overwhelmed by it. The frame of mind necessary for that result had been lacking.

Now, however, after five minutes of solitude on the depressing platform of Market Blandings Station, he was what the spiritualists call a sensitive subject. He had reached that depth of gloom and bodily discomfort when a sudden smile has all the effect of strong liquor and good news administered simultaneously, warming the blood and comforting the soul, and generally turning the world from a bleak desert into a land flowing with milk and honey.

It is not too much to say that he reeled before Joan's smile. It was so entirely unexpected. He clutched Mr. Peters' steamer trunk in his emotion. All his resolutions to be cold and distant were swept away. He had the feeling that in a friendless universe here was somebody who was fond of him and glad to see him.

A smile of such importance demands analysis, and in this case repays it; for many things lay behind this smile of Joan Valentine's on the platform of Market Blandings Station.

In the first place, she had had another of her swift changes of mood, and had once again tucked away hostility into its corner. She had thought it over and had come to the conclusion that as she had no logical grievance against Ashe for anything he had done to be distant to him was the behavior of a cat. Consequently she resolved, when they should meet again, to resume her attitude of good-fellowship. That in itself would have been enough to make her smile.

There was another reason, however, which had nothing to do with Ashe. While she had been tucking Aline into the automobile she met the eye of the driver of that vehicle and had perceived a curious look in it—a look of amazement and sheer terror. A moment, later, when Aline called the driver Freddie, she had understood. No wonder the Honorable Freddie had looked as though he had seen a ghost.

It would be a relief to the poor fellow when, as he undoubtedly would do in the course of the drive, he inquired of Aline the name of her maid and was told that it was Simpson. He would mutter something about "Reminds me of a girl I used to know," and would brood on the remarkable way in which Nature produces doubles. But he had a bad moment, and it was partly at the recollection of his face that Joan smiled.

A third reason was because the sight of the Honorable Freddie had reminded her that R. Jones had said he had written her poetry. That thought, too, had contributed toward the smile which so dazzled Ashe.

Ashe, not being miraculously intuitive, accepted the easier explanation that she smiled because she was glad to be in his company; and this thought, coming on top of his mood of despair and general dissatisfaction with everything mundane, acted on him like some powerful chemical.

In every man's life there is generally one moment to which in later years he can look back and say: "In this moment I fell in love!" Such a moment came to Ashe now.

Betwixt the stirrup and the ground,
Mercy I asked; mercy I found.

So sings the poet and so it was with Ashe.

In the almost incredibly brief time it took the small but sturdy porter to roll a milk can across the platform and hump it, with a clang, against other milk cans similarly treated a moment before, Ashe fell in love.

The word is so loosely used, to cover a thousand varying shades of emotion—from the volcanic passion of an Antony for a Cleopatra to the tepid preference of a grocer's assistant for the Irish maid at the second house on Main Street, as opposed to the Norwegian maid at the first house past the post office—the mere statement that Ashe fell in love is not a sufficient description of his feelings as he stood grasping Mr. Peters' steamer trunk. Analysis is required.

From his fourteenth year onward Ashe had been in love many times. His sensations in the case of Joan were neither the terrific upheaval that had caused him, in his fifteenth year, to collect twenty-eight photographs of the heroine of the road company of a musical comedy which had visited the Hayling Opera House, nor the milder flame that had caused him, when at college, to give up smoking for a week and try to read the complete works of Ella Wheeler Wilcox.

His love was something that lay between these two poles.

He did not wish the station platform of Market Blandings to become suddenly congested with red Indians so that he might save Joan's life; and he did not wish to give up anything at all. But he was conscious—to the very depths of his being—that a future in which Joan did not figure would be so insupportable as not to bear considering; and in the immediate present he very strongly favored the idea of clasping Joan in his arms and kissing her until further notice.

Mingled with these feelings was an excited gratitude to her for coming to him like this, with that electric smile on her face; a stunned realization that she was a thousand times prettier than he had ever imagined; and a humility that threatened to make him loose his clutch on the steamer trunk and roll about at her feet, yapping like a dog.

Gratitude, so far as he could dissect his tangled emotion was the predominating ingredient of his mood. Only once in his life had he felt so passionately grateful to any human being. On that occasion, too, the object of his gratitude had been feminine.

Years before, when a boy in his father's home in distant Hayling, Massachusetts, those in authority had commanded that he—in his eleventh year and as shy as one can be only at that interesting age—should rise in the presence of a roomful of strangers, adult guests, and recite "The Wreck of the Hesperus."

He had risen. He had blushed. He had stammered. He had contrived to whisper: "It was the Schooner Hesperus." And then, in a corner of the room, a little girl, for no properly explained reason, had burst out crying. She had yelled, she had bellowed, and would not be comforted; and in the ensuing confusion Ashe had escaped to the woodpile at the bottom of the garden, saved by a miracle.

All his life he had remembered the gratitude he had felt for that little timely girl, and never until now had he experienced any other similar spasm. But as he looked at Joan he found himself renewing that emotion of fifteen years ago.

She was about to speak. In a sort of trance he watched her lips part. He waited almost reverently for the first words she should speak to him in her new role of the only authentic goddess.

"Isn't it a shame?" she said. "I've just put a penny in the chocolate slot machine—and it's empty! I've a good mind to write to the company."

Ashe felt as though he were listening to the strains of some grand sweet anthem.

The small but sturdy porter, weary of his work among the milk cans, or perhaps—let us not do him an injustice even in thought—having finished it, approached them.

"The cart from the castle's here."

In the gloom beyond him there gleamed a light which had not been there before. The meditative snort of a horse supported his statement. He began to deal as authoritatively with Mr. Peters' steamer trunk as he had dealt with the milk cans.

"At last!" said Joan. "I hope it's a covered cart. I'm frozen. Let's go and see."

Ashe followed her with the gait of an automaton.

Cold is the ogre that drives all beautiful things into hiding. Below the surface of a frost-bound garden there lurk hidden bulbs, which are only biding their time to burst forth in a riot of laughing color; but shivering Nature dare not put forth her flowers until the ogre has gone. Not otherwise does cold suppress love. A man in an open cart on an English Spring night may continue to be in love; but love is not the emotion uppermost in his bosom. It shrinks within him and waits for better times.

The cart was not a covered cart. It was open to the four winds of heaven, of which the one at present active proceeded from the bleak east. To this fact may be attributed Ashe's swift recovery from the exalted mood into which Joan's smile had thrown him, his almost instant emergence from the trance. Deep down in him he was aware that his attitude toward Joan had not changed, but his conscious self was too fully occupied with the almost hopeless task of keeping his blood circulating, to permit of thoughts of love. Before the cart had traveled twenty yards he was a mere chunk of frozen misery.

After an eternity of winding roads, darkened cottages, and black fields and hedges, the cart turned in at a massive iron gate, which stood open giving entrance to a smooth gravel drive. Here the way ran for nearly a mile through an open park of great trees and was then swallowed in the darkness of dense shrubberies. Presently to the left appeared lights, at first in ones and twos, shining out and vanishing again; then, as the shrubberies ended and the smooth lawns and terraces began, blazing down on the travelers from a score of windows, with the heartening effect of fires on a winter night.

Against the pale gray sky Blandings Castle stood out like a mountain. It was a noble pile, of Early Tudor building. Its history is recorded in England's history books and Viollet-le-Duc has written of its architecture. It dominated the surrounding country.

The feature of it which impressed Ashe most at this moment, however, was the fact that it looked warm; and for the first time since the drive began he found himself in a mood that approximated cheerfulness. It was a little early to begin feeling cheerful, he discovered, for the journey was by no means over. Arrived within sight of the castle, the cart began a detour, which, ten minutes later, brought it under an arch and over cobblestones to the rear of the building, where it eventually pulled up in front of a great door.

Ashe descended painfully and beat his feet against the cobbles. He helped Joan to climb down. Joan was apparently in a gentle glow. Women seem impervious to cold.

The door opened. Warm, kitcheny scents came through it. Strong men hurried out to take down the trunks, while fair women, in the shape of two nervous scullery maids, approached Joan and Ashe, and bobbed curtsies. This under more normal conditions would have been enough to unman Ashe; but in his frozen state a mere curtsying scullery maid expended herself harmlessly on him. He even acknowledged the greeting with a kindly nod.

The scullery maids, it seemed, were acting in much the same capacity as the attaches of royalty. One was there to conduct Joan to the presence of Mrs. Twemlow, the housekeeper; the other to lead Ashe to where Beach, the butler, waited to do honor to the valet of the castle's most important guest.

After a short walk down a stone-flagged passage Joan and her escort turned to the right. Ashe's objective appeared to be located to the left. He parted from Joan with regret. Her moral support would have been welcome.

Presently his scullery maid stopped at a door and tapped thereon. A fruity voice, like old tawny port made audible, said: "Come in!" Ashe's guide opened the door.

"The gentleman, Mr. Beach," said she, and scuttled away to the less rarefied atmosphere of the kitchen.

Ashe's first impression of Beach, the butler, was one of tension. Other people, confronted for the first time with Beach, had felt the same. He had that strained air of being on the very point of bursting that one sees in bullfrogs and toy balloons. Nervous and imaginative men, meeting Beach, braced themselves involuntarily, stiffening their muscles for the explosion. Those who had the pleasure of more intimate acquaintance with him soon passed this stage, just as people whose homes are on the slopes of Mount Vesuvius become immune to fear of eruptions.

As far back as they could remember Beach had always looked as though an apoplectic fit were a matter of minutes; but he never had apoplexy and in time they came to ignore the possibility of it. Ashe, however, approaching him with a fresh eye, had the feeling that this strain could not possibly continue and that within a very short space of time the worst must happen. The prospect of this did much to rouse him from the coma into which he had been frozen by the rigors of the journey.

Butlers as a class seem to grow less and less like anything human in proportion to the magnificence of their surroundings. There is a type of butler employed in the comparatively modest homes of small country gentlemen who is practically a man and a brother; who hobnobs with the local tradesmen, sings a good comic song at the village inn, and in times of crisis will even turn to and work the pump when the water supply suddenly fails.

The greater the house the more does the butler diverge from this type. Blandings Castle was one of the more important of England's show places, and Beach accordingly had acquired a dignified inertia that almost qualified him for inclusion in the vegetable kingdom. He moved—when he moved at all—slowly. He distilled speech with the air of one measuring out drops of some precious drug. His heavy-lidded eyes had the fixed expression of a statue's.

With an almost imperceptible wave of a fat white hand, he conveyed to Ashe that he desired him to sit down. With a stately movement of his other hand, he picked up a kettle, which simmered on the hob. With an inclination of his head, he called Ashe's attention to a decanter on the table.

In another moment Ashe was sipping a whisky toddy, with the feeling that he had been privileged to assist at some mystic rite. Mr. Beach, posting himself before the fire and placing his hands behind his back, permitted speech to drip from him.

"I have not the advantage of your name, Mr.—"

Ashe introduced himself. Beach acknowledged the information with a half bow.

"You must have had a cold ride, Mr. Marson. The wind is in the east."

Ashe said yes; the ride had been cold.

"When the wind is in the east," continued Mr. Beach, letting each syllable escape with apparent reluctance, "I suffer from my feet."

"I beg your pardon?"

"I suffer from my feet," repeated the butler, measuring out the drops. "You are a young man, Mr. Marson. Probably you do not know what it is to suffer from your feet." He surveyed Ashe, his whisky toddy and the wall beyond him, with heavy-lidded inscrutability. "Corns!" he said.

Ashe said he was sorry.

"I suffer extremely from my feet—not only corns. I have but recently recovered from an ingrowing toenail. I suffered greatly from my ingrowing toenail. I suffer from swollen joints."

Ashe regarded this martyr with increasing disfavor. It is the flaw in the character of many excessively healthy young men that, though kind-hearted enough in most respects, they listen with a regrettable feeling of impatience to the confessions of those less happily situated as regards the ills of the flesh. Rightly or wrongly, they hold that these statements should be reserved for the ear of the medical profession, and other and more general topics selected for conversation with laymen.

"I'm sorry," he said hastily. "You must have had a bad time. Is there a large house party here just now?"

"We are expecting," said Mr. Beach, "a number of guests. We shall in all probability sit down thirty or more to dinner."

"A responsibility for you," said Ashe ingratiatingly, well pleased to be quit of the feet topic.

Mr. Beach nodded.

"You are right, Mr. Marson. Few persons realize the responsibilities of a man in my position. Sometimes, I can assure you, it preys on my mind, and I suffer from nervous headaches."

Ashe began to feel like a man trying to put out a fire which, as fast as he checks it at one point, breaks out at another.

"Sometimes when I come off duty everything gets blurred. The outlines of objects grow indistinct and misty. I have to sit down in a chair. The pain is excruciating."

"But it helps you to forget the pain in your feet."

"No, no. I suffer from my feet simultaneously."

Ashe gave up the struggle.

"Tell me all about your feet," he said.

And Mr. Beach told him all about his feet.

The pleasantest functions must come to an end, and the moment arrived when the final word on the subject of swollen joints was spoken. Ashe, who had resigned himself to a permanent contemplation of the subject, could hardly believe he heard correctly when, at the end of some ten minutes, his companion changed the conversation.

"You have been with Mr. Peters some time, Mr. Marson?"

"Eh? Oh! Oh, no only since last Wednesday."

"Indeed! Might I inquire whom you assisted before that?"

For a moment Ashe did what he would not have believed himself capable of doing—regretted that the topic of feet was no longer under discussion. The question placed him in an awkward position. If he lied and credited himself with a lengthy experience as a valet, he risked exposing himself. If he told the truth and confessed that this was his maiden effort in the capacity of gentleman's gentleman, what would the butler think? There were objections to each course, but to tell the truth was the easier of the two; so he told it.

"Your first situation?" said Mr. Beach. "Indeed!"

"I was—er—doing something else before I met Mr. Peters," said Ashe.

Mr. Beach was too well-bred to be inquisitive, but his eyebrows were not.

"Ah!" he said. "?" cried his eyebrows. "?—?—?"

Ashe ignored the eyebrows.

"Something different," he said.

There was an awkward silence. Ashe appreciated its awkwardness. He was conscious of a grievance against Mr. Peters. Why could not Mr. Peters have brought him down here as his secretary? To be sure, he had advanced some objection to that course in their conversation at the offices of Mainprice, Mainprice & Boole; but merely a silly, far-fetched objection. He wished he had had the sense to fight the point while there was time; but at the moment when they were arranging plans he had been rather tickled by the thought of becoming a valet. The notion had a pleasing musical-comedy touch about it. Why had he not foreseen the complications that must ensue? He could tell by the look on his face that this confounded butler was waiting for him to give a full explanation. What would he think if he withheld it? He would probably suppose that Ashe had been in prison.

Well, there was nothing to be done about it. If Beach was suspicious, he must remain suspicious. Fortunately the suspicions of a butler do not matter much.

Mr. Beach's eyebrows were still mutely urging him to reveal all, but Ashe directed his gaze at that portion of the room which Mr. Beach did not fill. He would be hanged if he was going to let himself be hypnotized by a pair of eyebrows into incriminating himself! He glared stolidly at the pattern of the wallpaper, which represented a number of birds of an unknown species seated on a corresponding number of exotic shrubs.

The silence was growing oppressive. Somebody had to break it soon. And as Mr. Beach was still confining himself to the language of the eyebrow and apparently intended to fight it out on that line if it took all Summer, Ashe himself broke it.

It seemed to him as he reconstructed the scene in bed that night that Providence must have suggested the subject to Mr. Peters' indigestion; for the mere mention of his employer's sufferings acted like magic on the butler.

"I might have had better luck while I was looking for a place," said Ashe. "I dare say you know how bad-tempered Mr. Peters is. He is dyspeptic."

"So," responded Mr. Beach, "I have been informed." He brooded for a space. "I, too," he proceeded, "suffer from my stomach. I have a weak stomach. The lining of my stomach is not what I could wish the lining of my stomach to be."

"Tell me," said Ashe gratefully, leaning forward in an attitude of attention, "all about the lining of your stomach."

It was a quarter of an hour later when Mr. Beach was checked in his discourse by the chiming of the little clock on the mantelpiece. He turned round and gazed at it with surprise not unmixed with displeasure.

"So late?" he said. "I shall have to be going about my duties. And you, also, Mr. Marson, if I may make the suggestion. No doubt Mr. Peters will be wishing to have your assistance in preparing for dinner. If you go along the passage outside you will come to the door that separates our portion of the house from the other. I must beg you to excuse me. I have to go to the cellar."

Following his directions Ashe came after a walk of a few yards to a green-baize door, which, swinging at his push, gave him a view of what he correctly took to be the main hall of the castle—a wide, comfortable space, ringed with settees and warmed by a log fire burning in a mammoth fireplace. On the right a broad staircase led to the upper regions.

It was at this point that Ashe realized the incompleteness of Mr. Beach's directions. Doubtless, the broad staircase would take him to the floor on which were the bedrooms; but how was he to ascertain, without the tedious process of knocking and inquiring at each door, which was the one assigned to Mr. Peters? It was too late to go back and ask the butler for further guidance; already he was on his way to the cellar in quest of the evening's wine.

As he stood irresolute a door across the hall opened and a man of his own age came out. Through the doorway, which the young man held open for an instant while he answered a question from somebody within, Ashe had a glimpse of glass-topped cases.

Could this be the museum—his goal? The next moment the door, opening a few inches more, revealed the outlying portions of an Egyptian mummy and brought certainty. It flashed across Ashe's mind that the sooner he explored the museum and located Mr. Peters' scarab, the better. He decided to ask Beach to take him there as soon as he had leisure.

Meantime the young man had closed the museum door and was crossing the hall. He was a wiry-haired, severe-looking young man, with a sharp nose and eyes that gleamed through rimless spectacles—none other, in fact than Lord Emsworth's private secretary, the Efficient Baxter. Ashe hailed him:

"I say, old man, would you mind telling me how I get to Mr. Peters' room? I've lost my bearings."

He did not reflect that this was hardly the way in which valets in the best society addressed their superiors. That is the worst of adopting what might be called a character part. One can manage the business well enough; it is the dialogue that provides the pitfalls.

Mr. Baxter would have accorded a hearty agreement to the statement that this was not the way in which a valet should have spoken to him; but at the moment he was not aware that Ashe was a valet. From his easy mode of address he assumed that he was one of the numerous guests who had been arriving at the castle all day. As he had asked for Mr. Peters, he fancied that Ashe must be the Honorable Freddie's American friend, George Emerson, whom he had not yet met. Consequently he replied with much cordiality that Mr. Peters' room was the second at the left on the second floor.

He said Ashe could not miss it. Ashe said he was much obliged.

"Awfully good of you," said Ashe.

"Not at all," said Mr. Baxter.

"You lose your way in a place like this," said Ashe.

"You certainly do," said Mr. Baxter.

Ashe went on his upward path and in a few moments was knocking at the door indicated. And sure enough it was Mr. Peters' voice that invited him to enter.

Mr. Peters, partially arrayed in the correct garb for gentlemen about to dine, was standing in front of the mirror, wrestling with his evening tie. As Ashe entered he removed his fingers and anxiously examined his handiwork. It proved unsatisfactory. With a yelp and an oath, he tore the offending linen from his neck.

"Damn the thing!"

It was plain to Ashe that his employer was in no sunny mood. There are few things less calculated to engender sunniness in a naturally bad-tempered man than a dress tie that will not let itself be pulled and twisted into the right shape. Even when things went well, Mr. Peters hated dressing for dinner. Words cannot describe his feelings when they went wrong.

There is something to be said in excuse for this impatience: It is a hollow mockery to be obliged to deck one's person as for a feast when that feast is to consist of a little asparagus and a few nuts.

Mr. Peters' eye met Ashe's in the mirror.

"Oh, it's you, is it? Come in, then. Don't stand staring. Close that door quick! Hustle! Don't scrape your feet on the floor. Try to look intelligent. Don't gape. Where have you been all this while? Why didn't you come before? Can you tie a tie? All right, then—do it!"

Somewhat calmed by the snow-white butterfly-shaped creation that grew under Ashe's fingers, he permitted himself to be helped into his coat. He picked up the remnant of a black cigar from the dressing-table and relit it.

"I've been thinking about you," he said.

"Yes?" said Ashe.

"Have you located the scarab yet?"

"No."

"What the devil have you been doing with yourself then? You've had time to collar it a dozen times."

"I have been talking to the butler."

"What the devil do you waste time talking to butlers for? I suppose you haven't even located the museum yet?"

"Yes; I've done that."

"Oh, you have, have you? Well, that's something. And how do you propose setting about the job?"

"The best plan would be to go there very late at night."

"Well, you didn't propose to stroll in in the afternoon, did you? How are you going to find the scarab when you do get in?"

Ashe had not thought of that. The deeper he went into this business the more things did there seem to be in it of which he had not thought.

"I don't know," he confessed.

"You don't know! Tell me, young man, are you considered pretty bright, as Englishmen go?"

"I am not English. I was born near Boston."

"Oh, you were, were you? You blanked bone-headed, bean-eating boob!" cried Mr. Peters, frothing over quite unexpectedly and waving his arms in a sudden burst of fury. "Then if you are an American why don't you show a little more enterprise? Why don't you put something over? Why do you loaf about the place as though you were supposed to be an ornament? I want results—and I want them quick!

"I'll tell you how you can recognize my scarab when you get into the museum. That shameless old green-goods man who sneaked it from me has had the gall, the nerve, to put it all by itself, with a notice as big as a circus poster alongside of it saying that it is a Cheops of the Fourth Dynasty, presented"—Mr. Peters choked—"presented by J. Preston Peters, Esquire! That's how you're going to recognize it."

Ashe did not laugh, but he nearly dislocated a rib in his effort to abstain from doing so. It seemed to him that this act on Lord Emsworth's part effectually disposed of the theory that Britons have no sense of humor. To rob a man of his choicest possession and then thank him publicly for letting you have it appealed to Ashe as excellent comedy.

"The thing isn't even in a glass case," continued Mr. Peters. "It's lying on an open tray on top of a cabinet of Roman coins. Anybody who was left alone for two minutes in the place could take it! It's criminal carelessness to leave a valuable scarab about like that. If Lord Jesse James was going to steal my Cheops he might at least have had the decency to treat it as though it was worth something."

"But it makes it easier for me to get it," said Ashe consolingly.

"It's got to be made easy if you are to get it!" snapped Mr. Peters. "Here's another thing: You say you are going to try for it late at night. Well, what are you going to do if anyone catches you prowling round at that time? Have you considered that?"

"No."

"You would have to say something, wouldn't you? You wouldn't chat about the weather, would you? You wouldn't discuss the latest play? You would have to think up some mighty good reason for being out of bed at that time, wouldn't you?"

"I suppose so."

"Oh, you do admit that, do you? Well, what you would say is this: You would explain that I had rung for you to come and read me to sleep. Do you understand?"

"You think that would be a satisfactory explanation of my being in the museum?"

"Idiot! I don't mean that you're to say it if you're caught actually in the museum. If you're caught in the museum the best thing you can do is to say nothing, and hope that the judge will let you off light because it's your first offense. You're to say it if you're found wandering about on your way there."

"It sounds thin to me."

"Does it? Well, let me tell you that it isn't so thin as you suppose, for it's what you will actually have to do most nights. Two nights out of three I have to be read to sleep. My indigestion gives me insomnia." As though to push this fact home, Mr. Peters suddenly bent double. "Oof!" he said. "Wow!" He removed the cigar from his mouth and inserted a digestive tabloid. "The lining of my stomach is all wrong," he added.

It is curious how trivial are the immediate causes that produce revolutions. If Mr. Peters had worded his complaint differently Ashe would in all probability have borne it without active protest. He had been growing more and more annoyed with this little person who buzzed and barked and bit at him, yet the idea of definite revolt had not occurred to him. But his sufferings at the hands of Beach, the butler, had reduced him to a state where he could endure no further mention of stomachic linings. There comes a time when our capacity for listening to detailed data about the linings of other people's stomachs is exhausted.

He looked at Mr. Peters sternly. He had ceased to be intimidated by the fiery little man and regarded him simply as a hypochondriac, who needed to be told a few useful facts.

"How do you expect not to have indigestion? You take no exercise and you smoke all day long."

The novel sensation of being criticized—and by a beardless youth at that—held Mr. Peters silent. He started convulsively, but he did not speak. Ashe, on his pet subject, became eloquent. In his opinion dyspeptics cumbered the earth. To his mind they had the choice between health and sickness, and they deliberately chose the latter.

"Your sort of man makes me angry. I know your type inside out. You overwork and shirk exercise, and let your temper run away with you, and smoke strong cigars on an empty stomach; and when you get indigestion as a natural result you look on yourself as a martyr, nourish a perpetual grouch, and make the lives of everybody you meet miserable. If you would put yourself into my hands for a month I would have you eating bricks and thriving on them. Up in the morning, Larsen Exercises, cold bath, a brisk rubdown, sharp walk—"

"Who the devil asked your opinion, you impertinent young hound?" inquired Mr. Peters.

"Don't interrupt—confound you!" shouted Ashe. "Now you have made me forget what I was going to say."

There was a tense silence. Then Mr. Peters began to speak:

"You—infernal—impudent—"

"Don't talk to me like that!"

"I'll talk to you just—"

Ashe took a step toward the door. "Very well, then," he said. "I'll quit! I'm through! You can get somebody else to do this job of yours for you."

The sudden sagging of Mr. Peters' jaw, the look of consternation that flashed on his face, told Ashe he had found the right weapon—that the game was in his hands. He continued with a feeling of confidence:

"If I had known what being your valet involved I wouldn't have undertaken the thing for a hundred thousand dollars. Just because you had some idiotic prejudice against letting me come down here as your secretary, which would have been the simple and obvious thing, I find myself in a position where at any moment I may be publicly rebuked by the butler and have the head stillroom maid looking at me as though I were something the cat had brought in."

His voice trembled with self-pity.

"Do you realize a fraction of the awful things you have let me in for? How on earth am I to remember whether I go in before the chef or after the third footman? I shan't have a peaceful minute while I'm in this place. I've got to sit and listen by the hour to a bore of a butler who seems to be a sort of walking hospital. I've got to steer my way through a complicated system of etiquette.

"And on top of all that you have the nerve, the insolence, to imagine that you can use me as a punching bag to work your bad temper off! You have the immortal rind to suppose that I will stand for being nagged and bullied by you whenever your suicidal way of living brings on an attack of indigestion! You have the supreme gall to fancy that you can talk as you please to me!

"Very well! I've had enough of it. I resign! If you want this scarab of yours recovered let somebody else do it. I've retired from business."

He took another step toward the door. A shaking hand clutched at his sleeve.

"My boy—my dear boy—be reasonable!"

Ashe was intoxicated with his own oratory. The sensation of bullyragging a genuine millionaire was new and exhilarating. He expanded his chest and spread his feet like a colossus.

"That's all very well," he said, coldly disentangling himself from the hand. "You can't get out of it like that. We have got to come to an understanding. The point is that if I am to be subjected to your—your senile malevolence every time you have a twinge of indigestion, no amount of money could pay me to stop on."

"My dear boy, it shall not occur again. I was hasty."

Mr. Peters, with agitated fingers, relit the stump of his cigar.

"Throw away that cigar!"

"My boy!"

"Throw it away! You say you were hasty. Of course you were hasty; and as long as you abuse your digestion you will go on being hasty. I want something better than apologies. If I am to stop here we must get to the root of things. You must put yourself in my hands as though I were your doctor. No more cigars. Every morning regular exercises."

"No, no!"

"Very well!"

"No; stop! Stop! What sort of exercises?"

"I'll show you to-morrow morning. Brisk walks."

"I hate walking."

"Cold baths."

"No, no!"

"Very well!"

"No; stop! A cold bath would kill me at my age."

"It would put new life into you. Do you consent to the cold baths? No? Very well!"

"Yes, yes, yes!"

"You promise?"

"Yes, yes!"

"All right, then."

The distant sound of the dinner gong floated in.

"We settled that just in time," said Ashe.

Mr. Peters regarded him fixedly.

"Young man," he said slowly, "if, after all this, you fail to recover my Cheops for me I'll—I'll—By George, I'll skin you!"

"Don't talk like that," said Ashe. "That's another thing you have got to remember. If my treatment is to be successful you must not let yourself think in that way. You must exercise self-control mentally. You must think beautiful thoughts."

"The idea of skinning you is a beautiful thought!" said Mr. Peters wistfully.

In order that their gayety might not be diminished—and the food turned to ashes in their mouths by the absence from the festive board of Mr. Beach, it was the custom for the upper servants at Blandings to postpone the start of their evening meal until dinner was nearly over above-stairs. This enabled the butler to take his place at the head of the table without fear of interruption, except for the few moments when coffee was being served.

Every night shortly before half-past eight—at which hour Mr. Beach felt that he might safely withdraw from the dining-room and leave Lord Emsworth and his guests to the care of Merridew, the under-butler, and James and Alfred, the footmen, returning only for a few minutes to lend tone and distinction to the distribution of cigars and liqueurs—those whose rank entitled them to do so made their way to the housekeeper's room, to pass in desultory conversation the interval before Mr. Beach should arrive, and a kitchen maid, with the appearance of one who has been straining at the leash and has at last managed to get free, opened the door, with the announcement: "Mr. Beach, if you please, dinner is served." On which Mr. Beach, extending a crooked elbow toward the housekeeper, would say, "Mrs. Twemlow!" and lead the way, high and disposedly, down the passage, followed in order of rank by the rest of the company, in couples, to the steward's room.

For Blandings was not one of those houses—or shall we say hovels?—where the upper servants are expected not only to feed but to congregate before feeding in the steward's room. Under the auspices of Mr. Beach and of Mrs. Twemlow, who saw eye to eye with him in these matters, things were done properly at the castle, with the correct solemnity. To Mr. Beach and Mrs. Twemlow the suggestion that they and their peers should gather together in the same room in which they were to dine would have been as repellent as an announcement from Lady Ann Warblington, the chatelaine, that the house party would eat in the drawing-room.

When Ashe, returning from his interview with Mr. Peters, was intercepted by a respectful small boy and conducted to the housekeeper's room, he was conscious of a sensation of shrinking inferiority akin to his emotions on his first day at school. The room was full and apparently on very cordial terms with itself. Everybody seemed to know everybody and conversation was proceeding in a manner reminiscent of an Old Home Week.

As a matter of fact, the house party at Blandings being in the main a gathering together of the Emsworth clan by way of honor and as a means of introduction to Mr. Peters and his daughter, the bride-of-the-house-to-be, most of the occupants of the housekeeper's room were old acquaintances and were renewing interrupted friendships at the top of their voices.

A lull followed Ashe's arrival and all eyes, to his great discomfort, were turned in his direction. His embarrassment was relieved by Mrs. Twemlow, who advanced to do the honors. Of Mrs. Twemlow little need be attempted in the way of pen portraiture beyond the statement that she went as harmoniously with Mr. Beach as one of a pair of vases or one of a brace of pheasants goes with its fellow. She had the same appearance of imminent apoplexy, the same air of belonging to some dignified and haughty branch of the vegetable kingdom.

"Mr. Marson, welcome to Blandings Castle!"

Ashe had been waiting for somebody to say this, and had been a little surprised that Mr. Beach had not done so. He was also surprised at the housekeeper's ready recognition of his identity, until he saw Joan in the throng and deduced that she must have been the source of information.

He envied Joan. In some amazing way she contrived to look not out of place in this gathering. He himself, he felt, had impostor stamped in large characters all over him.

Mrs. Twemlow began to make the introductions—a long and tedious process, which she performed relentlessly, without haste and without scamping her work. With each member of the aristocracy of his new profession Ashe shook hands, and on each member he smiled, until his facial and dorsal muscles were like to crack under the strain. It was amazing that so many high-class domestics could be collected into one moderate-sized room.

"Miss Simpson you know," said Mrs. Twemlow, and Ashe was about to deny the charge when he perceived that Joan was the individual referred to. "Mr. Judson, Mr. Marson. Mr. Judson is the Honorable Frederick's gentleman."

"You have not the pleasure of our Freddie's acquaintance as yet, I take it, Mr. Marson?" observed Mr. Judson genially, a smooth-faced, lazy-looking young man. "Freddie repays inspection."

"Mr. Marson, permit me to introduce you to Mr. Ferris, Lord Stockheath's gentleman."
Mr. Ferris, a dark, cynical man, with a high forehead, shook Ashe by the hand.

"Happy to meet you, Mr. Marson."

"Miss Willoughby, this is Mr. Marson, who will take you in to dinner. Miss Willoughby is Lady Mildred Mant's lady. As of course you are aware, Lady Mildred, our eldest daughter, married Colonel Horace Mant, of the Scots Guards."

Ashe was not aware, and he was rather surprised that Mrs. Twemlow should have a daughter whose name was Lady Mildred; but reason, coming to his rescue, suggested that by our she meant the offspring of the Earl of Emsworth and his late countess. Miss Willoughby was a light-hearted damsel, with a smiling face and chestnut hair, done low over her forehead.

Since etiquette forbade that he should take Joan in to dinner, Ashe was glad that at least an apparently pleasant substitute had been provided. He had just been introduced to an appallingly statuesque lady of the name of Chester, Lady Ann Warblington's own maid, and his somewhat hazy recollections of Joan's lecture on below-stairs precedence had left him with the impression that this was his destined partner. He had frankly quailed at the prospect of being linked to so much aristocratic hauteur.

When the final introduction had been made conversation broke out again. It dealt almost exclusively, so far as Ashe could follow it, with the idiosyncrasies of the employers of those present. He took it that this happened down the entire social scale below stairs. Probably the lower servants in the servants' hall discussed the upper servants in the room, and the still lower servants in the housemaids' sitting-room discussed their superiors of the servants' hall, and the stillroom gossiped about the housemaids' sitting-room.

He wondered which was the bottom circle of all, and came to the conclusion that it was probably represented by the small respectful boy who had acted as his guide a short while before. This boy, having nobody to discuss anybody with, presumably sat in solitary meditation, brooding on the odd-job man.

He thought of mentioning this theory to Miss Willoughby, but decided that it was too abstruse for her, and contented himself with speaking of some of the plays he had seen before leaving London. Miss Willoughby was an enthusiast on the drama; and, Colonel Mant's military duties keeping him much in town, she had had wide opportunities of indulging her tastes. Miss Willoughby did not like the country. She thought it dull.

"Don't you think the country dull, Mr. Marson?"

"I shan't find it dull here," said Ashe; and he was surprised to discover, through the medium of a pleased giggle, that he was considered to have perpetrated a compliment.

Mr. Beach appeared in due season, a little distrait, as becomes a man who has just been engaged on important and responsible duties.

"Alfred spilled the hock!" Ashe heard him announce to Mrs. Twemlow in a bitter undertone. "Within half an inch of his lordship's arm he spilled it."

Mrs. Twemlow murmured condolences. Mr. Beach's set expression was of one who is wondering how long the strain of existence can be supported.

"Mr. Beach, if you please, dinner is served."

The butler crushed down sad thoughts and crooked his elbow.

"Mrs. Twemlow!"

Ashe, miscalculating degrees of rank in spite of all his caution, was within a step of leaving the room out of his proper turn; but the startled pressure of Miss Willoughby's hand on his arm warned him in time. He stopped, to allow the statuesque Miss Chester to sail out under escort of a wizened little man with a horseshoe pin in his tie, whose name, in company with nearly all the others that had been spoken to him since he came into the room, had escaped Ashe's memory.

"You were nearly making a bloomer!" said Miss Willoughby brightly. "You must be absent-minded, Mr. Marson—like his lordship."

"Is Lord Emsworth absent-minded?"

Miss Willoughby laughed.

"Why, he forgets his own name sometimes! If it wasn't for Mr. Baxter, goodness knows what would happen to him."

"I don't think I know Mr. Baxter."

"You will if you stay here long. You can't get away from him if you're in the same house. Don't tell anyone I said so; but he's the real master here. His lordship's secretary he calls himself; but he's really everything rolled into one—like the man in the play."

Ashe, searching in his dramatic memories for such a person in a play, inquired whether Miss Willoughby meant Pooh-Bah, in "The Mikado," of which there had been a revival in London recently.

Miss Willoughby did mean Pooh-Bah.

"But Nosy Parker is what I call him," she said. "He minds everybody's business as well as his own."

The last of the procession trickled into the steward's room. Mr. Beach said grace somewhat patronizingly. The meal began.

"You've seen Miss Peters, of course, Mr. Marson?" said Miss Willoughby, resuming conversation with the soup.

"Just for a few minutes at Paddington."

"Oh! You haven't been with Mr. Peters long, then?"

Ashe began to wonder whether everybody he met was going to ask him this dangerous question.

"Only a day or so."

"Where were you before that?"

Ashe was conscious of a prickly sensation. A little more of this and he might as well reveal his true mission at the castle and have done with it.

"Oh, I was—that is to say—"

"How are you feeling after the journey, Mr. Marson?" said a voice from the other side of the table; and Ashe, looking up gratefully, found Joan's eyes looking into his with a curiously amused expression.

He was too grateful for the interruption to try to account for this. He replied that he was feeling very well, which was not the case. Miss Willoughby's interest was diverted to a discussion of the defects of the various railroad systems of Great Britain.

At the head of the table Mr. Beach had started an intimate conversation with Mr. Ferris, the valet of Lord Stockheath, the Honorable Freddie's "poor old Percy"—a cousin, Ashe had gathered, of Aline Peters' husband-to-be. The butler spoke in more measured tones even than usual, for he was speaking of tragedy.

"We were all extremely sorry, Mr. Ferris, to read of your misfortune."

Ashe wondered what had been happening to Mr. Ferris.

"Yes, Mr. Beach," replied the valet, "it's a fact we made a pretty poor show." He took a sip from his glass. "There is no concealing the fact—I have never tried to conceal it—that poor Percy is not bright."

Miss Chester entered the conversation.

"I couldn't see where the girl—what's her name? was so very pretty. All the papers had pieces where it said she was attractive, and what not; but she didn't look anything special to me from her photograph in the Mirror. What his lordship could see in her I can't understand."

"The photo didn't quite do her justice, Miss Chester. I was present in court, and I must admit she was svelte—decidedly svelte. And you must recollect that Percy, from childhood up, has always been a highly susceptible young nut. I speak as one who knows him."

Mr. Beach turned to Joan.

"We are speaking of the Stockheath breach-of-promise case, Miss Simpson, of which you doubtless read in the newspapers. Lord Stockheath is a nephew of ours. I fancy his lordship was greatly shocked at the occurrence."

"He was," chimed in Mr. Judson from down the table. "I happened to overhear him speaking of it to young Freddie. It was in the library on the morning when the judge made his final summing up and slipped it into Lord Stockheath so proper. 'If ever anything of this sort happens to you, you young scalawag,' he says to Freddie—"

Mr. Beach coughed. "Mr. Judson!"

"Oh, it's all right, Mr. Beach; we're all in the family here, in a manner of speaking. It wasn't as though I was telling it to a lot of outsiders. I'm sure none of these ladies or gentlemen will let it go beyond this room?"

The company murmured virtuous acquiescence.

"He says to Freddie: 'You young scalawag, if ever anything of this sort happens to you, you can pack up and go off to Canada, for I'll have nothing more to do with you!'—or words to that effect. And Freddie says: 'Oh, dash it all, gov'nor, you know—what?'"

However short Mr. Judson's imitation of his master's voice may have fallen of histrionic perfection, it pleased the company. The room shook with mirth.

"Mr. Judson is clever, isn't he, Mr. Marson?" whispered Miss Willoughby, gazing with adoring eyes at the speaker.

Mr. Beach thought it expedient to deflect the conversation. By the unwritten law of the room every individual had the right to speak as freely as he wished about his own personal employer; but Judson, in his opinion, sometimes went a trifle too far.

"Tell me, Mr. Ferris," he said, "does his lordship seem to bear it well?"

"Oh, Percy is bearing it well enough."

Ashe noted as a curious fact that, though the actual valet of any person under discussion spoke of him almost affectionately by his Christian name, the rest of the company used the greatest ceremony and gave him his title with all respect. Lord Stockheath was Percy to Mr. Ferris, and the Honorable Frederick Threepwood was Freddie to Mr. Judson; but to Ferris, Mr. Judson's Freddie was the Honorable Frederick, and to Judson Mr. Ferris' Percy was Lord Stockheath. It was rather a pleasant form of etiquette, and struck Ashe as somehow vaguely feudal.

"Percy," went on Mr. Ferris, "is bearing it like a little Briton—the damages not having come out of his pocket! It's his old father—who had to pay them—that's taking it to heart. You might say he's doing himself proud. He says it's brought on his gout again, and that's why he's gone to Droitwich instead of coming here. I dare say Percy isn't sorry."

"It has been," said Mr. Beach, summing up, "a most unfortunate occurrence. The modern tendency of the lower classes to get above themselves is becoming more marked every day. The young female in this case was, I understand, a barmaid. It is deplorable that our young men should allow themselves to get into such entanglements."

"The wonder to me," said the irrepressible Mr. Judson, "is that more of these young chaps don't get put through it. His lordship wasn't so wide of the mark when he spoke like that to Freddie in the library that time. I give you my word, it's a mercy young Freddie hasn't been up against it! When we were in London, Freddie and I," he went on, cutting through Mr. Beach's disapproving cough, "before what you might call the crash, when his lordship cut off supplies and had him come back and live here, Freddie was asking for it—believe me! Fell in love with a girl in the chorus of one of the theaters. Used to send me to the stage door with notes and flowers every night for weeks, as regular as clockwork.

"What was her name? It's on the tip of my tongue. Funny how you forget these things! Freddie was pretty far gone. I recollect once, happening to be looking round his room in his absence, coming on a poem he had written to her. It was hot stuff—very hot! If that girl has kept those letters it's my belief we shall see Freddie following in Lord Stockheath's footsteps."

There was a hush of delighted horror round the table.

"Goo'," said Miss Chester's escort with unction. "You don't say so, Mr. Judson! It wouldn't half make them look silly if the Honorable Frederick was sued for breach just now, with the wedding coming on!"

"There is no danger of that."

It was Joan's voice, and she had spoken with such decision that she had the ear of the table immediately. All eyes looked in her direction. Ashe was struck with her expression. Her eyes were shining as though she were angry; and there was a flush on her face. A phrase he had used in the train came back to him. She looked like a princess in disguise.

"What makes you say that, Miss Simpson?" inquired Judson, annoyed. He had been at pains to make the company's flesh creep, and it appeared to be Joan's aim to undo his work.

It seemed to Ashe that Joan made an effort of some sort as though she were pulling herself together and remembering where she was.

"Well," she said, almost lamely, "I don't think it at all likely that he proposed marriage to this girl."

"You never can tell," said Judson. "My impression is that Freddie did. It's my belief that there's something on his mind these days. Before he went to London with his lordship the other day he was behaving very strange. And since he came back it's my belief that he has been brooding. And I happen to know he followed the affair of Lord Stockheath pretty closely, for he clipped the clippings out of the paper. I found them myself one day when I happened to be going through his things."

Beach cleared his throat—his mode of indicating that he was about to monopolize the conversation.

"And in any case, Miss Simpson," he said solemnly, "with things come to the pass they have come to, and the juries—drawn from the lower classes—in the nasty mood they're in, it don't seem hardly necessary in these affairs for there to have been any definite promise of marriage. What with all this socialism rampant, they seem so happy at the idea of being able to do one of us an injury that they give heavy damages without it. A few ardent expressions, and that's enough for them. You recollect the Havant case, and when young Lord Mount Anville was sued? What it comes to is that anarchy is getting the upper hand, and the lower classes are getting above themselves. It's all these here cheap newspapers that does it. They tempt the lower classes to get above themselves.

"Only this morning I had to speak severe to that young fellow, James, the footman. He was a good young fellow once and did his work well, and had a proper respect for people; but now he's gone all to pieces. And why? Because six months ago he had the rheumatism, and had the audacity to send his picture and a testimonial, saying that it had cured him of awful agonies, to Walkinshaw's Supreme Ointment, and they printed it in half a dozen papers; and it has been the ruin of James. He has got above himself and don't care for nobody."

"Well, all I can say is," resumed Judson, "that I hope to goodness nothing won't happen to Freddie of that kind; for it's not every girl that would have him."

There was a murmur of assent to this truth.

"Now your Miss Peters," said Judson tolerantly—"she seems a nice little thing."

"She would be pleased to hear you say so," said Joan.

"Joan Valentine!" cried Judson, bringing his hands down on the tablecloth with a bang. "I've just remembered it. That was the name of the girl Freddie used to write the letters and poems to; and that's who it is I've been trying all along to think you reminded me of, Miss Simpson. You're the living image of Freddie's Miss Joan Valentine."

Ashe was not normally a young man of particularly ready wit; but on this occasion it may have been that the shock of this revelation, added to the fact that something must be done speedily if Joan's discomposure was not to become obvious to all present, quickened his intelligence. Joan, usually so sure of herself, so ready of resource, had gone temporarily to pieces. She was quite white, and her eyes met Ashe's with almost a hunted expression.

If the attention of the company was to be diverted, something drastic must be done. A mere verbal attempt to change the conversation would be useless. Inspiration descended on Ashe.

In the days of his childhood in Hayling, Massachusetts, he had played truant from Sunday school again and again in order to frequent the society of one Eddie Waffles, the official bad boy of the locality. It was not so much Eddie's charm of conversation which had attracted him—though that had been great—as the fact that Eddie, among his other accomplishments, could give a lifelike imitation of two cats fighting in a back yard; and Ashe felt that he could never be happy until he had acquired this gift from the master.

In course of time he had done so. It might be that his absences from Sunday school in the cause of art had left him in later years a trifle shaky on the subject of the Kings of Judah, but his hard-won accomplishment had made him in request at every smoking concert at Oxford; and it saved the situation now.

"Have you ever heard two cats fighting in a back yard?" he inquired casually of his neighbor, Miss Willoughby.

The next moment the performance was in full swing. Young Master Waffles, who had devoted considerable study to his subject, had conceived the combat of his imaginary cats in a broad, almost Homeric, vein. The unpleasantness opened with a low gurgling sound, answered by another a shade louder and possibly more querulous. A momentary silence was followed by a long-drawn note, like rising wind, cut off abruptly and succeeded by a grumbling mutter. The response to this was a couple of sharp howls. Both parties to the contest then indulged in a discontented whining, growing louder and louder until the air was full of electric menace. And then, after another sharp silence, came war, noisy and overwhelming.

Standing at Master Waffles' side, you could follow almost every movement of that intricate fray, and mark how now one and now the other of the battlers gained a short-lived advantage. It was a great fight. Shrewd blows were taken and given, and in the eye of the imagination you could see the air thick with flying fur. Louder and louder grew the din; and then, at its height, it ceased in one crescendo of tumult, and all was still, save for a faint, angry moaning.

Such was the cat fight of Master Eddie Waffles; and Ashe, though falling short of the master, as a pupil must, rendered it faithfully and with energy.

To say that the attention of the company was diverted from Mr. Judson and his remarks by the extraordinary noises which proceeded from Ashe's lips would be to offer a mere shadowy suggestion of the sensation caused by his efforts. At first, stunned surprise, then consternation, greeted him. Beach, the butler, was staring as one watching a miracle, nearer apparently to apoplexy than ever. On the faces of the others every shade of emotion was to be seen.

That this should be happening in the steward's room at Blandings Castle was scarcely less amazing than if it had taken place in a cathedral. The upper servants, rigid in their seats, looked at each other, like Cortes' soldiers—"with a wild surmise."

The last faint moan of feline defiance died away and silence fell on the room. Ashe turned to Miss Willoughby.

"Just like that!" he said. "I was telling Miss Willoughby," he added apologetically to Mrs. Twemlow, "about the cats in London. They were a great trial."

For perhaps three seconds his social reputation swayed to and fro in the balance, while the company pondered on what he had done. It was new; but it was humorous—or was it vulgar? There is nothing the English upper servant so abhors as vulgarity. That was what the steward's room was trying to make up its mind about.

Then Miss Willoughby threw her shapely head back and the squeal of her laughter smote the ceiling. And at that the company made its decision. Everybody laughed. Everybody urged Ashe to give an encore. Everybody was his friend and admirer—everybody but Beach, the butler. Beach, the butler, was shocked to his very core. His heavy-lidded eyes rested on Ashe with disapproval. It seemed to Beach, the butler, that this young man Marson had got above himself.

Ashe found Joan at his side. Dinner was over and the diners were making for the housekeeper's room.

"Thank you, Mr. Marson. That was very good of you and very clever." Her eyes twinkled. "But what a terrible chance you took! You have made yourself a popular success, but you might just as easily have become a social outcast. As it is, I am afraid Mr. Beach did not approve."

"I'm afraid he didn't. In a minute or so I'm going to fawn on him and make all well."

Joan lowered her voice.

"It was quite true, what that odious little man said. Freddie Threepwood did write me letters. Of course I destroyed them long ago."

"But weren't you running the risk in coming here that he might recognize you? Wouldn't that make it rather unpleasant for you?"

"I never met him, you see. He only wrote to me. When he came to the station to meet us this evening he looked startled to see me; so I suppose he remembers my appearance. But Aline will have told him that my name is Simpson."

"That fellow Judson said he was brooding. I think you ought to put him out of his misery."

"Mr. Judson must have been letting his imagination run away with him. He is out of his misery. He sent a horrid fat man named Jones to see me in London about the letters, and I told him I had destroyed them. He must have let him know that by this time."

"I see."

They went into the housekeeper's room. Mr. Beach was standing before the fire. Ashe went up to him. It was not an easy matter to mollify Mr. Beach. Ashe tried the most tempting topics. He mentioned swollen feet—he dangled the lining of Mr. Beach's stomach temptingly before his eyes; but the butler was not to be softened. Only when Ashe turned the conversation to the subject of the museum did a flicker of animation stir him.

Mr. Beach was fond and proud of the Blandings Castle museum. It had been the means of getting him into print for the first and only time in his life. A year before, a representative of the Intelligencer and Echo, from the neighboring town of Blatchford, had come to visit the castle on behalf of his paper; and he had begun one section of his article with the words: "Under the auspices of Mr. Beach, my genial cicerone, I then visited his lordship's museum—" Mr. Beach treasured the clipping in a special writing-desk.

He responded almost amiably to Ashe's questions. Yes; he had seen the scarab—he pronounced it scayrub—which Mr. Peters had presented to his lordship. He understood that his lordship thought very highly of Mr. Peters' scayrub. He had overheard Mr. Baxter telling his lordship that it was extremely valuable.

"Mr. Beach," said Ashe, "I wonder whether you would take me to see Lord Emsworth's museum?"

Mr. Beach regarded him heavily.

"I shall be pleased to take you to see his lordship's museum," he replied.

One can attribute only to the nervous mental condition following the interview he had had with Ashe in his bedroom the rash act Mr. Peters attempted shortly after dinner.

Mr. Peters, shortly after dinner, was in a dangerous and reckless mood. He had had a wretched time all through the meal. The Blandings chef had extended himself in honor of the house party, and had produced a succession of dishes, which in happier days Mr. Peters would have devoured eagerly. To be compelled by considerations of health to pass these by was enough to damp the liveliest optimist. Mr. Peters had suffered terribly. Occasions of feasting and revelry like the present were for him so many battlefields, on which greed fought with prudence.

All through dinner he brooded on Ashe's defiance and the horrors which were to result from that defiance. One of Mr. Peters' most painful memories was of a two weeks' visit he had once paid to Mr.

Muldoon in his celebrated establishment at White Plains. He had been persuaded to go there by a brother millionaire whom, until then, he had always regarded as a friend. The memory of Mr. Muldoon's cold shower baths and brisk system of physical exercise still lingered.

The thought that under Ashe's rule he was to go through privately very much what he had gone through in the company of a gang of other unfortunates at Muldoon's froze him with horror. He knew those health cranks who believed that all mortal ailments could be cured by cold showers and brisk walks. They were all alike and they nearly killed you. His worst nightmare was the one where he dreamed he was back at Muldoon's, leading his horse up that endless hill outside the village.

He would not stand it! He would be hanged if he'd stand it! He would defy Ashe. But if he defied Ashe, Ashe would go away; and then whom could he find to recover his lost scarab?

Mr. Peters began to appreciate the true meaning of the phrase about the horns of a dilemma. The horns of this dilemma occupied his attention until the end of the dinner. He shifted uneasily from one to the other and back again. He rose from the table in a thoroughly overwrought condition of mind. And then, somehow, in the course of the evening, he found himself alone in the hall, not a dozen feet from the unlocked museum door.

It was not immediately that he appreciated the significance of this fact. He had come to the hall because its solitude suited his mood. It was only after he had finished a cigar—Ashe could not stop his smoking after dinner—that it suddenly flashed on him that he had ready at hand a solution of all his troubles. A brief minute's resolute action and the scarab would be his again, and the menace of Ashe a thing of the past. He glanced about him. Yes; he was alone.

Not once since the removal of the scarab had begun to exercise his mind had Mr. Peters contemplated for an instant the possibility of recovering it himself. The prospect of the unpleasantness that would ensue had been enough to make him regard such an action as out of the question. The risk was too great to be considered for a moment; but here he was, in a position where the risk was negligible!

Like Ashe, he had always visualized the recovery of his scarab as a thing of the small hours, a daring act to be performed when sleep held the castle in its grip. That an opportunity would be presented to him of walking in quite calmly and walking out again with the Cheops in his pocket, had never occurred to him as a possibility.

Yet now this chance was presenting itself in all its simplicity, and all he had to do was to grasp it. The door of the museum was not even closed. He could see from where he stood that it was ajar.

He moved cautiously in its direction—not in a straight line as one going to a museum, but circuitously as one strolling without an aim. From time to time he glanced over his shoulder. He reached the door, hesitated, and passed it. He turned, reached the door again—and again passed it. He stood for a moment darting his eyes about the hall; then, in a burst of resolution, he dashed for the door and shot in like a rabbit.

At the same moment the Efficient Baxter, who, from the shelter of a pillar on the gallery that ran around two-thirds of the hall, had been eyeing the peculiar movements of the distinguished guest with considerable interest for some minutes, began to descend the stairs.

Rupert Baxter, the Earl of Emsworth's indefatigable private secretary, was one of those men whose chief characteristic is a vague suspicion of their fellow human beings. He did not suspect them of this or that definite crime; he simply suspected them. He prowled through life as we are told the hosts of Midian prowled.

His powers in this respect were well-known at Blandings Castle. The Earl of Emsworth said: "Baxter is invaluable—positively invaluable." The Honorable Freddie said: "A chappie can't take a step in this bally house without stumbling over that damn feller, Baxter!" The manservant and the maidservant within the gates, like Miss Willoughby, employing that crisp gift for characterization which is the property of the English lower orders, described him as a Nosy Parker.

Peering over the railing of the balcony and observing the curious movements of Mr. Peters, who, as a matter of fact, while making up his mind to approach the door, had been backing and filling about the hall in a quaint serpentine manner like a man trying to invent a new variety of the tango, the Efficient Baxter had found himself in some way—why, he did not know—of what, he could not say—but in some nebulous way, suspicious.

He had not definitely accused Mr. Peters in his mind of any specific tort or malfeasance. He had merely felt that something fishy was toward. He had a sixth sense in such matters.

But when Mr. Peters, making up his mind, leaped into the museum, Baxter's suspicions lost their vagueness and became crystallized. Certainty descended on him like a bolt from the skies. On oath, before a notary, the Efficient Baxter would have declared that J. Preston Peters was about to try to purloin the scarab.

Lest we should seem to be attributing too miraculous powers of intuition to Lord Emsworth's secretary, it should be explained that the mystery which hung about that curio had exercised his mind not a little since his employer had given it to him to place in the museum. He knew Lord Emsworth's power of forgetting and he did not believe his account of the transaction. Scarab maniacs like Mr. Peters did not give away specimens from their collections as presents. But he had not divined the truth of what had happened in London.

The conclusion at which he had arrived was that Lord Emsworth had bought the scarab and had forgotten all about it. To support this theory was the fact that the latter had taken his check book to London with him. Baxter's long acquaintance with the earl had left him with the conviction that there was no saying what he might not do if left loose in London with a check book.

As to Mr. Peters' motive for entering the museum, that, too, seemed completely clear to the secretary. He was a curio enthusiast himself and he had served collectors in a secretarial capacity; and he knew, both from experience and observation, that strange madness which may at any moment afflict the collector, blotting out morality and the nice distinction between meum and tuum, as with a sponge. He knew that collectors who would not steal a loaf if they were starving might—and did—fall before the temptation of a coveted curio.

He descended the stairs three at a time, and entered the museum at the very instant when Mr. Peters' twitching fingers were about to close on his treasure. He handled the delicate situation with eminent tact. Mr. Peters, at the sound of his step, had executed a backward leap, which was as good as a confession of guilt, and his face was rigid with dismay; but the Efficient Baxter pretended not to notice these phenomena. His manner, when he spoke, was easy and unembarrassed.

"Ah! Taking a look at our little collection, Mr. Peters? You will see that we have given the place of honor to your Cheops. It is certainly a fine specimen—a wonderfully fine specimen."

Mr. Peters was recovering slowly. Baxter talked on, to give him time. He spoke of Mut and Bubastis, of Ammon and the Book of the Dead. He directed the other's attention to the Roman coins.

He was touching on some aspects of the Princess Gilukhipa of Mitanni, in whom his hearer could scarcely fail to be interested, when the door opened and Beach, the butler, came in, accompanied by Ashe. In the bustle of the interruption Mr. Peters escaped, glad to be elsewhere, and questioning for the first time in his life the dictum that if you want a thing well done you must do it yourself.

"I was not aware, sir," said Beach, the butler, "that you were in occupation of the museum. I would not have intruded; but this young man expressed a desire to examine the exhibits, and I took the liberty of conducting him."

"Come in, Beach—come in," said Baxter.

The light fell on Ashe's face, and he recognized him as the cheerful young man who had inquired the way to Mr. Peters' room before dinner and who, he had by this time discovered, was not the Honorable Freddie's friend, George Emerson—or, indeed, any other of the guests of the house. He felt suspicious.

"Oh, Beach!"

"Sir?"

"Just a moment."

He drew the butler into the hall, out of earshot.

"Beach, who is that man?"

"Mr. Peters' valet, sir."

"Mr. Peters' valet!"

"Yes, sir."

"Has he been in service long?" asked Baxter, remembering that a mere menial had addressed him as "old man."

Beach lowered his voice. He and the Efficient Baxter were old allies, and it seemed right to Beach to confide in him.

"He has only just joined Mr. Peters, sir; and he has never been in service before. He told me so himself, and I was unable to elicit from him any information as to his antecedents. His manner struck me, sir, as peculiar. It crossed my mind to wonder whether Mr. Peters happened to be aware of this. I should dislike to do any young man an injury; but it might be anyone coming to a gentleman without a character, like this young man. Mr. Peters might have been deceived, sir."

The Efficient Baxter's manner became distraught. His mind was working rapidly.

"Should he be informed, sir?"

"Eh! Who?"

"Mr. Peters, sir—in case he should have been deceived?"

"No, no; Mr. Peters knows his own business."

"Far from me be it to appear officious, sir; but—"

"Mr. Peters probably knows all about him. Tell me, Beach, who was it suggested this visit to the museum? Did you?"

"It was at the young man's express desire that I conducted him, sir."

The Efficient Baxter returned to the museum without a word. Ashe, standing in the middle of the room, was impressing the topography of the place on his memory. He was unaware of the piercing stare of suspicion that was being directed at him from behind.

He did not see Baxter. He was not even thinking of Baxter; but Baxter was on the alert. Baxter was on the warpath. Baxter knew!

CHAPTER VI

Among the compensations of advancing age is a wholesome pessimism, which, though it takes the fine edge off of whatever triumphs may come to us, has the admirable effect of preventing Fate from working off on us any of those gold bricks, coins with strings attached, and unhatched chickens, at which ardent youth snatches with such enthusiasm, to its subsequent disappointment. As we emerge from the twenties we grow into a habit of mind that looks askance at Fate bearing gifts. We miss, perhaps, the occasional prize, but we also avoid leaping light-heartedly into traps.

Ashe Marson had yet to reach the age of tranquil mistrust; and when Fate seemed to be treating him kindly he was still young enough to accept such kindnesses on their face value and rejoice at them.

As he sat on his bed at the end of his first night in Castle Blandings, he was conscious to a remarkable degree that Fortune was treating him well. He had survived—not merely without discredit, but with positive triumph—the initiatory plunge into the etiquette maelstrom of life below stairs. So far from doing the wrong thing and drawing down on himself the just scorn of the steward's room, he had been the life and soul of the party. Even if to-morrow, in an absent-minded fit, he should anticipate the groom of the chambers in the march to the table, he would be forgiven; for the humorist has his privileges.

So much for that. But that was only a part of Fortune's kindnesses. To have discovered on the first day of their association the correct method of handling and reducing to subjection his irascible employer was an even greater boon. A prolonged association with Mr. Peters on the lines in which their acquaintance had begun would have been extremely trying. Now, by virtue of a fortunate stand at the outset, he had spiked the millionaire's guns.

Thirdly, and most important of all, he had not only made himself familiar with the locality and surroundings of the scarab, but he had seen, beyond the possibility of doubt, that the removal of it and the earning of the five thousand dollars would be the simplest possible task. Already he was spending the money in his mind. And to such lengths had optimism led him that, as he sat on his bed reviewing the events of the day, his only doubt was whether to get the scarab at once or to let it remain where it was until he had the opportunity of doing Mr. Peters' interior good on the lines he had mapped out in their conversation; for, of course, directly he had restored the scarab to its rightful owner and pocketed the reward, his position as healer and trainer to the millionaire would cease automatically.

He was sorry for that, because it troubled him to think that a sick man would not be made well; but, on the whole, looking at it from every aspect, it would be best to get the scarab as soon as possible and leave Mr. Peters' digestion to look after itself. Being twenty-six and an optimist, he had no suspicion that Fate might be playing with him; that Fate might have unpleasant surprises in store; that Fate even now was preparing to smite him in his hour of joy with that powerful weapon, the Efficient Baxter.

He looked at his watch. It was five minutes to one. He had no idea whether they kept early hours at Blandings Castle or not, but he deemed it prudent to give the household another hour in which to settle down. After which he would just trot down and collect the scarab.

The novel he had brought down with him from London fortunately proved interesting. Two o'clock came before he was ready for it. He slipped the book into his pocket and opened the door.

All was still—still and uncommonly dark. Along the corridor on which his room was situated the snores of sleeping domestics exploded, growled and twittered in the air. Every menial on the list seemed to be snoring, some in one key, some in another, some defiantly, some plaintively; but the main fact was that they were all snoring somehow, thus intimating that, so far as this side of the house was concerned, the coast might be considered clear and interruption of his plans a negligible risk.

Researches made at an earlier hour had familiarized him with the geography of the place. He found his way to the green-baize door without difficulty and, stepping through, was in the hall, where the remains of the log fire still glowed a fitful red. This, however, was the only illumination, and it was fortunate that he did not require light to guide him to the museum.

He knew the direction and had measured the distance. It was precisely seventeen steps from where he stood. Cautiously, and with avoidance of noise, he began to make the seventeen steps.

He was beginning the eleventh when he bumped into somebody— somebody soft—somebody whose hand, as it touched his, felt small and feminine.

The fragment of a log fell on the ashes and the fire gave a dying spurt. Darkness succeeded the sudden glow. The fire was out. That little flame had been its last effort before expiring, but it had been enough to enable him to recognize Joan Valentine.

"Good Lord!" he gasped.

His astonishment was short-lived. Next moment the only thing that surprised him was the fact that he was not more surprised. There was something about this girl that made the most bizarre happenings seem right and natural. Ever since he had met her his life had changed from an orderly succession of uninteresting days to a strange carnival of the unexpected, and use was accustoming him to it. Life had taken on the quality of a dream, in which anything might happen and in which everything that did happen was to be accepted with the calmness natural in dreams.

It was strange that she should be here in the pitch-dark hall in the middle of the night; but—after all—no stranger than that he should be. In this dream world in which he now moved it had to be taken for granted that people did all sorts of odd things from all sorts of odd motives.

"Hello!" he said.

"Don't be alarmed."

"No, no!"

"I think we are both here for the same reason."

"You don't mean to say—"

"Yes; I have come here to earn the five thousand dollars, too, Mr. Marson. We are rivals."

In his present frame of mind it seemed so simple and intelligible to Ashe that he wondered whether he was really hearing it the first time. He had an odd feeling that he had known this all along.

"You are here to get the scarab?"

"Exactly."

Ashe was dimly conscious of some objection to this, but at first it eluded him. Then he pinned it down.

"But you aren't a young man of good appearance," he said.

"I don't know what you mean. But Aline Peters is an old friend of mine. She told me her father would give a large reward to whoever recovered the scarab; so I—"

"Look out!" whispered Ashe. "Run! There's somebody coming!"

There was a soft footfall on the stairs, a click, and above Ashe's head a light flashed out. He looked round. He was alone, and the green-baize door was swaying gently to and fro.

"Who's that? Who's there?" said a voice.

The Efficient Baxter was coming down the broad staircase.

A general suspicion of mankind and a definite and particular suspicion of one individual made a bad opiate. For over an hour sleep had avoided the Efficient Baxter with an unconquerable coyness. He had tried all the known ways of wooing slumber, but they had failed him, from the counting of sheep downward. The events of the night had whipped his mind to a restless activity. Try as he might to lose consciousness, the recollection of the plot he had discovered surged up and kept him wakeful.

It is the penalty of the suspicious type of mind that it suffers from its own activity. From the moment he detected Mr. Peters in the act of rifling the museum and marked down Ashe as an accomplice, Baxter's repose was doomed. Nor poppy nor mandragora, nor all the drowsy sirups of the world, could ever medicine him to that sweet sleep which he owed yesterday.

But it was the recollection that on previous occasions of wakefulness hot whisky and water had done the trick, which had now brought him from his bed and downstairs. His objective was the decanter on the table of the smoking-room, which was one of the rooms opening on the gallery that looked down on the hall. Hot water he could achieve in his bedroom by means of his stove.

So out of bed he had climbed and downstairs he had come; and here he was, to all appearances, just in time to foil the very plot on which he had been brooding. Mr. Peters might be in bed, but there in the hall below him stood the accomplice, not ten paces from the museum's door. He arrived on the spot at racing speed and confronted Ashe.

"What are you doing here?"

And then, from the Baxter viewpoint, things began to go wrong. By all the rules of the game, Ashe, caught, as it were, red-handed, should have wilted, stammered and confessed all; but Ashe was fortified by that philosophic calm which comes to us in dreams, and, moreover, he had his story ready.

"Mr. Peters rang for me, sir."

He had never expected to feel grateful to the little firebrand who employed him, but he had to admit that the millionaire, in their late conversation, had shown forethought. The thought struck him that but for Mr. Peters' advice he might by now be in an extremely awkward position; for his was not a swiftly inventive mind.

"Rang for you? At half-past two in the morning!"

"To read to him, sir."

"To read to him at this hour?"

"Mr. Peters suffers from insomnia, sir. He has a weak digestion and pain sometimes prevents him from sleeping. The lining of his stomach is not at all what it should be."

"I don't believe a word of it."

With that meekness which makes the good man wronged so impressive a spectacle, Ashe produced and exhibited his novel.

"Here is the book I am about to read to him. I think, sir, if you will excuse me, I had better be going to his room. Good night, sir."

He proceeded to mount the stairs. He was sorry for Mr. Peters, so shortly about to be roused from a refreshing slumber; but these were life's tragedies and must be borne bravely.

The Efficient Baxter dogged him the whole way, sprinting silently in his wake and dodging into the shadows whenever the light of an occasional electric bulb made it inadvisable to keep to the open. Then abruptly he gave up the pursuit. For the first time his comparative impotence in this silent conflict on which he had embarked was made manifest to him, and he perceived that on mere suspicion, however strong, he could do nothing. To accuse Mr. Peters of theft or to accuse him of being accessory to a theft was out of the question.

Yet his whole being revolted at the thought of allowing the sanctity of the museum to be violated. Officially its contents belonged to Lord Emsworth, but ever since his connection with the castle he had been put in charge of them, and he had come to look on them as his own property. If he was only a collector by proxy he had, nevertheless, the collector's devotion to his curios, beside which the lioness' attachment to her cubs is tepid; and he was prepared to do anything to retain in his possession a scarab toward which he already entertained the feelings of a life proprietor.

No—not quite anything! He stopped short at the idea of causing unpleasantness between the father of the Honorable Freddie and the father of the Honorable Freddie's fiancee. His secretarial position at the castle was a valuable one and he was loath to jeopardize it.

There was only one way in which this delicate affair could be brought to a satisfactory conclusion. It was obvious from what he had seen that night that Mr. Peters' connection with the attempt on the scarab was to be merely sympathetic, and that the actual theft was to be accomplished by Ashe. His only course, therefore, was to catch Ashe actually in the museum. Then Mr. Peters need not appear in the matter at all. Mr. Peters' position in those circumstances would be simply that of a man who had happened to employ, through no fault of his own, a valet who happened to be a thief.

He had made a mistake, he perceived, in locking the door of the museum. In future he must leave it open, as a trap is open; and he must stay up nights and keep watch. With these reflections, the Efficient Baxter returned to his room.

Meantime Ashe had entered Mr. Peters' bedroom and switched on the light. Mr. Peters, who had just succeeded in dropping off to sleep, sat up with a start.

"I've come to read to you," said Ashe.

Mr. Peters emitted a stifled howl, in which wrath and self-pity were nicely blended.

"You fool, don't you know I have just managed to get to sleep?"

"And now you're awake again," said Ashe soothingly. "Such is life! A little rest, a little folding of the hands in sleep, and then bing!—off we go again. I hope you will like this novel. I dipped into it and it seems good."

"What do you mean by coming in here at this time of night? Are you crazy?"

"It was your suggestion; and, by the way, I must thank you for it. I apologize for calling it thin. It worked like a charm. I don't think he believed it—in fact, I know he didn't; but it held him. I couldn't have thought up anything half so good in an emergency."

Mr. Peters' wrath changed to excitement.

"Did you get it? Have you been after my—my Cheops?"

"I have been after your Cheops, but I didn't get it. Bad men were abroad. That fellow with the spectacles, who was in the museum when I met you there this evening, swooped down from nowhere, and I had to tell him that you had rung for me to read to you. Fortunately I had this novel on me. I think he followed me upstairs to see whether I really did come to your room."

Mr. Peters groaned miserably.

"Baxter," he said; "He's a man named Baxter—Lord Emsworth's private secretary; and he suspects us. He's the man we—I mean you—have got to look out for."

"Well, never mind. Let's be happy while we can. Make yourself comfortable and I'll start reading. After all, what could be pleasanter than a little literature in the small hours? Shall I begin?"

Ashe Marson found Joan Valentine in the stable yard after breakfast the next morning, playing with a retriever puppy. "Will you spare me a moment of your valuable time?"

"Certainly, Mr. Marson."

"Shall we walk out into the open somewhere—where we can't be overheard?"

"Perhaps it would be better."

They moved off.

"Request your canine friend to withdraw," said Ashe. "He prevents me from marshaling my thoughts."

"I'm afraid he won't withdraw."

"Never mind. I'll do my best in spite of him. Tell me, was I dreaming or did I really meet you in the hall this morning at about twenty minutes after two?"

"You did."

"And did you really tell me that you had come to the castle to steal—"

"Recover."

"—Recover Mr. Peters' scarab?"

"I did."

"Then it's true?"

"It is."

Ashe scraped the ground with a meditative toe.

"This," he said, "seems to me to complicate matters somewhat."

"It complicates them abominably!"

"I suppose you were surprised when you found that I was on the same game as yourself."

"Not in the least."

"You weren't!"

"I knew it directly I saw the advertisement in the Morning Post. And I hunted up the Morning Post directly you had told me that you had become Mr. Peters' valet."

"You have known all along!"

"I have."

Ashe regarded her admiringly.

"You're wonderful!"

"Because I saw through you?"

"Partly that; but chiefly because you had the pluck to undertake a thing like this."

"You undertook it."

"But I'm a man."

"And I'm a woman. And my theory, Mr. Marson, is that a woman can do nearly everything better than a man. What a splendid test case this would make to settle the Votes-for-Women question once and for all! Here we are—you and I—a man and a woman, each trying for the same thing and each starting with equal chances. Suppose I beat you? How about the inferiority of women then?"

"I never said women were inferior."

"You did with your eyes."

"Besides, you're an exceptional woman."

"You can't get out of it with a compliment. I'm an ordinary woman and I'm going to beat a real man."

Ashe frowned.

"I don't like to think of ourselves as working against each other."

"Why not?"

"Because I like you."

"I like you, Mr. Marson; but we must not let sentiment interfere with business. You want Mr. Peters' five thousand dollars. So do I."

"I hate the thought of being the instrument to prevent you from getting the money."

"You won't be. I shall be the instrument to prevent you from getting it. I don't like that thought, either; but one has got to face it."

"It makes me feel mean."

"That's simply your old-fashioned masculine attitude toward the female, Mr. Marson. You look on woman as a weak creature, to be shielded and petted. We aren't anything of the sort. We're terrors! We're as hard as nails. We're awful creatures. You mustn't let my sex interfere with your trying to get this reward. Think of me as though I were another man. We're up against each other in a fair fight, and I don't want any special privileges. If you don't do your best from now onward I shall never forgive you. Do you understand?"

"I suppose so."

"And we shall need to do our best. That little man with the glasses is on his guard. I was listening to you last night from behind the door. By the way, you shouldn't have told me to run away and then have stayed yourself to be caught. That is an example of the sort of thing I mean. It was chivalry—not business."

"I had a story ready to account for my being there. You had not."

"And what a capital story it was! I shall borrow it for my own use. If I am caught I shall say I had to read Aline to sleep because she suffers from insomnia. And I shouldn't wonder if she did—poor girl! She doesn't get enough to eat. She is being starved—poor child! I heard one of the footmen say that she refused everything at dinner last night. And, though she vows it isn't, my belief is that it's all because she is afraid to make a stand against her old father. It's a shame!"

"She is a weak creature, to be shielded and petted," said Ashe solemnly.

Joan laughed.

"Well, yes; you caught me there. I admit that poor Aline is not a shining example of the formidable modern woman; but—" She stopped. "Oh, bother! I've just thought of what I ought to have said—the good repartee that would have crushed you. I suppose it's too late now?"

"Not at all. I'm like that myself—only it is generally the next day when I hit the right answer. Shall we go back? . . . She is a weak creature, to be shielded and petted."

"Thank you so much," said Joan gratefully. "And why is she a weak creature? Because she has allowed herself to be shielded and petted; because she has permitted man to give her special privileges, and generally—No; it isn't so good as I thought it was going to be."

"It should be crisper," said Ashe critically. "It lacks the punch."

"But it brings me back to my point, which is that I am not going to imitate her and forfeit my independence of action in return for chivalry. Try to look at it from my point of view, Mr. Marson. I know you need the money just as much as I do. Well, don't you think I should feel a little mean if I thought you were not trying your hardest to get it, simply because you didn't think it would be fair to try your hardest against a woman? That would cripple me. I should not feel as though I had the right to do anything. It's too important a matter for you to treat me like a child and let me win to avoid disappointing me. I want the money; but I don't want it handed to me."

"Believe me," said Ashe earnestly, "it will not be handed to you. I have studied the Baxter question more deeply than you have, and I can assure you that Baxter is a menace. What has put him so firmly on the right scent I don't know; but he seems to have divined the exact state of affairs in its entirety—so far as I am concerned, that is to say. Of course he has no idea you are mixed up in the business; but I am afraid his suspicion of me will hit you as well. What I mean is that, for some time to come, I fancy that man proposes to camp out on the rug in front of the museum door. It would be madness for either of us to attempt to go there at present."

"It is being made very hard for us, isn't it? And I thought it was going to be so simple."

"I think we should give him at least a week to simmer down."

"Fully that."

"Let us look on the bright side. We are in no hurry. Blandings Castle is quite as comfortable as Number Seven Arundell Street, and the commissariat department is a revelation to me. I had no idea English servants did themselves so well. And, as for the social side, I love it; I revel in it. For the first time in my life I feel as though I am somebody. Did you observe my manner toward the kitchen maid who waited on us at dinner last night? A touch of the old noblesse about it, I fancy. Dignified but not unkind, I think. And I can keep it up. So far as I am concerned, let this life continue indefinitely."

"But what about Mr. Peters? Don't you think there is danger he may change his mind about that five thousand dollars if we keep him waiting too long?"

"Not a chance of it. Being almost within touch of the scarab has had the worst effect on him. It has intensified the craving. By the way, have you seen the scarab?"

"Yes; I got Mrs. Twemlow to take me to the museum while you were talking to the butler. It was dreadful to feel that it was lying there in the open waiting for somebody to take it, and not be able to do anything."

"I felt exactly the same. It isn't much to look at, is it? If it hadn't been for the label I wouldn't have believed it was the thing for which Peters was offering five thousand dollars' reward. But that's his affair. A thing is worth what somebody will give for it. Ours not to reason why; ours but to elude Baxter and gather it in."

"Ours, indeed! You speak as though we were partners instead of rivals."

Ashe uttered an exclamation. "You've hit it! Why not? Why any cutthroat competition? Why shouldn't we form a company? It would solve everything."

Joan looked thoughtful.

"You mean divide the reward?"

"Exactly—into two equal parts."

"And the labor?"

"The labor?"

"How shall we divide that?"

Ashe hesitated.

"My idea," he said, "was that I should do what I might call the rough work; and—"

"You mean you should do the actual taking of the scarab?"

"Exactly. I would look after that end of it."

"And what would my duties be?"

"Well, you—you would, as it were—how shall I put it? You would, so to speak, lend moral support."

"By lying snugly in bed, fast asleep?"

Ashe avoided her eye.

"Well, yes—er—something on those lines."

"While you ran all the risks?"

"No, no. The risks are practically nonexistent."

"I thought you said just now that it would be madness for either of us to attempt to go to the museum at present." Joan laughed. "It won't do, Mr. Marson. You remind me of an old cat I once had. Whenever he killed a mouse he would bring it into the drawing-room and lay it affectionately at my feet. I would reject the corpse with horror and turn him out, but back he would come with his loathsome gift. I simply couldn't make him understand that he was not doing me a kindness. He thought highly of his mouse and it was beyond him to realize that I did not want it.

"You are just the same with your chivalry. It's very kind of you to keep offering me your dead mouse; but honestly I have no use for it. I won't take favors just because I happen to be a female. If we are going to form this partnership I insist on doing my fair share of the work and running my fair share of the risks—the practically nonexistent risks."

"You're very—resolute."

"Say pig-headed; I shan't mind. Certainly I am! A girl has got to be, even nowadays, if she wants to play fair. Listen, Mr. Marson; I will not have the dead mouse. I do not like dead mice. If you attempt to work off your dead mouse on me this partnership ceases before it has begun. If we are to work together we are going to make alternate attempts to get the scarab. No other arrangement will satisfy me."

"Then I claim the right to make the first one."

"You don't do anything of the sort. We toss up for first chance, like little ladies and gentlemen. Have you a coin? I will spin, and you call."

Ashe made a last stand.

"This is perfectly—"

"Mr. Marson!"

Ashe gave in. He produced a coin and handed it to her gloomily.

"Under protest," he said.

"Head or tail?" said Joan, unmoved.

Ashe watched the coin gyrating in the sunshine.

"Tail!" he cried.

The coin stopped rolling.

"Tail it is," said Joan. "What a nuisance! Well, never mind—I'll get my chance if you fail."

"I shan't fail," said Ashe fervently. "If I have to pull the museum down I won't fail. Thank heaven, there's no chance now of your doing anything foolish!"

"Don't be too sure. Well, good luck, Mr. Marson!"

"Thank you, partner."

They shook hands.

As they parted at the door, Joan made one further remark: "There's just one thing, Mr. Marson."

"Yes?"

"If I could have accepted the mouse from anyone I should certainly have accepted it from you."

CHAPTER VII

It is worthy of record, in the light of after events, that at the beginning of their visit it was the general opinion of the guests gathered together at Blandings Castle that the place was dull. The house party had that air of torpor which one sees in the saloon passengers of an Atlantic liner—that appearance of resignation to an enforced idleness and a monotony to be broken only by meals. Lord Emsworth's guests gave the impression, collectively, of being just about to yawn and look at their watches.

This was partly the fault of the time of year, for most house parties are dull if they happen to fall between the hunting and the shooting seasons, but must be attributed chiefly to Lord Emsworth's extremely sketchy notions of the duties of a host.

A host has no right to interne a regiment of his relations in his house unless he also invites lively and agreeable outsiders to meet them. If he does commit this solecism the least he can do is to work himself to the bone in the effort to invent amusements and diversions for his victims. Lord Emsworth had failed badly in both these matters. With the exception of Mr. Peters, his daughter Aline and George Emerson, there was nobody in the house who did not belong to the clan; and, as for his exerting himself to entertain, the company was lucky if it caught a glimpse of its host at meals.

Lord Emsworth belonged to the people-who-like-to-be-left-alone- to-amuse-themselves-when-they-come-to-a-place school of hosts. He pottered about the garden in an old coat—now uprooting a weed, now wrangling with the autocrat from Scotland, who was theoretically in his service as head gardener—dreamily satisfied, when he thought of them at all, that his guests were as perfectly happy as he was.

Apart from his son Freddie, whom he had long since dismissed as a youth of abnormal tastes, from whom nothing reasonable was to be expected, he could not imagine anyone not being content merely to be at Blandings when the buds were bursting on the trees.

A resolute hostess might have saved the situation; but Lady Ann Warblington's abilities in that direction stopped short at leaving everything to Mrs. Twemlow and writing letters in her bedroom. When Lady Ann Warblington was not writing letters in her bedroom—which was seldom, for she had an apparently inexhaustible correspondence—she was nursing sick headaches in it. She was one of those hostesses whom a guest never sees except when he goes into the library and espies the tail of her skirt vanishing through the other door.

As for the ordinary recreations of the country house, the guests could frequent the billiard room, where they were sure to find Lord Stockheath playing a hundred up with his cousin, Algernon Wooster—a spectacle of the liveliest interest—or they could, if fond of golf, console themselves for the absence of links in the neighborhood with the exhilarating pastime of clock golf; or they could stroll about the terraces with such of their relations as they happened to be on speaking terms with at the moment, and abuse their host and the rest of their relations.

This was the favorite amusement; and after breakfast, on a morning ten days after Joan and Ashe had formed their compact, the terraces were full of perambulating couples. Here, Colonel Horace Mant, walking with the Bishop of Godalming, was soothing that dignitary by clothing in soldierly words thoughts that the latter had not been able to crush down, but which his holy office scarcely permitted him to utter.

There, Lady Mildred Mant, linked to Mrs. Jack Hale, of the collateral branch of the family, was saying things about her father in his capacity of host and entertainer, that were making her companion feel like another woman. Farther on, stopping occasionally to gesticulate, could be seen other Emsworth relations and connections. It was a typical scene of quiet, peaceful English family life.

Leaning on the broad stone balustrade of the upper terrace, Aline Peters and George Emerson surveyed the malcontents. Aline gave a little sigh, almost inaudible; but George's hearing was good.

"I was wondering when you are going to admit it," he said, shifting his position so that he faced her.

"Admit what?"

"That you can't stand the prospect; that the idea of being stuck for life with this crowd, like a fly on fly paper, is too much for you; that you are ready to break off your engagement to Freddie and come away and marry me and live happily ever after."

"George!"

"Well, wasn't that what it meant? Be honest!"

"What what meant?"

"That sigh."

"I didn't sigh. I was just breathing."

"Then you can breathe in this atmosphere! You surprise me!" He raked the terraces with hostile eyes. "Look at them! Look at them—crawling round like doped beetles. My dear girl, it's no use your pretending that this sort of thing wouldn't kill you. You're pining away already. You're thinner and paler since you came here. Gee! How we shall look back at this and thank our stars that we're out of it when we're back in old New York, with the elevated rattling and the street cars squealing over the points, and something doing every step you take. I shall call you on the 'phone from the office and have you meet me down town somewhere, and we'll have a bite to eat and go to some show, and a bit of supper afterward and a dance or two; and then go home to our cozy—"

"George, you mustn't—really!"

"Why mustn't I?"

"It's wrong. You can't talk like that when we are both enjoying the hospitality—"

A wild laugh, almost a howl, disturbed the talk of the most adjacent of the perambulating relations. Colonel Horace Mant, checked in mid-sentence, looked up resentfully at the cause of the interruption.

"I wish somebody would tell me whether it's that American fellow, Emerson, or young Freddie who's supposed to be engaged to Miss Peters. Hanged if you ever see her and Freddie together, but she and Emerson are never to be found apart. If my respected father-in-law had any sense I should have thought he would have had sense enough to stop that."

"You forget, my dear Horace," said the bishop charitably; "Miss Peters and Mr. Emerson have known each other since they were children."

"They were never nearly such children as Emsworth is now," snorted the colonel. "If that girl isn't in love with Emerson I'll be—I'll eat my hat."

"No, no," said the bishop. "No, no! Surely not, Horace. What were you saying when you broke off?"

"I was saying that if a man wanted his relations never to speak to each other again for the rest of their lives the best thing he could do would be to herd them all together in a dashed barrack of a house a hundred miles from anywhere, and then go off and spend all his time prodding dashed flower beds with a spud—dash it!"

"Just so; just so. So you were. Go on, Horace; I find a curious comfort in your words."

On the terrace above them Aline was looking at George with startled eyes.

"George!"

"I'm sorry; but you shouldn't spring these jokes on me so suddenly. You said enjoying! Yes—reveling in it, aren't we!"

"It's a lovely old place," said Aline defensively.

"And when you've said that you've said everything. You can't live on scenery and architecture for the rest of your life. There's the human element to be thought of. And you're beginning—"

"There goes father," interrupted Aline. "How fast he is walking! George, have you noticed a sort of difference in father these last few days?"

"I haven't. My specialty is keeping an eye on the rest of the Peters family."

"He seems better somehow. He seems to have almost stopped smoking—and I'm very glad, for those cigars were awfully bad for him. The doctor expressly told him he must stop them, but he wouldn't pay any attention to him. And he seems to take so much more exercise. My bedroom is next to his, you know, and every morning I can hear things going on through the wall—father dancing about and puffing a good deal. And one morning I met his valet going in with a pair of Indian clubs. I believe father is really taking himself in hand at last."

George Emerson exploded.

"And about time, too! How much longer are you to go on starving yourself to death just to give him the resolution to stick to his dieting? It maddens me to see you at dinner. And it's killing you. You're getting pale and thin. You can't go on like this."

A wistful look came over Aline's face.

"I do get a little hungry sometimes—late at night generally."

"You want somebody to take care of you and look after you. I'm the man. You may think you can fool me; but I can tell. You're weakening on this Freddie proposition. You're beginning to see that it won't do. One of these days you're going to come to me and say: 'George, you were right. I take the count. Me for the quiet sneak to the station, without anybody knowing, and the break for London, and the wedding at the registrar's.' Oh, I know! I couldn't have loved you all this time and not know. You're weakening."

The trouble with these supermen is that they lack reticence. They do not know how to omit. They expand their chests and whoop. And a girl, even the mildest and sweetest of girls—even a girl like Aline Peters—cannot help resenting the note of triumph. But supermen despise tact. As far as one can gather, that is the chief difference between them and the ordinary man.

A little frown appeared on Aline's forehead and she set her mouth mutinously.

"I'm not weakening at all," she said, and her voice was—for her—quite acid. "You—you take too much for granted."

George was contemplating the landscape with a conqueror's eye.

"You are beginning to see that it is impossible—this Freddie foolishness."

"It is not foolishness," said Aline pettishly, tears of annoyance in her eyes. "And I wish you wouldn't call him Freddie."

"He asked me to. He asked me to!"

Aline stamped her foot.

"Well, never mind. Please don't do it."

"Very well, little girl," said George softly. "I wouldn't do anything to hurt you."

The fact that it never even occurred to George Emerson he was being offensively patronizing shows the stern stuff of which these supermen are made.

The Efficient Baxter bicycled broodingly to Market Blandings for tobacco. He brooded for several reasons. He had just seen Aline Peters and George Emerson in confidential talk on the upper terrace, and that was one thing which exercised his mind, for he suspected George Emerson. He suspected him nebulously as a snake in the grass; as an influence working against the orderly progress of events concerning the marriage that had been arranged and would shortly take place between Miss Peters and the Honorable Frederick Threepwood.

It would be too much to say that he had any idea that George was putting in such hard and consistent work in his serpentine role; indeed if he could have overheard the conversation just recorded it is probable that Rupert Baxter would have had heart failure; but he had observed the intimacy between the two as he observed most things in his immediate neighborhood, and he disapproved of it. It was all very well to say that George Emerson had known Aline Peters since she was a child. If that was so, then in the opinion of the Efficient Baxter he had known her quite long enough and ought to start making the acquaintance of somebody else.

He blamed the Honorable Freddie. If the Honorable Freddie had been a more ardent lover he would have spent his time with Aline, and George Emerson would have taken his proper place as one of the crowd at the back of the stage. But Freddie's view of the matter seemed to be that he had done all that could be expected of a chappie in getting engaged to the girl, and that now he might consider himself at liberty to drop her for a while.

So Baxter, as he bicycled to Market Blandings for tobacco, brooded on Freddie, Aline Peters and George Emerson. He also brooded on Mr. Peters and Ashe Marson. Finally he brooded in a general way, because he had had very little sleep the past week.

The spectacle of a young man doing his duty and enduring considerable discomforts while doing it is painful; but there is such uplift in it, it affords so excellent a moral picture, that I cannot omit a short description of the manner in which Rupert Baxter had spent the nights which had elapsed since his meeting with Ashe in the small hours in the hall.

In the gallery which ran above the hall there was a large chair, situated a few paces from the great staircase. On this, in an overcoat—for the nights were chilly—and rubber-soled shoes, the Efficient Baxter had sat, without missing a single night, from one in the morning until daybreak, waiting, waiting, waiting. It had been an ordeal to try the stoutest determination. Nature had never intended Baxter for a night bird. He loved his bed. He knew that doctors held that insufficient sleep made a man pale and sallow, and he had always aimed at the peach-bloom complexion which comes from a sensible eight hours between the sheets.

One of the King Georges of England—I forget which—once said that a certain number of hours' sleep each night—I cannot recall at the moment how many—made a man something, which for the time being has slipped my memory. Baxter agreed with him. It went against all his instincts to sit up in this fashion; but it was his duty and he did it.

It troubled him that, as night after night went by and Ashe, the suspect, did not walk into the trap so carefully laid for him, he found an increasing difficulty in keeping awake. The first two or three of his series of vigils he had passed in an unimpeachable wakefulness, his chin resting on the rail of the gallery and his ears alert for the slightest sound; but he had not been able to maintain this standard of excellence.

On several occasions he had caught himself in the act of dropping off, and the last night he had actually wakened with a start to find it quite light. As his last recollection before that was of an inky darkness impenetrable to the eye, dismay gripped him with a sudden clutch and he ran swiftly down to the museum. His relief on finding that the scarab was still there had been tempered by thoughts of what might have been.

Baxter, then, as he bicycled to Market Blandings for tobacco, had good reason to brood. Having bought his tobacco and observed the life and thought of the town for half an hour—it was market day and the normal stagnation of the place was temporarily relieved and brightened by pigs that eluded their keepers, and a bull calf which caught a stout farmer at the psychological moment when he was tying his shoe lace and lifted him six feet—he made his way to the Emsworth Arms, the most respectable of the eleven inns the citizens of Market Blandings contrived in some miraculous way to support.

In English country towns, if the public houses do not actually outnumber the inhabitants, they all do an excellent trade. It is only when they are two to one that hard times hit them and set the innkeepers to blaming the government.

It was not the busy bar, full to overflowing with honest British yeomen—many of them in a similar condition—that Baxter sought. His goal was the genteel dining-room on the first floor, where a bald and shuffling waiter, own cousin to a tortoise, served luncheon to those desiring it. Lack of sleep had reduced Baxter to a condition where the presence and chatter of the house party were insupportable. It was his purpose to lunch at the Emsworth Arms and take a nap in an armchair afterward.

He had relied on having the room to himself, for Market Blandings did not lunch to a great extent; but to his annoyance and disappointment the room was already occupied by a man in brown tweeds.

Occupied is the correct word, for at first sight this man seemed to fill the room. Never since almost forgotten days when he used to frequent circuses and side shows, had Baxter seen a fellow human being so extraordinarily obese. He was a man about fifty years old, gray-haired, of a mauve complexion, and his general appearance suggested joviality.

To Baxter's chagrin, this person engaged him in conversation directly he took his seat at the table. There was only one table in the room, as is customary in English inns, and it had the disadvantage that it collected those seated at it into one party. It was impossible for Baxter to withdraw into himself and ignore this person's advances.

It is doubtful whether he could have done it, however, had they been separated by yards of floor, for the fat man was not only naturally talkative but, as appeared from his opening remarks, speech had been dammed up within him for some time by lack of a suitable victim.

"Morning!" he began; "nice day. Good for the farmers. I'll move up to your end of the table if I may, sir. Waiter, bring my beef to this gentleman's end of the table."

He creaked into a chair at Baxter's side and resumed:

"Infernally quiet place, this, sir. I haven't found a soul to speak to since I arrived yesterday afternoon except deaf-and-dumb rustics. Are you making a long stay here?"

"I live outside the town."

"I pity you. Wouldn't care to do it myself. Had to come here on business and shan't be sorry when it's finished. I give you my word I couldn't sleep a wink last night because of the quiet. I was just dropping off when a beast of a bird outside the window gave a chirrup, and it brought me up with a jerk as though somebody had fired a gun. There's a damned cat somewhere near my room that mews. I lie in bed waiting for the next mew, all worked up.

"Heaven save me from the country! It may be all right for you, if you've got a comfortable home and a pal or two to chat with after dinner; but you've no conception what it's like in this infernal town—I suppose it calls itself a town. What a hole! There's a church down the street. I'm told it's Norman or something. Anyway, it's old. I'm not much of a man for churches as a rule, but I went and took a look at it.

"Then somebody told me there was a fine view from the end of High Street; so I went and took a look at that. And now, so far as I can make out, I've done the sights and exhausted every possibility of entertainment the town has to provide—unless there's another church. I'm so reduced that I'll go and see the Methodist Chapel, if there is one."

Fresh air, want of sleep and the closeness of the dining-room combined to make Baxter drowsy. He ate his lunch in a torpor, hardly replying to his companion's remarks, who, for his part, did not seem to wish or to expect replies. It was enough for him to be talking.

"What do people do with themselves in a place like this? When they want amusement, I mean. I suppose it's different if you've been brought up to it. Like being born color-blind or something. You don't notice. It's the visitor who suffers. They've no enterprise in this sort of place. There's a bit of land just outside here that would make a sweet steeplechase course; natural barriers; everything. It hasn't occurred to 'em to do anything with it. It makes you despair of your species—that sort of thing. Now if I—"

Baxter dozed. With his fork still impaling a piece of cold beef, he dropped into that half-awake, half-asleep state which is Nature's daytime substitute for the true slumber of the night. The fat man, either not noticing or not caring, talked on. His voice was a steady drone, lulling Baxter to rest.

Suddenly there was a break. Baxter sat up, blinking. He had a curious impression that his companion had said "Hello, Freddie!" and that the door had just opened and closed.

"Eh?" he said.

"Yes?" said the fat man.

"What did you say?"

"I was speaking of—"

"I thought you said, 'Hello, Freddie!'"

His companion eyed him indulgently.

"I thought you were dropping off when I looked at you. You've been dreaming. What should I say, 'Hello, Freddie!' for?"

The conundrum was unanswerable. Baxter did not attempt to answer it. But there remained at the back of his mind a quaint idea that he had caught sight, as he woke, of the Honorable Frederick Threepwood, his face warningly contorted, vanishing through the doorway. Yet what could the Honorable Freddie be doing at the Emsworth Arms?

A solution of the difficulty occurred to him: he had dreamed he had seen Freddie and that had suggested the words which, reason pointed out, his companion could hardly have spoken. Even if the Honorable Freddie should enter the room, this fat man, who was apparently a drummer of some kind, would certainly not know who he was, nor would he address him so familiarly.

Yes, that must be the explanation. After all, the quaintest things happened in dreams. Last night, when he had fallen asleep in his chair, he had dreamed that he was sitting in a glass case in the museum, making faces at Lord Emsworth, Mr. Peters, and Beach, the butler, who were trying to steal him, under the impression that he was a scarab of the reign of Cheops of the Fourth Dynasty—a thing he would never have done when awake. Yes; he must certainly have been dreaming.

In the bedroom into which he had dashed to hide himself, on discovering that the dining-room was in possession of the Efficient Baxter, the Honorable Freddie sat on a rickety chair, scowling. He elaborated a favorite dictum of his:

"You can't take a step anywhere without stumbling over that damn feller, Baxter!"

He wondered whether Baxter had seen him. He wondered whether Baxter had recognized him. He wondered whether Baxter had heard R. Jones say, "Hello, Freddie!"

He wondered, if such should be the case, whether R. Jones' presence of mind and native resource had been equal to explaining away the remark.

CHAPTER VIII

"'Put the butter or drippings in a kettle on the range, and when hot add the onions and fry them; add the veal and cook until brown. Add the water, cover closely, and cook very slowly until the meat is tender; then add the seasoning and place the potatoes on top of the meat. Cover and cook until the potatoes are tender, but not falling to pieces.'"

"Sure," said Mr. Peters—"not falling to pieces. That's right. Go on."

"'Then add the cream and cook five minutes longer'" read Ashe.

"Is that all?"

"That's all of that one."

Mr. Peters settled himself more comfortably in bed.

"Read me the piece where it tells about curried lobster."

Ashe cleared his throat.

"'Curried Lobster,'" he read. "'Materials: Two one-pound lobsters, two teaspoonfuls lemon juice, half a spoonful curry powder, two tablespoonfuls butter, a tablespoonful flour, one cupful scalded milk, one cupful cracker crumbs, half teaspoonful salt, quarter teaspoonful pepper.'"

"Go on."

"'Way of Preparing: Cream the butter and flour and add the scalded milk; then add the lemon juice, curry powder, salt and pepper. Remove the lobster meat from the shells and cut into half-inch cubes.'"

"Half-inch cubes," sighed Mr. Peters wistfully. "Yes?"

"'Add the latter to the sauce.'"

"You didn't say anything about the latter. Oh, I see; it means the half-inch cubes. Yes?"

"'Refill the lobster shells, cover with buttered crumbs, and bake until the crumbs are brown. This will serve six persons.'"

"And make them feel an hour afterward as though they had swallowed a live wild cat," said Mr. Peters ruefully.

"Not necessarily," said Ashe. "I could eat two portions of that at this very minute and go off to bed and sleep like a little child."

Mr. Peters raised himself on his elbow and stared at him. They were in the millionaire's bedroom, the time being one in the morning, and Mr. Peters had expressed a wish that Ashe should read him to sleep. He had voted against Ashe's novel and produced from the recesses of his suitcase a much-thumbed cookbook. He explained that since his digestive misfortunes had come on him he had derived a certain solace from its perusal.

It may be that to some men sorrow's crown of sorrow is remembering happier things; but Mr. Peters had not found that to be the case. In his hour of affliction it soothed him to read of Hungarian Goulash and escaloped brains, and to remember that he, too, the nut-and-grass eater of today, had once dwelt in Arcadia.

The passage of the days, which had so sapped the stamina of the efficient Baxter, had had the opposite effect on Mr. Peters. His was one of those natures that cannot deal in half measures. Whatever he did, he did with the same driving energy. After the first passionate burst of resistance he had settled down into a model pupil in Ashe's one-man school of physical culture. It had been the same, now that he came to look back on it, at Muldoon's.

Now that he remembered, he had come away from White Plains hoping, indeed, never to see the place again, but undeniably a different man physically. It was not the habit of Professor Muldoon to let his patients loaf; but Mr. Peters, after the initial plunge, had needed no driving. He had worked hard at his cure then, because it was the job in hand. He worked hard now, under the guidance of Ashe, because, once he had begun, the thing interested and gripped him.

Ashe, who had expected continued reluctance, had been astonished and delighted at the way in which the millionaire had behaved. Nature had really intended Ashe for a trainer; he identified himself so thoroughly with his man and rejoiced at the least signs of improvement.

In Mr. Peters' case there had been distinct improvement already. Miracles do not happen nowadays, and it was too much to expect one who had maltreated his body so consistently for so many years to become whole in a day; but to an optimist like Ashe signs were not wanting that in due season Mr. Peters would rise on stepping-stones of his dead self to higher things, and though never soaring into the class that devours lobster a la Newburg and smiles after it, might yet prove himself a devil of a fellow among the mutton chops.

"You're a wonder!" said Mr. Peters. "You're fresh, and you have no respect for your elders and betters; but you deliver the goods. That's the point. Why, I'm beginning to feel great! Say, do you know I felt a new muscle in the small of my back this morning? They are coming out on me like a rash."

"That's the Larsen Exercises. They develop the whole body."

"Well, you're a pretty good advertisement for them if they need one. What were you before you came to me—a prize-fighter?"

"That's the question everybody I have met since I arrived here has asked me. I believe it made the butler think I was some sort of crook when I couldn't answer it. I used to write stories— detective stories."

"What you ought to be doing is running a place over here in England like Muldoon has back home. But you will be able to write one more story out of this business here, if you want to. When are you going to have another try for my scarab?"

"To-night."

"To-night? How about Baxter?"

"I shall have to risk Baxter."

Mr. Peters hesitated. He had fallen out of the habit of being magnanimous during the past few years, for dyspepsia brooks no divided allegiance and magnanimity has to take a back seat when it has its grip on you.

"See here," he said awkwardly; "I've been thinking this over lately—and what's the use? It's a queer thing; and if anybody had told me a week ago that I should be saying it I wouldn't have believed him; but I am beginning to like you. I don't want to get you into trouble. Let the old scarab go. What's a scarab anyway? Forget about it and stick on here as my private Muldoon. If it's the five thousand that's worrying you, forget that too. I'll give it to you as your fee."

Ashe was astounded. That it could really be his peppery employer who spoke was almost unbelievable. Ashe's was a friendly nature and he could never be long associated with anyone without trying to establish pleasant relations; but he had resigned himself in the present case to perpetual warfare.

He was touched; and if he had ever contemplated abandoning his venture, this, he felt, would have spurred him on to see it through. This sudden revelation of the human in Mr. Peters was like a trumpet call.

"I wouldn't think of it," he said. "It's great of you to suggest such a thing; but I know just how you feel about the thing, and I'm going to get it for you if I have to wring Baxter's neck. Probably Baxter will have given up waiting as a bad job by now if he has been watching all this while. We've given him ten nights to cool off. I expect he is in bed, dreaming pleasant dreams. It's nearly two o'clock. I'll wait another ten minutes and then go down." He picked up the cookbook. "Lie back and make yourself comfortable, and I'll read you to sleep first."

"You're a good boy," said Mr. Peters drowsily.

"Are you ready? 'Pork Tenderloin Larded. Half pound fat pork—'" A faint smile curved Mr. Peters' lips. His eyes were closed and he breathed softly. Ashe went on in a low voice: "'four large pork tenderloins, one cupful cracker crumbs, one cupful boiling water, two tablespoonfuls butter, one teaspoonful salt, half teaspoonful pepper, one teaspoonful poultry seasoning.'"

A little sigh came from the bed.

"'Way of Preparing: Wipe the tenderloins with a damp cloth. With a sharp knife make a deep pocket lengthwise in each tenderloin. Cut your pork into long thin strips and, with a needle, lard each tenderloin. Melt the butter in the water, add the seasoning and the cracker crumbs, combining all thoroughly. Now fill each pocket in the tenderloin with this stuffing. Place the tenderloins—'"

A snore sounded from the pillows, punctuating the recital like a mark of exclamation. Ashe laid down the book and peered into the darkness beyond the rays of the bed lamp. His employer slept.

Ashe switched off the light and crept to the door. Out in the passage he stopped and listened. All was still. He stole downstairs.

George Emerson sat in his bedroom in the bachelors' wing of the castle smoking a cigarette. A light of resolution was in his eyes. He glanced at the table beside his bed and at what was on that table, and the light of resolution flamed into a glare of fanatic determination. So might a medieval knight have looked on the eve of setting forth to rescue a maiden from a dragon.

His cigarette burned down. He looked at his watch, put it back, and lit another cigarette. His aspect was the aspect of one waiting for the appointed hour. Smoking his second cigarette, he resumed his meditations. They had to do with Aline Peters.

George Emerson was troubled about Aline Peters. Watching over her, as he did, with a lover's eye, he had perceived that about her which distressed him. On the terrace that morning she had been abrupt to him—what in a girl of less angelic disposition one might have called snappy. Yes, to be just, she had snapped at him. That meant something. It meant that Aline was not well. It meant what her pallor and tired eyes meant—that the life she was leading was doing her no good.

Eleven nights had George dined at Blandings Castle, and on each of the eleven nights he had been distressed to see the manner in which Aline, declining the baked meats, had restricted herself to the miserable vegetable messes which were all that doctor's orders permitted to her suffering father. George's pity had its limits. His heart did not bleed for Mr. Peters. Mr. Peters' diet was his own affair. But that Aline should starve herself in this fashion, purely by way of moral support for her parent, was another matter.

George was perhaps a shade material. Himself a robust young man and taking what might be called an outsize in meals, he attached perhaps too much importance to food as an adjunct to the perfect life. In his survey of Aline he took a line through his own requirements; and believing that eleven such dinners as he had seen Aline partake of would have killed him he decided that his loved one was on the point of starvation.

No human being, he held, could exist on such Barmecide feasts. That Mr. Peters continued to do so did not occur to him as a flaw in his reasoning. He looked on Mr. Peters as a sort of machine. Successful business men often give that impression to the young. If George had been told that Mr. Peters went along on gasoline, like an automobile, he would not have been much surprised. But that Aline—his Aline—should have to deny herself the exercise of that mastication of rich meats which, together with the gift of speech, raises man above the beasts of the field—That was what tortured George.

He had devoted the day to thinking out a solution of the problem. Such was the overflowing goodness of Aline's heart that not even he could persuade her to withdraw her moral support from her father and devote herself to keeping up her strength as she should do. It was necessary to think of some other plan.

And then a speech of hers had come back to him. She had said—poor child:

"I do get a little hungry sometimes—late at night generally."

The problem was solved. Food should be brought to her late at night.

On the table by his bed was a stout sheet of packing paper. On this lay, like one of those pictures in still life that one sees on suburban parlor walls, a tongue, some bread, a knife, a fork, salt, a corkscrew and a small bottle of white wine.

It is a pleasure, when one has been able hitherto to portray George's devotion only through the medium of his speeches, to produce these comestibles as Exhibit A, to show that he loved Aline with no common love; for it had not been an easy task to get them there. In a house of smaller dimensions he would have raided the larder without shame, but at Blandings Castle there was no saying where the larder might be. All he knew was that it lay somewhere beyond that green-baize door opening on the hall, past which he was wont to go on his way to bed. To prowl through the maze of the servants' quarters in search of it was impossible. The only thing to be done was to go to Market Blandings and buy the things.

Fortune had helped him at the start by arranging that the Honorable Freddie, also, should be going to Market Blandings in the little runabout, which seated two. He had acquiesced in George's suggestion that he, George, should occupy the other seat, but with a certain lack of enthusiasm it seemed to George. He had not volunteered any reason as to why he was going to Market Blandings in the little runabout, and on arrival there had betrayed an unmistakable desire to get rid of George at the earliest opportunity.

As this had suited George to perfection, he being desirous of getting rid of the Honorable Freddie at the earliest opportunity, he had not been inquisitive, and they had parted on the outskirts of the town without mutual confidences.

George had then proceeded to the grocer's, and after that to another of the Market Blandings inns, not the Emsworth Arms, where he had bought the white wine. He did not believe in the local white wine, for he was a young man with a palate and mistrusted country cellars, but he assumed that, whatever its quality, it would cheer Aline in the small hours.

He had then tramped the whole five miles back to the castle with his purchases. It was here that his real troubles began and the quality of his love was tested. The walk, to a heavily laden man, was bad enough; but it was as nothing compared with the ordeal of smuggling the cargo up to his bedroom. Superhuman though he was, George was alive to the delicacy of the situation. One cannot convey food and drink to one's room in a strange house without, if detected, seeming to cast a slur on the table of the host. It was as one who carries dispatches through an enemy's lines that George took cover, emerged from cover, dodged, ducked and ran; and the moment when he sank down on his bed, the door locked behind him, was one of the happiest of his life.

The recollection of that ordeal made the one he proposed to embark on now seem slight in comparison. All he had to do was to go to Aline's room on the other side of the house, knock softly on the door until signs of wakefulness made themselves heard from within, and then dart away into the shadows whence he had come, and so back to bed. He gave Aline credit for the intelligence that would enable her, on finding a tongue, some bread, a knife, a fork, salt, a corkscrew and a bottle of white wine on the mat, to know what to do with them—and perhaps to guess whose was the loving hand that had laid them there.

The second clause, however, was not important, for he proposed to tell her whose was the hand next morning. Other people might hide their light under a bushel—not George Emerson.

It only remained now to allow time to pass until the hour should be sufficiently advanced to insure safety for the expedition. He looked at his watch again. It was nearly two. By this time the house must be asleep.

He gathered up the tongue, the bread, the knife, the fork, the salt, the corkscrew and the bottle of white wine, and left the room. All was still. He stole downstairs.

On his chair in the gallery that ran round the hall, swathed in an overcoat and wearing rubber-soled shoes, the Efficient Baxter sat and gazed into the darkness. He had lost the first fine careless rapture, as it were, which had helped him to endure these vigils, and a great weariness was on him. He found difficulty in keeping his eyes open, and when they were open the darkness seemed to press on them painfully. Take him for all in all, the Efficient Baxter had had about enough of it.

Time stood still. Baxter's thoughts began to wander. He knew that this was fatal and exerted himself to drag them back. He tried to concentrate his mind on some one definite thing. He selected the scarab as a suitable object, but it played him false. He had hardly concentrated on the scarab before his mind was straying off to ancient Egypt, to Mr. Peters' dyspepsia, and on a dozen other branch lines of thought.

He blamed the fat man at the inn for this. If the fat man had not thrust his presence and conversation on him he would have been able to enjoy a sound sleep in the afternoon, and would have come fresh to his nocturnal task. He began to muse on the fat man. And by a curious coincidence whom should he meet a few moments later but this same man!

It happened in a somewhat singular manner, though it all seemed perfectly logical and consecutive to Baxter. He was climbing up the outer wall of Westminster Abbey in his pyjamas and a tall hat, when the fat man, suddenly thrusting his head out of a window which Baxter had not noticed until that moment, said, "Hello, Freddie!"

Baxter was about to explain that his name was not Freddie when he found himself walking down Piccadilly with Ashe Marson. Ashe said to him: "Nobody loves me. Everybody steals my grapefruit!" And the pathos of it cut the Efficient Baxter like a knife. He was on the point of replying; when Ashe vanished and Baxter discovered that he was not in Piccadilly, as he had supposed, but in an aeroplane with Mr. Peters, hovering over the castle.

Mr. Peters had a bomb in his hand, which he was fondling with loving care. He explained to Baxter that he had stolen it from the Earl of Emsworth's museum. "I did it with a slice of cold beef and a pickle," he explained; and Baxter found himself realizing that that was the only way. "Now watch me drop it," said Mr. Peters, closing one eye and taking aim at the castle. "I have to do this by the doctor's orders."

He loosed the bomb and immediately Baxter was lying in bed watching it drop. He was frightened, but the idea of moving did not occur to him. The bomb fell very slowly, dipping and fluttering like a feather. It came closer and closer. Then it struck with a roar and a sheet of flame.

Baxter woke to a sound of tumult and crashing. For a moment he hovered between dreaming and waking, and then sleep passed from him, and he was aware that something noisy and exciting was in progress in the hall below.

Coming down to first causes, the only reason why collisions of any kind occur is because two bodies defy Nature's law that a given spot on a given plane shall at a given moment of time be occupied by only one body.

There was a certain spot near the foot of the great staircase which Ashe, coming downstairs from Mr. Peters' room, and George Emerson, coming up to Aline's room, had to pass on their respective routes. George reached it at one minute and three seconds after two a.m., moving silently but swiftly; and Ashe, also maintaining a good rate of speed, arrived there at one minute and four seconds after the hour, when he ceased to walk and began to fly, accompanied by George Emerson, now going down. His arms were round George's neck and George was clinging to his waist.

In due season they reached the foot of the stairs and a small table, covered with occasional china and photographs in frames, which lay adjacent to the foot of the stairs. That—especially the occasional china—was what Baxter had heard.

George Emerson thought it was a burglar. Ashe did not know what it was, but he knew he wanted to shake it off; so he insinuated a hand beneath George's chin and pushed upward. George, by this time parted forever from the tongue, the bread, the knife, the fork, the salt, the corkscrew and the bottle of white wine, and having both hands free for the work of the moment, held Ashe with the left and punched him in the ribs with the right.

Ashe, removing his left arm from George's neck, brought it up as a reinforcement to his right, and used both as a means of throttling George. This led George, now permanently underneath, to grasp Ashe's ears firmly and twist them, relieving the pressure on his throat and causing Ashe to utter the first vocal sound of the evening, other than the explosive Ugh! that both had emitted at the instant of impact.

Ashe dislodged George's hands from his ears and hit George in the ribs with his elbow. George kicked Ashe on the left ankle. Ashe rediscovered George's throat and began to squeeze it afresh; and a pleasant time was being had by all when the Efficient Baxter, whizzing down the stairs, tripped over Ashe's legs, shot forward and cannoned into another table, also covered with occasional china and photographs in frames.

The hall at Blandings Castle was more an extra drawing-room than a hall; and, when not nursing a sick headache in her bedroom, Lady Ann Warblington would dispense afternoon tea there to her guests. Consequently it was dotted pretty freely with small tables. There were, indeed, no fewer than five more in various spots, waiting to be bumped into and smashed.

The bumping into and smashing of small tables, however, is a task that calls for plenty of time, a leisured pursuit; and neither George nor Ashe, a third party having been added to their little affair, felt a desire to stay on and do the thing properly. Ashe was strongly opposed to being discovered and called on to account for his presence there at that hour; and George, conscious of the tongue and its adjuncts now strewn about the hall, had a similar prejudice against the tedious explanations that detection must involve.

As though by mutual consent each relaxed his grip. They stood panting for an instant; then, Ashe in the direction where he supposed the green-baize door of the servants' quarters to be, George to the staircase that led to his bedroom, they went away from that place.

They had hardly done so when Baxter, having disassociated himself from the contents of the table he had upset, began to grope his way toward the electric-light switch, the same being situated near the foot of the main staircase. He went on all fours, as a safer method of locomotion, though slower, than the one he had attempted before.

Noises began to make themselves heard on the floors above. Roused by the merry crackle of occasional china, the house party was bestirring itself to investigate. Voices sounded, muffled and inquiring.

Meantime Baxter crawled steadily on his hands and knees toward the light switch. He was in much the same condition as one White Hope of the ring is after he has put his chin in the way of the fist of a rival member of the Truck Drivers' Union. He knew that he was still alive. More he could not say. The mists of sleep, which still shrouded his brain, and the shake-up he had had from his encounter with the table, a corner of which he had rammed with the top of his head, combined to produce a dreamlike state.

And so the Efficient Baxter crawled on; and as he crawled his hand, advancing cautiously, fell on something—something that was not alive; something clammy and ice-cold, the touch of which filled him with a nameless horror.

To say that Baxter's heart stood still would be physiologically inexact. The heart does not stand still. Whatever the emotions of its owner, it goes on beating. It would be more accurate to say that Baxter felt like a man taking his first ride in an express elevator, who has outstripped his vital organs by several floors and sees no immediate prospect of their ever catching up with him again. There was a great cold void where the more intimate parts of his body should have been. His throat was dry and contracted. The flesh of his back crawled, for he knew what it was he had touched.

Painful and absorbing as had been his encounter with the table, Baxter had never lost sight of the fact that close beside him a furious battle between unseen forces was in progress. He had heard the bumping and the thumping and the tense breathing even as he picked occasional china from his person. Such a combat, he had felt, could hardly fail to result in personal injury to either the party of the first part or the party of the second part, or both. He knew now that worse than mere injury had happened, and that he knelt in the presence of death.

There was no doubt that the man was dead. Insensibility alone could never have produced this icy chill. He raised his head in the darkness, and cried aloud to those approaching. He meant to cry: "Help! Murder!" But fear prevented clear articulation. What he shouted was: "Heh! Mer!" On which, from the neighborhood of the staircase, somebody began to fire a revolver.

The Earl of Emsworth had been sleeping a sound and peaceful sleep when the imbroglio began downstairs. He sat up and listened. Yes; undoubtedly burglars! He switched on his light and jumped out of bed. He took a pistol from a drawer, and thus armed went to look into the matter. The dreamy peer was no poltroon.

It was quite dark when he arrived on the scene of conflict, in the van of a mixed bevy of pyjamaed and dressing-gowned relations. He was in the van because, meeting these relations in the passage above, he had said to them: "Let me go first. I have a pistol." And they had let him go first. They were, indeed, awfully nice about it, not thrusting themselves forward or jostling or anything, but behaving in a modest and self-effacing manner that was pretty to watch.

When Lord Emsworth said, "Let me go first," young Algernon Wooster, who was on the very point of leaping to the fore, said, "Yes, by Jove! Sound scheme, by Gad!"—and withdrew into the background; and the Bishop of Godalming said: "By all means, Clarence undoubtedly; most certainly precede us."

When his sense of touch told him he had reached the foot of the stairs, Lord Emsworth paused. The hall was very dark and the burglars seemed temporarily to have suspended activities. And then one of them, a man with a ruffianly, grating voice, spoke. What it was he said Lord Emsworth could not understand. It sounded like "Heh! Mer!"—probably some secret signal to his confederates. Lord Emsworth raised his revolver and emptied it in the direction of the sound.

Extremely fortunately for him, the Efficient Baxter had not changed his all-fours attitude. This undoubtedly saved Lord Emsworth the worry of engaging a new secretary. The shots sang above Baxter's head one after the other, six in all, and found other billets than his person. They disposed themselves as follows: The first shot broke a window and whistled out into the night; the second shot hit the dinner gong and made a perfectly extraordinary noise, like the Last Trump; the third, fourth and fifth shots embedded themselves in the wall; the sixth and final shot hit a life-size picture of his lordship's grandmother in the face and improved it out of all knowledge.

One thinks no worse of Lord Emsworth's grandmother because she looked like Eddie Foy, and had allowed herself to be painted, after the heavy classic manner of some of the portraits of a hundred years ago, in the character of Venus—suitably draped, of course, rising from the sea; but it was beyond the possibility of denial that her grandson's bullet permanently removed one of Blandings Castle's most prominent eyesores.

Having emptied his revolver, Lord Emsworth said, "Who is there? Speak!" in rather an aggrieved tone, as though he felt he had done his part in breaking the ice, and it was now for the intruder to exert himself and bear his share of the social amenities.

The Efficient Baxter did not reply. Nothing in the world could have induced him to speak at that moment, or to make any sound whatsoever that might betray his position to a dangerous maniac who might at any instant reload his pistol and resume the fusillade. Explanations, in his opinion, could be deferred until somebody had the presence of mind to switch on the lights. He flattened himself on the carpet and hoped for better things. His cheek touched the corpse beside him; but though he winced and shuddered he made no outcry. After those six shots he was through with outcries.

A voice from above, the bishop's voice, said: "I think you have killed him, Clarence."

Another voice, that of Colonel Horace Mant, said: "Switch on those dashed lights! Why doesn't somebody? Dash it!"

The whole strength of the company began to demand light.

When the lights came, it was from the other side of the hall. Six revolver shots, fired at quarter past two in the morning, will rouse even sleeping domestics. The servants' quarters were buzzing like a hive. Shrill feminine screams were puncturing the air. Mr. Beach, the butler, in a suit of pink silk pajamas, of which no one would have suspected him, was leading a party of men servants down the stairs—not so much because he wanted to lead them as because they pushed him.

The passage beyond the green-baize door became congested, and there were cries for Mr. Beach to open it and look through and see what was the matter; but Mr. Beach was smarter than that and wriggled back so that he no longer headed the procession. This done, he shouted:

"Open that door there! Open that door! Look and see what the matter is."

Ashe opened the door. Since his escape from the hall he had been lurking in the neighborhood of the green-baize door and had been engulfed by the swirling throng. Finding himself with elbowroom for the first time, he pushed through, swung the door open and switched on the lights.

They shone on a collection of semi-dressed figures, crowding the staircase; on a hall littered with china and glass; on a dented dinner gong; on an edited and improved portrait of the late Countess of Emsworth; and on the Efficient Baxter, in an overcoat and rubber-soled shoes, lying beside a cold tongue. At no great distance lay a number of other objects—a knife, a fork, some bread, salt, a corkscrew and a bottle of white wine.

Using the word in the sense of saying something coherent, the Earl of Emsworth was the first to speak. He peered down at his recumbent secretary and said:

"Baxter! My dear fellow—what the devil?"

The feeling of the company was one of profound disappointment. They were disgusted at the anticlimax. For an instant, when the Efficient one did not move, a hope began to stir; but as soon as it was seen that he was not even injured, gloom reigned. One of two things would have satisfied them— either a burglar or a corpse. A burglar would have been welcome, dead or alive; but, if Baxter proposed to fill the part adequately it was imperative that he be dead. He had disappointed them deeply by turning out to be the object of their quest. That he should not have been even grazed was too much.

There was a cold silence as he slowly raised himself from the floor. As his eyes fell on the tongue, he started and remained gazing fixedly at it. Surprise paralyzed him.

Lord Emsworth was also looking at the tongue and he leaped to a not unreasonable conclusion. He spoke coldly and haughtily; for he was not only annoyed, like the others, at the anticlimax, but offended. He knew that he was not one of your energetic hosts who exert themselves unceasingly to supply their guests with entertainment; but there was one thing on which, as a host, he did pride himself—in the material matters of life he did his guests well; he kept an admirable table.

"My dear Baxter," he said in the tones he usually reserved for the correction of his son Freddie, "if your hunger is so great that you are unable to wait for breakfast and have to raid my larder in the middle of the night, I wish to goodness you would contrive to make less noise about it. I do not grudge you the food—help yourself when you please—but do remember that people who have not such keen appetites as yourself like to sleep during the night. A far better plan, my dear fellow, would be to have sandwiches or buns—or whatever you consider most sustaining— sent up to your bedroom."

Not even the bullets had disordered Baxter's faculties so much as this monstrous accusation. Explanations pushed and jostled one another in his fermenting brain, but he could not utter them. On every side he met gravely reproachful eyes. George Emerson was looking at him in pained disgust. Ashe Marson's face was the face of one who could never have believed this had he not seen it with his own eyes. The scrutiny of the knife-and-shoe boy was unendurable.

He stammered. Words began to proceed from him, tripping and stumbling over each other. Lord Emsworth's frigid disapproval did not relax.

"Pray do not apologize, Baxter. The desire for food is human. It is your boisterous mode of securing and conveying it that I deprecate. Let us all go to bed."

"But, Lord Emsworth—"

"To bed!" repeated his lordship firmly.

The company began to stream moodily upstairs. The lights were switched off. The Efficient Baxter dragged himself away. From the darkness in the direction of the servants' door a voice spoke.

"Greedy pig!" said the voice scornfully.

It sounded like the fresh young voice of the knife-and-shoe boy, but Baxter was too broken to investigate. He continued his retreat without pausing.

"Stuffin' of 'isself at all hours!" said the voice.

There was a murmur of approval from the unseen throng of domestics.

CHAPTER IX

As we grow older and realize more clearly the limitations of human happiness, we come to see that the only real and abiding pleasure in life is to give pleasure to other people. One must assume that the Efficient Baxter had not reached the age when this comes home to a man, for the fact that he had given genuine pleasure to some dozens of his fellow-men brought him no balm.

There was no doubt about the pleasure he had given. Once they had got over their disappointment at finding that he was not a dead burglar, the house party rejoiced whole-heartedly at the break in the monotony of life at Blandings Castle. Relations who had not been on speaking terms for years forgot their quarrels and strolled about the grounds in perfect harmony, abusing Baxter. The general verdict was that he was insane.

"Don't tell me that young fellow's all there," said Colonel Horace Mant; "because I know better. Have you noticed his eye? Furtive! Shifty! Nasty gleam in it. Besides—dash it!—did you happen to take a look at the hall last night after he had been there? It was in ruins, my dear sir—absolute dashed ruins. It was positively littered with broken china and tables that had been bowled over. Don't tell me that was just an accidental collision in the dark.

"My dear sir, the man must have been thrashing about—absolutely thrashing about, like a dashed salmon on a dashed hook. He must have had a paroxysm of some kind—some kind of a dashed fit. A doctor could give you the name for it. It's a well-known form of insanity. Paranoia—isn't that what they call it? Rush of blood to the head, followed by a general running amuck.

"I've heard fellows who have been in India talk of it. Natives get it. Don't know what they're doing, and charge through the streets taking cracks at people with dashed whacking great knives. Same with this young man, probably in a modified form at present. He ought to be in a home. One of these nights, if this grows on him, he will be massacring Emsworth in his bed."

"My dear Horace!" The Bishop of Godalming's voice was properly horror-stricken; but there was a certain unctuous relish in it.

"Take my word for it! Though, mind you, I don't say they aren't well suited. Everyone knows that Emsworth has been, to all practical intents and purposes, a dashed lunatic for years. What was it that young fellow Emerson, Freddie's American friend, was saying, the other day about some acquaintance of his who is not quite right in the head? Nobody in the house—is that it? Something to that effect, at any rate. I felt at the time it was a perfect description of Emsworth."

"My dear Horace! Your father-in-law! The head of the family!"

"A dashed lunatic, my dear sir—head of the family or no head of the family. A man as absent-minded as he is has no right to call himself sane. Nobody in the house—I recollect it now—nobody in the house except gas, and that has not been turned on. That's Emsworth!"

The Efficient Baxter, who had just left his presence, was feeling much the same about his noble employer. After a sleepless night he had begun at an early hour to try and corner Lord Emsworth in order to explain to him the true inwardness of last night's happenings. Eventually he had tracked him to the museum, where he found him happily engaged in painting a cabinet of birds' eggs. He was seated on a small stool, a large pot of red paint on the floor beside him, dabbing at the cabinet with a dripping brush. He was absorbed and made no attempt whatever to follow his secretary's remarks.

For ten minutes Baxter gave a vivid picture of his vigil and the manner in which it had been interrupted.

"Just so; just so, my dear fellow," said the earl when he had finished. "I quite understand. All I say is, if you do require additional food in the night let one of the servants bring it to your room before bedtime; then there will be no danger of these disturbances. There is no possible objection to your eating a hundred meals a day, my good Baxter, provided you do not rouse the whole house over them. Some of us like to sleep during the night."

"But, Lord Emsworth! I have just explained—It was not—I was not—"

"Never mind, my dear fellow; never mind. Why make such an important thing of it? Many people like a light snack before actually retiring. Doctors, I believe, sometimes recommend it. Tell me, Baxter, how do you think the museum looks now? A little brighter? Better for the dash of color? I think so. Museums are generally such gloomy places."

"Lord Emsworth, may I explain once again?"

The earl looked annoyed.

"My dear Baxter, I have told you that there is nothing to explain. You are getting a little tedious. What a deep, rich red this is, and how clean new paint smells! Do you know, Baxter, I have been longing to mess about with paint ever since I was a boy! I recollect my old father beating me with a walking stick. . . .

That would be before your time, of course. By the way, if you see Freddie, will you tell him I want to speak to him? He probably is in the smoking-room. Send him to me here."

It was an overwrought Baxter who delivered the message to the Honorable Freddie, who, as predicted, was in the smoking-room, lounging in a deep armchair.

There are times when life presses hard on a man, and it pressed hard on Baxter now. Fate had played him a sorry trick. It had put him in a position where he had to choose between two courses, each as disagreeable as the other. He must either face a possible second fiasco like that of last night, or else he must abandon his post and cease to mount guard over his threatened treasure.

His imagination quailed at the thought of a repetition of last night's horrors. He had been badly shaken by his collision with the table and even more so by the events that had followed it. Those revolver shots still rang in his ears.

It was probably the memory of those shots that turned the scale. It was unlikely he would again become entangled with a man bearing a tongue and the other things—he had given up in despair the attempt to unravel the mystery of the tongue; it completely baffled him—but it was by no means unlikely that if he spent another night in the gallery looking on the hall he might not again become a target for Lord Emsworth's irresponsible firearm. Nothing, in fact, was more likely; for in the disturbed state of the public mind the slightest sound after nightfall would be sufficient cause for a fusillade.

He had actually overheard young Algernon Wooster telling Lord Stockheath he had a jolly good mind to sit on the stairs that night with a shotgun, because it was his opinion that there was a jolly sight more in this business than there seemed to be; and what he thought of the bally affair was that there was a gang of some kind at work, and that that feller—what's-his-name?—that feller Baxter was some sort of an accomplice.

With these things in his mind Baxter decided to remain that night in the security of his bedroom. He had lost his nerve. He formed this decision with the utmost reluctance, for the thought of leaving the road to the museum clear for marauders was bitter in the extreme. If he could have overheard a conversation between Joan Valentine and Ashe Marson it is probable he would have risked Lord Emsworth's revolver and the shotgun of the Honorable Algernon Wooster.

Ashe, when he met Joan and recounted the events of the night, at which Joan, who was a sound sleeper, had not been present, was inclined to blame himself as a failure. True, fate had been against him, but the fact remained that he had achieved nothing. Joan, however, was not of this opinion.

"You have done wonders," she said. "You have cleared the way for me. That is my idea of real teamwork. I'm so glad now that we formed our partnership. It would have been too bad if I had got all the advantage of your work and had jumped in and deprived you of the reward. As it is, I shall go down and finish the thing off to-night with a clear conscience."

"You can't mean that you dream of going down to the museum to-night!"

"Of course I do."

"But it's madness!"

"On the contrary, to-night is the one night when there ought to be no risk at all."

"After what happened last night?"

"Because of what happened last night. Do you imagine Mr. Baxter will dare to stir from his bed after that? If ever there was a chance of getting this thing finished, it will be to-night."

"You're quite right. I never looked at it in that way. Baxter wouldn't risk a second disaster. I'll certainly make a success of it this time."

Joan raised her eyebrows.

"I don't quite understand you, Mr. Marson. Do you propose to try to get the scarab to-night?"

"Yes. It will be as easy as—"

"Are you forgetting that, by the terms of our agreement, it is my turn?"

"You surely don't intend to hold me to that?"

"Certainly I do."

"But, good heavens, consider my position! Do you seriously expect me to lie in bed while you do all the work, and then to take a half share in the reward?"

"I do."

"It's ridiculous!"

"It's no more ridiculous than that I should do the same. Mr. Marson, there's no use in our going over all this again. We settled it long ago."

Joan refused to discuss the matter further, leaving Ashe in a condition of anxious misery comparable only to that which, as night began to draw near, gnawed the vitals of the Efficient Baxter.

Breakfast at Blandings Castle was an informal meal. There was food and drink in the long dining-hall for such as were energetic enough to come down and get it; but the majority of the house party breakfasted in their rooms, Lord Emsworth, whom nothing in the world would have induced to begin the day in the company of a crowd of his relations, most of whom he disliked, setting them the example.

When, therefore, Baxter, yielding to Nature after having remained awake until the early morning, fell asleep at nine o'clock, nobody came to rouse him. He did not ring his bell, so he was not disturbed; and he slept on until half past eleven, by which time, it being Sunday morning and the house party including one bishop and several of the minor clergy, most of the occupants of the place had gone off to church.

Baxter shaved and dressed hastily, for he was in state of nervous apprehension. He blamed himself for having lain in bed so long. When every minute he was away might mean the loss of the scarab, he had passed several hours in dreamy sloth. He had wakened with a presentiment. Something told him the scarab had been stolen in the night, and he wished now that he had risked all and kept guard.

The house was very quiet as he made his way rapidly to the hall. As he passed a window he perceived Lord Emsworth, in an un-Sabbatarian suit of tweeds and bearing a garden fork—which must have pained the bishop—bending earnestly over a flower bed; but he was the only occupant of the grounds, and indoors there was a feeling of emptiness. The hall had that Sunday-morning air of wanting to be left to itself, and disapproving of the entry of anything human until lunch time, which can be felt only by a guest in a large house who remains at home when his fellows have gone to church.

The portraits on the walls, especially the one of the Countess of Emsworth in the character of Venus rising from the sea, stared at Baxter as he entered, with cold reproof. The very chairs seemed distant and unfriendly; but Baxter was in no mood to appreciate their attitude. His conscience slept. His mind was occupied, to the exclusion of all other things, by the scarab and its probable fate. How disastrously remiss it had been of him not to keep guard last night! Long before he opened the museum door he was feeling the absolute certainty that the worst had happened.

It had. The card which announced that here was an Egyptian scarab of the reign of Cheops of the Fourth Dynasty, presented by J. Preston Peters, Esquire, still lay on the cabinet in its wonted place; but now its neat lettering was false and misleading. The scarab was gone.

For all that he had expected this, for all his premonition of disaster, it was an appreciable time before the Efficient Baxter rallied from the blow. He stood transfixed, goggling at the empty place.

Then his mind resumed its functions. All, he perceived, was not yet lost. Baxter the watchdog must retire, to be succeeded by Baxter the sleuthhound. He had been unable to prevent the theft of the scarab, but he might still detect the thief.

For the Doctor Watsons of this world, as opposed to the Sherlock Holmeses, success in the province of detective work must always be, to a very large extent, the result of luck. Sherlock Holmes can extract a clew from a wisp of straw or a flake of cigar ash; but Doctor Watson has to have it taken out for him and dusted, and exhibited clearly, with a label attached.

The average man is a Doctor Watson. We are wont to scoff in a patronizing manner at that humble follower of the great investigator; but as a matter of fact we should have been just as dull ourselves. We should not even have risen to the modest height of a Scotland Yard bungler.

Baxter was a Doctor Watson. What he wanted was a clew; but it is so hard for the novice to tell what is a clew and what is not. And then he happened to look down—and there on the floor was a clew that nobody could have overlooked.

Baxter saw it, but did not immediately recognize it for what it was. What he saw, at first, was not a clew, but just a mess. He had a tidy soul and abhorred messes, and this was a particularly messy mess. A considerable portion of the floor was a sea of red paint. The can from which it had flowed was lying on its side—near the wall. He had noticed that the smell of paint had seemed particularly pungent, but had attributed this to a new freshet of energy on the part of Lord Emsworth. He had not perceived that paint had been spilled.

"Pah!" said Baxter.

Then suddenly, beneath the disguise of the mess, he saw the clew. A footmark! No less. A crimson footmark on the polished wood! It was as clear and distinct as though it had been left there for the purpose of assisting him. It was a feminine footmark, the print of a slim and pointed shoe.

This perplexed Baxter. He had looked on the siege of the scarab as an exclusively male affair. But he was not perplexed long. What could be simpler than that Mr. Peters should have enlisted female aid? The female of the species is more deadly than the male. Probably she makes a better purloiner of scarabs. At any rate, there the footprint was, unmistakably feminine.

Inspiration came to him. Aline Peters had a maid! What more likely than that secretly she should be a hireling of Mr. Peters, on whom he had now come to look as a man of the blackest and most sinister character? Mr. Peters was a collector; and when a collector makes up his mind to secure a treasure, he employs, Baxter knew, every possible means to that end.

Baxter was now in a state of great excitement. He was hot on the scent and his brain was working like a buzz saw in an ice box. According to his reasoning, if Aline Peters' maid had done this thing there should be red paint in the hall marking her retreat, and possibly a faint stain on the stairs leading to the servants' bedrooms.

He hastened from the museum and subjected the hall to a keen scrutiny. Yes; there was red paint on the carpet. He passed through the green-baize door and examined the stairs. On the bottom step there was a faint but conclusive stain of crimson!

He was wondering how best to follow up this clew when he perceived Ashe coming down the stairs. Ashe, like Baxter, and as the result of a night disturbed by anxious thoughts, had also overslept himself.

There are moments when the giddy excitement of being right on the trail causes the amateur—or Watsonian—detective to be incautious. If Baxter had been wise he would have achieved his object—the getting a glimpse of Joan's shoes—by a devious and snaky route. As it was, zeal getting the better of prudence, he rushed straight on. His early suspicion of Ashe had been temporarily obscured. Whatever Ashe's claims to be a suspect, it had not been his footprint Baxter had seen in the museum.

"Here, you!" said the Efficient Baxter excitedly.

"Sir?"

"The shoes!"

"I beg your pardon?"

"I wish to see the servants' shoes. Where are they?"

"I expect they have them on, sir."

"Yesterday's shoes, man—yesterday's shoes. Where are they?"

"Where are the shoes of yesteryear?" murmured Ashe. "I should say at a venture, sir, that they would be in a large basket somewhere near the kitchen. Our genial knife-and-shoe boy collects them, I believe, at early dawn."

"Would they have been cleaned yet?"

"If I know the lad, sir—no."

"Go and bring that basket to me. Bring it to me in this room."

The room to which he referred was none other than the private sanctum of Mr. Beach, the butler, the door of which, standing open, showed it to be empty. It was not Baxter's plan, excited as he was, to risk being discovered sifting shoes in the middle of a passage in the servants' quarters.

Ashe's brain was working rapidly as he made for the shoe cupboard, that little den of darkness and smells, where Billy, the knife-and-shoe boy, better known in the circle in which he moved as Young Bonehead, pursued his menial tasks. What exactly was at the back of the Efficient Baxter's mind prompting these maneuvers he did not know; but that there was something he was certain.

He had not yet seen Joan this morning, and he did not know whether or not she had carried out her resolve of attempting to steal the scarab on the previous night; but this activity and mystery on the part of their enemy must have some sinister significance. He gathered up the shoe basket thoughtfully. He staggered back with it and dumped it down on the floor of Mr. Beach's room. The Efficient Baxter stooped eagerly over it. Ashe, leaning against the wall, straightened the creases in his clothes and flicked disgustedly at an inky spot which the journey had transferred from the basket to his coat.

"We have here, sir," he said, "a fair selection of our various foot coverings."

"You did not drop any on your way?"

"Not one, sir."

The Efficient Baxter uttered a grunt of satisfaction and bent once more to his task. Shoes flew about the room. Baxter knelt on the floor beside the basket, and dug like a terrier at a rat hole. At last he made a find and with an exclamation of triumph rose to his feet. In his hand he held a shoe.

"Put those back," he said.

Ashe began to pick up the scattered footgear.

"That's the lot, sir," he said, rising.

"Now come with me. Leave the basket there. You can carry it back when you return."

"Shall I put back that shoe, sir?"

"Certainly not. I shall take this one with me."

"Shall I carry it for you, sir?"

Baxter reflected.

"Yes. I think that would be best."

Trouble had shaken his nerve. He was not certain that there might not be others besides Lord Emsworth in the garden; and it occurred to him that, especially after his reputation for eccentric conduct had been so firmly established by his misfortunes that night in the hall, it might cause comment should he appear before them carrying a shoe.

Ashe took the shoe and, doing so, understood what before had puzzled him. Across the toe was a broad splash of red paint. Though he had nothing else to go on, he saw all. The shoe he held was a female shoe. His own researches in the museum had made him aware of the presence there of red paint. It was not difficult to build up on these data a pretty accurate estimate of the position of affairs.

"Come with me," said Baxter.

He left the room. Ashe followed him.

In the garden Lord Emsworth, garden fork in hand, was dealing summarily with a green young weed that had incautiously shown its head in the middle of a flower bed. He listened to Baxter's statement with more interest than he usually showed in anybody's statements. He resented the loss of the scarab, not so much on account of its intrinsic worth as because it had been the gift of his friend Mr. Peters.

"Indeed!" he said, when Baxter had finished. "Really? Dear me! It certainly seems—It is extremely suggestive. You are certain there was red paint on this shoe?"

"I have it with me. I brought it on purpose to show you." He looked at Ashe, who stood in close attendance. "The shoe!"

Lord Emsworth polished his glasses and bent over the exhibit.

"Ah!" he said. "Now let me look at—This, you say, is the—Just so; just so! Just—My dear Baxter, it may be that I have not examined this shoe with sufficient care, but—Can you point out to me exactly where this paint is that you speak of?"

The Efficient Baxter stood staring at the shoe with wild, fixed stare. Of any suspicion of paint, red or otherwise, it was absolutely and entirely innocent!

The shoe became the center of attraction, the center of all eyes. The Efficient Baxter fixed it with the piercing glare of one who feels that his brain is tottering. Lord Emsworth looked at it with a mildly puzzled expression. Ashe Marson examined it with a sort of affectionate interest, as though he were waiting for it to do a trick of some kind. Baxter was the first to break the silence.

"There was paint on this shoe," he said vehemently. "I tell you there was a splash of red paint across the toe. This man here will bear me out in this. You saw paint on this shoe?"

"Paint, sir?"

"What! Do you mean to tell me you did not see it?"

"No, sir; there was no paint on this shoe."

"This is ridiculous. I saw it with my own eyes. It was a broad splash right across the toe."

Lord Emsworth interposed.

"You must have made a mistake, my dear Baxter. There is certainly no trace of paint on this shoe. These momentary optical delusions are, I fancy, not uncommon. Any doctor will tell you—"

"I had an aunt, your lordship," said Ashe chattily, "who was remarkably subject—"

"It is absurd! I cannot have been mistaken," said Baxter. "I am positively certain the toe of this shoe was red when I found it."

"It is quite black now, my dear Baxter."

"A sort of chameleon shoe," murmured Ashe.

The goaded secretary turned on him.

"What did you say?"

"Nothing, sir."

Baxter's old suspicion of this smooth young man came surging back to him.

"I strongly suspect you of having had something to do with this."

"Really, Baxter," said the earl, "that is surely the least probable of solutions. This young man could hardly have cleaned the shoe on his way from the house. A few days ago, when painting in the museum, I inadvertently splashed some paint on my own shoe. I can assure you it does not brush off. It needs a very systematic cleaning before all traces are removed."

"Exactly, your lordship," said Ashe. "My theory, if I may—"

"Yes?"

"My theory, your lordship, is that Mr. Baxter was deceived by the light-and-shade effects on the toe of the shoe. The morning sun, streaming in through the window, must have shone on the shoe in such a manner as to give it a momentary and fictitious aspect of redness. If Mr. Baxter recollects, he did not look long at the shoe. The picture on the retina of the eye consequently had not time to fade. I myself remember thinking at the moment that the shoe appeared to have a certain reddish tint. The mistake—"

"Bah!" said Baxter shortly.

Lord Emsworth, now thoroughly bored with the whole affair and desiring nothing more than to be left alone with his weeds and his garden fork, put in his word. Baxter, he felt, was curiously irritating these days. He always seemed to be bobbing up. The Earl of Emsworth was conscious of a strong desire to be free from his secretary's company. He was efficient, yes—invaluable indeed—he did not know what he should do without Baxter; but there was no denying that his company tended after a while to become a trifle tedious. He took a fresh grip on his garden fork and shifted it about in the air as a hint that the interview had lasted long enough.

"It seems to me, my dear fellow," he said, "the only explanation that will square with the facts. A shoe that is really smeared with red paint does not become black of itself in the course of a few minutes."

"You are very right, your lordship," said Ashe approvingly. "May I go now, your lordship?"

"Certainly—certainly; by all means."

"Shall I take the shoe with me, your lordship?"

"If you do not want it, Baxter."

The secretary passed the fraudulent piece of evidence to Ashe without a word; and the latter, having included both gentlemen in a kindly smile, left the garden.

On returning to the butler's room, Ashe's first act was to remove a shoe from the top of the pile in the basket. He was about to leave the room with it, when the sound of footsteps in the passage outside halted him.

"I do not in the least understand why you wish me to come here, my dear Baxter," said a voice, "and you are completely spoiling my morning, but—"

For a moment Ashe was at a loss. It was a crisis that called for swift action, and it was a little hard to know exactly what to do. It had been his intention to carry the paint-splashed shoe back to his own room, there to clean it at his leisure; but it appeared that his strategic line of retreat was blocked. Plainly, the possibility—nay, the certainty—that Ashe had substituted another shoe for the one with the incriminating splash of paint on it had occurred to the Efficient Baxter almost directly the former had left the garden.

The window was open. Ashe looked out. There were bushes below. It was a makeshift policy, and one which did not commend itself to him as the ideal method, but it seemed the only thing to be done, for already the footsteps had reached the door. He threw the shoe out of window, and it sank beneath the friendly surface of the long grass round a wisteria bush.

Ashe turned, relieved, and the next moment the door opened and Baxter walked in, accompanied—with obvious reluctance—by his bored employer.

Baxter was brisk and peremptory.

"I wish to look at those shoes again," he said coldly.

"Certainly, sir," said Ashe.

"I can manage without your assistance," said Baxter.

"Very good, sir."

Leaning against the wall, Ashe watched him with silent interest, as he burrowed among the contents of the basket, like a terrier digging for rats. The Earl of Emsworth took no notice of the proceedings. He yawned plaintively, and pottered about the room. He was one of Nature's potterers.

The scrutiny of the man whom he had now placed definitely as a malefactor irritated Baxter. Ashe was looking at him in an insufferably tolerant manner, as if he were an indulgent father brooding over his infant son while engaged in some childish frolic. He lodged a protest.

"Don't stand there staring at me!"

"I was interested in what you were doing, sir."

"Never mind! Don't stare at me in that idiotic way."

"May I read a book, sir?"

"Yes, read if you like."

"Thank you, sir."

Ashe took a volume from the butler's slenderly stocked shelf. The shoe-expert resumed his investigations in the basket. He went through it twice, but each time without success. After the second search he stood up and looked wildly about the room. He was as certain as he could be of anything that the missing piece of evidence was somewhere within those four walls. There was very little cover in the room, even for so small a fugitive as a shoe. He raised the tablecloth and peered beneath the table.

"Are you looking for Mr. Beach, sir?" said Ashe. "I think he has gone to church."

Baxter, pink with his exertions, fastened a baleful glance upon him.

"You had better be careful," he said.

At this point the Earl of Emsworth, having done all the pottering possible in the restricted area, yawned like an alligator.

"Now, my dear Baxter—" he began querulously.

Baxter was not listening. He was on the trail. He had caught sight of a small closet in the wall, next to the mantelpiece, and it had stimulated him.

"What is in this closet?"

"That closet, sir?"

"Yes, this closet." He rapped the door irritably.

"I could not say, sir. Mr. Beach, to whom the closet belongs, possibly keeps a few odd trifles there. A ball of string, perhaps. Maybe an old pipe or something of that kind. Probably nothing of value or interest."

"Open it."

"It appears to be locked, sir—"

"Unlock it."

"But where is the key?"

Baxter thought for a moment.

"Lord Emsworth," he said, "I have my reasons for thinking that this man is deliberately keeping the contents of this closet from me. I am convinced that the shoe is in there. Have I your leave to break open the door?"

The earl looked a little dazed, as if he were unequal to the intellectual pressure of the conversation.

"Now, my dear Baxter," said the earl impatiently, "please tell me once again why you have brought me in here. I cannot make head or tail of what you have been saying. Apparently you accuse this young man of keeping his shoes in a closet. Why should you suspect him of keeping his shoes in a closet? And if he wishes to do so, why on earth should not he keep his shoes in a closet? This is a free country."

"Exactly, your lordship," said Ashe approvingly. "You have touched the spot."

"It all has to do with the theft of your scarab, Lord Emsworth. Somebody got into the museum and stole the scarab."

"Ah, yes; ah, yes—so they did. I remember now. You told me. Bad business that, my dear Baxter. Mr. Peters gave me that scarab. He will be most deucedly annoyed if it's lost. Yes, indeed."

"Whoever stole it upset the can of red paint and stepped in it."

"Devilish careless of them. It must have made the dickens of a mess. Why don't people look where they are walking?"

"I suspect this man of shielding the criminal by hiding her shoe in this closet."

"Oh, it's not his own shoes that this young man keeps in closets?"

"It is a woman's shoe, Lord Emsworth."

"The deuce it is! Then it was a woman who stole the scarab? Is that the way you figure it out? Bless my soul, Baxter, one wonders what women are coming to nowadays. It's all this movement, I suppose. The Vote, and all that—eh? I recollect having a chat with the Marquis of Petersfield some time ago. He is in the Cabinet, and he tells me it is perfectly infernal the way these women carry on. He said sometimes it got to such a pitch, with them waving banners and presenting petitions, and throwing flour and things at a fellow, that if he saw his own mother coming toward him, with a hand behind her back, he would run like a rabbit. Told me so himself."

"So," said the Efficient Baxter, cutting in on the flow of speech, "what I wish to do is to break open this closet."

"Eh? Why?"

"To get the shoe."

"The shoe? . . . Ah, yes, I recollect now. You were telling me."

"If your lordship has no objection."

"Objection, my dear fellow? None in the world. Why should I have any objection? Let me see! What is it you wish to do?"

"This," said Baxter shortly.

He seized the poker from the fireplace and delivered two rapid blows on the closet door. The wood was splintered. A third blow smashed the flimsy lock. The closet, with any skeletons it might contain, was open for all to view.

It contained a corkscrew, a box of matches, a paper-covered copy of a book entitled "Mary, the Beautiful Mill-Hand," a bottle of embrocation, a spool of cotton, two pencil-stubs, and other useful and entertaining objects. It contained, in fact, almost everything except a paint-splashed shoe, and Baxter gazed at the collection in dumb disappointment.

"Are you satisfied now, my dear Baxter," said the earl, "or is there any more furniture that you would like to break? You know, this furniture breaking is becoming a positive craze with you, my dear fellow. You ought to fight against it. The night before last, I don't know how many tables broken in the hall; and now this closet. You will ruin me. No purse can stand the constant drain."

Baxter did not reply. He was still trying to rally from the blow. A chance remark of Lord Emsworth's set him off on the trail once more. Lord Emsworth, having said his say, had dismissed the affair from his mind and begun to potter again. The course of his pottering had brought him to the fireplace, where a little pile of soot on the fender caught his eye. He bent down to inspect it.

"Dear me!" he said. "I must remember to tell Beach to have his chimney swept. It seems to need it badly."

No trumpet-call ever acted more instantaneously on old war-horse than this simple remark on the Efficient Baxter. He was still convinced that Ashe had hidden the shoe somewhere in the room, and, now that the closet had proved an alibi, the chimney was the only spot that remained unsearched. He dived forward with a rush, nearly knocking Lord Emsworth off his feet, and thrust an arm up into the unknown. The startled peer, having recovered his balance, met Ashe's respectfully pitying gaze.

"We must humor him," said the gaze, more plainly than speech.

Baxter continued to grope. The chimney was a roomy chimney, and needed careful examination. He wriggled his hand about clutchingly. From time to time soot fell in gentle showers.

"My dear Baxter!"

Baxter was baffled. He withdrew his hand from the chimney, and straightened himself. He brushed a bead of perspiration from his face with the back of his hand. Unfortunately, he used the sooty hand, and the result was too much for Lord Emsworth's politeness. He burst into a series of pleased chuckles.

"Your face, my dear Baxter! Your face! It is positively covered with soot—positively! You must go and wash it. You are quite black. Really, my dear fellow, you present rather an extraordinary appearance. Run off to your room."

Against this crowning blow the Efficient Baxter could not stand up. It was the end.

"Soot!" he murmured weakly. "Soot!"

"Your face is covered, my dear fellow—quite covered."

"It certainly has a faintly sooty aspect, sir," said Ashe.

His voice roused the sufferer to one last flicker of spirit.

"You will hear more of this," he said. "You will—"

At this moment, slightly muffled by the intervening door and passageway, there came from the direction of the hall a sound like the delivery of a ton of coal. A heavy body bumped down the stairs, and a voice which all three recognized as that of the Honorable Freddie uttered an oath that lost itself in a final crash and a musical splintering sound, which Baxter for one had no difficulty in recognizing as the dissolution of occasional china.

Even if they had not so able a detective as Baxter with them, Lord Emsworth and Ashe would have been at no loss to guess what had happened. Doctor Watson himself could have deduced it from the evidence. The Honorable Freddie had fallen downstairs.

With a little ingenuity this portion of the story of Mr. Peters' scarab could be converted into an excellent tract, driving home the perils, even in this world, of absenting one's self from church on Sunday morning. If the Honorable Freddie had gone to church he would not have been running down the great staircase at the castle at this hour; and if he had not been running down the great staircase at the castle at that hour he would not have encountered Muriel.

Muriel was a Persian cat belonging to Lady Ann Warblington. Lady Ann had breakfasted in bed and lain there late, as she rather fancied she had one of her sick headaches coming on. Muriel had left her room in the wake of the breakfast tray, being anxious to be present at the obsequies of a fried sole that had formed Lady Ann's simple morning meal, and had followed the maid who bore it until she had reached the hall.

At this point the maid, who disliked Muriel, stopped and made a noise like an exploding pop bottle, at the same time taking a little run in Muriel's direction and kicking at her with a menacing foot. Muriel, wounded and startled, had turned in her tracks and sprinted back up the staircase at the exact moment when the Honorable Freddie, who for some reason was in a great hurry, ran lightly down.

There was an instant when Freddie could have saved himself by planting a number-ten shoe on Muriel's spine, but even in that crisis he bethought him that he hardly stood solid enough with the authorities to risk adding to his misdeeds the slaughter of his aunt's favorite cat, and he executed a rapid swerve. The spared cat proceeded on her journey upstairs, while Freddie, touching the staircase at intervals, went on down.

Having reached the bottom, he sat amid the occasional china, like Marius among the ruins of Carthage, and endeavored to ascertain the extent of his injuries. He had a dazed suspicion that he was irretrievably fractured in a dozen places. It was in this attitude that the rescue party found him. He gazed up at them with silent pathos.

"In the name of goodness, Frederick," said Lord Emsworth peevishly, "what do you imagine you are doing?"

Freddie endeavored to rise, but sank back again with a stifled howl.

"It was that bally cat of Aunt Ann's," he said. "It came legging it up the stairs. I think I've broken my leg."

"You have certainly broken everything else," said his father unsympathetically. "Between you and Baxter, I wonder there's a stick of furniture standing in the house."

"Thanks, old chap," said Freddie gratefully as Ashe stepped forward and lent him an arm. "I think my bally ankle must have got twisted. I wish you would give me a hand up to my room."

"And, Baxter, my dear fellow," said Lord Emsworth, "you might telephone to Doctor Bird, in Market Blandings, and ask him to be good enough to drive out. I am sorry, Freddie," he added, "that you should have met with this accident; but—but everything is so—so disturbing nowadays that I feel—I feel most disturbed."

Ashe and the Honorable Freddie began to move across the hall—Freddie hopping, Ashe advancing with a sort of polka step. As they reached the stairs there was a sound of wheels outside and the vanguard of the house party, returned from church, entered the house.

"It's all very well to give it out officially that Freddie has fallen downstairs and sprained his ankle," said Colonel Horace Mant, discussing the affair with the Bishop of Godalming later in the afternoon; "but it's my firm belief that that fellow Baxter did precisely as I said he would—ran amuck and inflicted dashed frightful injuries on young Freddie. When I got into the house there was Freddie being helped up the stairs, while Baxter, with his face covered with soot, was looking after him with a sort of evil grin. What had he smeared his face with soot for, I should like to know, if he were perfectly sane?

"The whole thing is dashed fishy and mysterious and the sooner I can get Mildred safely out of the place, the better I shall be pleased. The fellow's as mad as a hatter!"

CHAPTER X

When Lord Emsworth, sighting Mr. Peters in the group of returned churchgoers, drew him aside and broke the news that the valuable scarab, so kindly presented by him to the castle museum, had been stolen in the night by some person unknown, he thought the millionaire took it exceedingly well. Though the stolen object no longer belonged to him, Mr. Peters no doubt still continued to take an affectionate interest in it and might have been excused had he shown annoyance that his gift had been so carelessly guarded.

Mr. Peters was, however, thoroughly magnanimous about the matter. He deprecated the notion that the earl could possibly have prevented this unfortunate occurrence. He quite understood. He was not in the least hurt. Nobody could have foreseen such a calamity. These things happened and one had to accept them. He himself had once suffered in much the same way, the gem of his collection having been removed almost beneath his eyes in the smoothest possible fashion.

Altogether, he relieved Lord Emsworth's mind very much; and when he had finished doing so he departed swiftly and rang for Ashe. When Ashe arrived he bubbled over with enthusiasm. He was lyrical in his praise. He went so far as to slap Ashe on the back. It was only when the latter disclaimed all credit for what had occurred that he checked the flow of approbation.

"It wasn't you who got it? Who was it, then?"

"It was Miss Peters' maid. It's a long story; but we were working in partnership. I tried for the thing and failed, and she succeeded."

It was with mixed feelings that Ashe listened while Mr. Peters transferred his adjectives of commendation to Joan. He admired Joan's courage, he was relieved that her venture had ended without disaster, and he knew that she deserved whatever anyone could find to say in praise of her enterprise: but, at first, though he tried to crush it down, he could not help feeling a certain amount of chagrin that a girl should have succeeded where he, though having the advantage of first chance, had failed. The terms of his partnership with Joan had jarred on him from the beginning.

A man may be in sympathy with the modern movement for the emancipation of woman and yet feel aggrieved when a mere girl proves herself a more efficient thief than himself. Woman is invading man's sphere more successfully every day; but there are still certain fields in which man may consider that he is rightfully entitled to a monopoly—and the purloining of scarabs in the watches of the night is surely one of them. Joan, in Ashe's opinion, should have played a meeker and less active part.

These unworthy emotions did not last long. Whatever his other shortcomings, Ashe possessed a just mind. By the time he had found Joan, after Mr. Peters had said his say, and dispatched him below stairs for that purpose, he had purged himself of petty regrets and was prepared to congratulate her wholeheartedly. He was, however, resolved that nothing should induce him to share in the reward. On that point, he resolved, he would refuse to be shaken.

"I have just left Mr. Peters," he began. "All is well. His check book lies before him on the table and he is trying to make his fountain pen work long enough to write a check. But there is just one thing I want to say—"

She interrupted him. To his surprise, she was eyeing him coldly and with disapproval.

"And there is just one thing I want to say," she said; "and that is, if you imagine I shall consent to accept a penny of the reward—"

"Exactly what I was going to say. Of course I couldn't dream of taking any of it."

"I don't understand you. You are certainly going to have it all. I told you when we made our agreement that I should only take my share if you let me do my share of the work. Now that you have broken that agreement, nothing could induce me to take it. I know you meant it kindly, Mr. Marson, but I simply can't feel grateful. I told you that ours was a business contract and that I wouldn't have any chivalry; and I thought that after you had given me your promise—"

"One moment," said Ashe, bewildered. "I can't follow this. What do you mean?"

"What do I mean? Why, that you went down to the museum last night before me and took the scarab, though you had promised to stay away and give me my chance."

"But I didn't do anything of the sort."

It was Joan's turn to look bewildered.

"But you have got the scarab, Mr. Marson?"

"Why, you have got it!"

"No!"

"But—but it has gone!"

"I know. I went down to the museum last night, as we had arranged; and when I got there there was no scarab. It had disappeared."

They looked at each other in consternation. Ashe was the first to speak.

"It was gone when you got to the museum?"

"There wasn't a trace of it. I took it for granted that you had been down before me. I was furious!"

"But this is ridiculous!" said Ashe. "Who can have taken it? There was nobody beside ourselves who knew Mr. Peters was offering the reward. What exactly happened last night?"

"I waited until one o'clock. Then I slipped down, got into the museum, struck a match, and looked for the scarab. It wasn't there. I couldn't believe it at first. I struck some more matches—quite a number—but it was no good. The scarab was gone; so I went back to bed and thought hard thoughts about you. It was silly of me. I ought to have known you would not break your word; but there didn't seem any other solution of the thing's disappearance.

"Well, somebody must have taken it; and the question is, what are we to do?" She laughed. "It seems to me that we were a little premature in quarreling about how we are to divide that reward. It looks as though there wasn't going to be any reward."

"Meantime," said Ashe gloomily, "I suppose I have got to go back and tell Peters. I expect it will break his heart."

CHAPTER XI

Blandings Castle dozed in the calm of an English Sunday afternoon. All was peace. Freddie was in bed, with orders from the doctor to stay there until further notice. Baxter had washed his face. Lord Emsworth had returned to his garden fork. The rest of the house party strolled about the grounds or sat in them, for the day was one of those late spring days that are warm with a premature suggestion of midsummer.

Aline Peters was sitting at the open window of her bedroom, which commanded an extensive view of the terraces. A pile of letters lay on the table beside her, for she had just finished reading her mail. The postman came late to the castle on Sundays and she had not been able to do this until luncheon was over.

Aline was puzzled. She was conscious of a fit of depression for which she could in no way account. She had a feeling that all was not well with the world, which was the more remarkable in that she was usually keenly susceptible to weather conditions and reveled in sunshine like a kitten. Yet here was a day nearly as fine as an American day—and she found no solace in it.

She looked down on the terrace; as she looked the figure of George Emerson appeared, walking swiftly. And at the sight of him something seemed to tell her that she had found the key to her gloom.

There are many kinds of walk. George Emerson's was the walk of mental unrest. His hands were clasped behind his back, his eyes stared straight in front of him from beneath lowering brows, and between his teeth was an unlighted cigar. No man who is not a professional politician holds an unlighted cigar in his mouth unless he wishes to irritate and baffle a ticket chopper in the subway, or because unpleasant meditations have caused him to forget he has it there. Plainly, then, all was not well with George Emerson.

Aline had suspected as much at luncheon; and looking back she realized that it was at luncheon her depression had begun. The discovery startled her a little. She had not been aware, or she had refused to admit to herself, that George's troubles bulked so large on her horizon. She had always told herself that she liked George, that George was a dear old friend, that George amused and stimulated her; but she would have denied she was so wrapped up in George that the sight of him in trouble would be enough to spoil for her the finest day she had seen since she left America.

There was something not only startling but shocking in the thought; for she was honest enough with herself to recognize that Freddie, her official loved one, might have paced the grounds of the castle chewing an unlighted cigar by the hour without stirring any emotion in her at all.

And she was to marry Freddie next month! This was surely a matter that called for thought. She proceeded, gazing down the while at the perambulating George, to give it thought.

Aline's was not a deep nature. She had never pretended to herself that she loved the Honorable Freddie in the sense in which the word is used in books. She liked him and she liked the idea of being connected with the peerage; her father liked the idea and she liked her father. And the combination of these likings had caused her to reply "Yes" when, last Autumn, Freddie, swelling himself out like an embarrassed frog and gulping, had uttered that memorable speech beginning, "I say, you know, it's like this, don't you know!"—and ending, "What I mean is, will you marry me—what?"

She had looked forward to being placidly happy as the Honorable Mrs. Frederick Threepwood. And then George Emerson had reappeared in her life, a disturbing element.

Until to-day she would have resented the suggestion that she was in love with George. She liked to be with him, partly because he was so easy to talk to, and partly because it was exciting to be continually resisting the will power he made no secret of trying to exercise. But to-day there was a difference. She had suspected it at luncheon and she realized it now. As she looked down at him from behind the curtain, and marked his air of gloom, she could no longer disguise it from herself.

She felt maternal—horribly maternal. George was in trouble and she wanted to comfort him.

Freddie, too, was in trouble. But did she want to comfort Freddie? No. On the contrary, she was already regretting her promise, so lightly given before luncheon, to go and sit with him that afternoon. A well-marked feeling of annoyance that he should have been so silly as to tumble downstairs and sprain his ankle was her chief sentiment respecting Freddie.

George Emerson continued to perambulate and Aline continued to watch him. At last she could endure it no longer. She gathered up her letters, stacked them in a corner of the dressing-table and left the room. George had reached the end of the terrace and turned when she began to descend the stone steps outside the front door. He quickened his pace as he caught sight of her. He halted before her and surveyed her morosely.

"I have been looking for you," he said.

"And here I am. Cheer up, George! Whatever is the matter? I've been sitting in my room looking at you, and you have been simply prowling. What has gone wrong?"

"Everything!"

"How do you mean—everything?"

"Exactly what I say. I'm done for. Read this."

Aline took the yellow slip of paper. "A cable," added George. "I got it this morning—mailed on from my rooms in London. Read it."

"I'm trying to. It doesn't seem to make sense."

George laughed grimly.

"It makes sense all right."

"I don't see how you can say that. 'Meredith elephant kangaroo—?'"

"Office cipher; I was forgetting. 'Elephant' means 'Seriously ill and unable to attend to duty.' Meredith is one of the partners in my firm in New York."

"Oh, I'm so sorry! Do you think he is very sick? Are you very fond of Mr. Meredith?"

"Meredith is a good fellow and I like him; but if it was simply a matter of his being ill I'm afraid I could manage to bear up under the news. Unfortunately 'kangaroo' means 'Return, without fail, by the next boat.'"

"You must return by the next boat?" Aline looked at him, in her eyes a slow-growing comprehension of the situation. "Oh!" she said at length.

"I put it stronger than that," said George.

"But—the next boat—That means on Wednesday."

"Wednesday morning, from Southampton. I shall have to leave here to-morrow."

Aline's eyes were fixed on the blue hills across the valley, but she did not see them. There was a mist between. She was feeling crushed and ill-treated and lonely. It was as though George was already gone and she left alone in an alien land.

"But, George!" she said; she could find no other words for her protest against the inevitable.

"It's bad luck," said Emerson quietly; "but I shouldn't wonder if it is not the best thing that really could have happened. It finishes me cleanly, instead of letting me drag on and make both of us miserable. If this cable hadn't come I suppose I should have gone on bothering you up to the day of your wedding. I should have fancied, to the last moment, that there was a chance for me; but this ends me with one punch.

"Even I haven't the nerve to imagine that I can work a miracle in the few hours before the train leaves to-morrow. I must just make the best of it. If we ever meet again—and I don't see why we should—you will be married. My particular brand of mental suggestion doesn't work at long range. I shan't hope to influence you by telepathy."

He leaned on the balustrade at her side and spoke in a low, level voice.

"This thing," he said, "coming as a shock, coming out of the blue sky without warning—Meredith is the last man in the world you would expect to crack up; he looked as fit as a dray horse the last time I saw him—somehow seems to have hammered a certain amount of sense into me. Odd it never struck me before; but I suppose I have been about the most bumptious, conceited fool that ever happened.

"Why I should have imagined that there was a sort of irresistible fascination in me, which was bound to make you break off your engagement and upset the whole universe simply to win the wonderful reward of marrying me, is more than I can understand. I suppose it takes a shock to make a fellow see exactly what he really amounts to. I couldn't think any more of you than I do; but, if I could, the way you have put up with my mouthing and swaggering and posing as a sort of superman, would make me do it. You have been wonderful!"

Aline could not speak. She felt as though her whole world had been turned upside down in the last quarter of an hour. This was a new George Emerson, a George at whom it was impossible to laugh, but an insidiously attractive George. Her heart beat quickly. Her mind was not clear; but dimly she realized that he had pulled down her chief barrier of defense and that she was more open to attack than she had ever been. Obstinacy, the automatic desire to resist the pressure of a will that attempted to overcome her own, had kept her cool and level-headed in the past. With masterfulness she had been able to cope. Humility was another thing altogether.

Soft-heartedness was Aline's weakness. She had never clearly recognized it, but it had been partly pity that had induced her to accept Freddie; he had seemed so downtrodden and sorry for himself during those Autumn days when they had first met. Prudence warned her that strange things might happen if once she allowed herself to pity George Emerson.

The silence lengthened. Aline could find nothing to say. In her present mood there was danger in speech.

"We have known each other so long," said Emerson, "and I have told you so often that I love you, we have come to make almost a joke of it, as though we were playing some game. It just happens that that is our way—to laugh at things; but I am going to say it once again, even though it has come to be a sort of catch phrase. I love you! I'm reconciled to the fact that I am done for, out of the running, and that you are going to marry somebody else; but I am not going to stop loving you.

"It isn't a question of whether I should be happier if I forgot you. I can't do it. It's just an impossibility—and that's all there is to it. Whatever I may be to you, you are part of me, and you always will be part of me. I might just as well try to go on living without breathing as living without loving you."

He stopped and straightened himself.

"That's all! I don't want to spoil a perfectly good Spring afternoon for you by pulling out the tragic stop. I had to say all that; but it's the last time. It shan't occur again. There will be no tragedy when I step into the train to-morrow. Is there any chance that you might come and see me off?"

Aline nodded.

"You will? That will be splendid! Now I'll go and pack and break it to my host that I must leave him. I expect, it will be news to him to learn that I am here. I doubt if he knows me by sight."

Aline stood where he had left her, leaning on the balustrade. In the fullness of time there came to her the recollection she had promised Freddie that shortly after luncheon she would sit with him.

The Honorable Freddie, draped in purple pyjamas and propped up with many pillows, was lying in bed, reading Gridley Quayle, Investigator. Aline's entrance occurred at a peculiarly poignant moment in the story and gave him a feeling of having been brought violently to earth from a flight in the clouds. It is not often an author has the good fortune to grip a reader as the author of Gridley Quayle gripped Freddie.

One of the results of his absorbed mood was that he greeted Aline with a stare of an even glassier quality than usual. His eyes were by nature a trifle prominent; and to Aline, in the overstrung condition in which her talk with George Emerson had left her, they seemed to bulge at her like a snail's. A man seldom looks his best in bed, and to Aline, seeing him for the first time at this disadvantage, the Honorable Freddie seemed quite repulsive. It was with a feeling of positive panic that she wondered whether he would want her to kiss him.

Freddie made no such demand. He was not one of your demonstrative lovers. He contented himself with rolling over in bed and dropping his lower jaw.

"Hello, Aline!"

Aline sat down on the edge of the bed.

"Well, Freddie?"

Her betrothed improved his appearance a little by hitching up his jaw. As though feeling that would be too extreme a measure, he did not close his mouth altogether; but he diminished the abyss. The Honorable Freddie belonged to the class of persons who move through life with their mouths always restfully open.

It seemed to Aline that on this particular afternoon a strange dumbness had descended on her. She had been unable to speak to George and now she could not think of anything to say to Freddie. She looked at him and he looked at her; and the clock on the mantel-piece went on ticking.

"It was that bally cat of Aunt Ann's," said Freddie at length, essaying light conversation. "It came legging it up the stairs and I took the most frightful toss. I hate cats! Do you hate cats? I knew a fellow in London who couldn't stand cats."

Aline began to wonder whether there was not something permanently wrong with her organs of speech. It should have been a simple matter to develop the cat theme, but she found herself unable to do so.

Her mind was concentrated, to the exclusion of all else, on the repellent nature of the spectacle provided by her loved one in pyjamas. Freddie resumed the conversation.

"I was just reading a corking book. Have you ever read these things? They come out every month, and they're corking. The fellow who writes them must be a corker. It beats me how he thinks of these things. They are about a detective—a chap called Gridley Quayle. Frightfully exciting!"

An obvious remedy for dumbness struck Aline.

"Shall I read to you, Freddie?"

"Right-ho! Good scheme! I've got to the top of this page."

Aline took the paper-covered book.

"'Seven guns covered him with deadly precision.' Did you get as far as that?"

"Yes; just beyond. It's a bit thick, don't you know! This chappie Quayle has been trapped in a lonely house, thinking he was going to see a pal in distress; and instead of the pal there pop out a whole squad of masked blighters with guns. I don't see how he's going to get out of it, myself; but I'll bet he does. He's a corker!"

If anybody could have pitied Aline more than she pitied herself, as she waded through the adventures of Mr. Quayle, it would have been Ashe Marson. He had writhed as he wrote the words and she writhed as she read them. The Honorable Freddie also writhed, but with tense excitement.

"What's the matter? Don't stop!" he cried as Aline's voice ceased.

"I'm getting hoarse, Freddie."

Freddie hesitated. The desire to remain on the trail with Gridley struggled with rudimentary politeness.

"How would it be—Would you mind if I just took a look at the rest of it myself? We could talk afterward, you know. I shan't be long."

"Of course! Do read if you want to. But do you really like this sort of thing, Freddie?"

"Me? Rather! Why—don't you?"

"I don't know. It seems a little—I don't know."

Freddie had become absorbed in his story. Aline did not attempt further analysis of her attitude toward Mr. Quayle; she relapsed into silence.

It was a silence pregnant with thought. For the first time in their relations, she was trying to visualize to herself exactly what marriage with this young man would mean. Hitherto, it struck her, she had really seen so little of Freddie that she had scarcely had a chance of examining him. In the crowded world outside he had always seemed a tolerable enough person. To-day, somehow, he was different. Everything was different to-day.

This, she took it, was a fair sample of what she might expect after marriage. Marriage meant—to come to essentials—that two people were very often and for lengthy periods alone together, dependent on each other for mutual entertainment. What exactly would it be like, being alone often and for lengthy periods with Freddie? Well, it would, she assumed, be like this.

"It's all right," said Freddie without looking up. "He did get out! He had a bomb on him, and he threatened to drop it and blow the place to pieces unless the blighters let him go. So they cheesed it. I knew he had something up his sleeve."

Like this! Aline drew a deep breath. It would be like this—forever and ever and ever—until she died. She bent forward and stared at him.

"Freddie," she said, "do you love me?" There was no reply. "Freddie, do you love me? Am I a part of you? If you hadn't me would it be like trying to go on living without breathing?"

The Honorable Freddie raised a flushed face and gazed at her with an absent eye.

"Eh? What?" he said. "Do I—Oh; yes, rather! I say, one of the blighters has just loosed a rattlesnake into Gridley Quayle's bedroom through the transom!"

Aline rose from her seat and left the room softly. The Honorable Freddie read on, unheeding.

Ashe Marson had not fallen far short of the truth in his estimate of the probable effect on Mr. Peters of the information that his precious scarab had once more been removed by alien hands and was now farther from his grasp than ever. A drawback to success in life is that failure, when it does come, acquires an exaggerated importance. Success had made Mr. Peters, in certain aspects of his character, a spoiled child.

At the moment when Ashe broke the news he would have parted with half his fortune to recover the scarab. Its recovery had become a point of honor. He saw it as the prize of a contest between his will and that of whatever malignant powers there might be ranged against him in the effort to show him that there were limits to what he could achieve. He felt as he had felt in the old days when people sneaked up on him in Wall Street and tried to loosen his grip on a railroad or a pet stock. He was suffering from that form of paranoia which makes men multimillionaires. Nobody would be foolish enough to become a multimillionaire if it were not for the desire to prove himself irresistible.

Mr. Peters obtained a small relief for his feelings by doubling the existing reward, and Ashe went off in search of Joan, hoping that this new stimulus, acting on their joint brains, might develop inspiration.

"Have any fresh ideas been vouchsafed to you?" he asked. "You may look on me as baffled."

Joan shook her head.

"Don't give up," she urged. "Think again. Try to realize what this means, Mr. Marson. Between us we have lost ten thousand dollars in a single night. I can't afford it. It is like losing a legacy. I absolutely refuse to give in without an effort and go back to writing duke-and-earl stories for Home Gossip."

"The prospect of tackling Gridley Quayle again—"

"Why, I was forgetting that you were a writer of detective stories. You ought to be able to solve this mystery in a moment. Ask yourself, 'What would Gridley Quayle have done?'"

"I can answer that. Gridley Quayle would have waited helplessly for some coincidence to happen to help him out."

"Had he no methods?"

"He was full of methods; but they never led him anywhere without the coincidence. However, we might try to figure it out. What time did you get to the museum?"

"One o'clock."

"And you found the scarab gone. What does that suggest to you?"

"Nothing. What does it suggest to you?"

"Absolutely nothing. Let us try again. Whoever took the scarab must have had special information that Peters was offering the reward."

"Then why hasn't he been to Mr. Peters and claimed it?"

"True! That would seem to be a flaw in the reasoning. Once again: Whoever took it must have been in urgent and immediate need of money."

"And how are we to find out who was in urgent and immediate need of money?"

"Exactly! How indeed?"

There was a pause.

"I should think your Mr. Quayle must have been a great comfort to his clients, wasn't he?" said Joan.

"Inductive reasoning, I admit, seems to have fallen down to a certain extent," said Ashe. "We must wait for the coincidence. I have a feeling that it will come." He paused. "I am very fortunate in the way of coincidences."

"Are you?"

Ashe looked about him and was relieved to find that they appeared to be out of earshot of their species. It was not easy to achieve this position at the castle if you happened to be there as a domestic servant. The space provided for the ladies and gentlemen attached to the guests was limited, and it was rarely that you could enjoy a stroll without bumping into a maid, a valet or a footman; but now they appeared to be alone. The drive leading to the back regions of the castle was empty. As far as the eye could reach there were no signs of servants—upper or lower. Nevertheless, Ashe lowered his voice.

"Was it not a strange coincidence," he said, "that you should have come into my life at all?"

"Not very," said Joan prosaically. "It was quite likely that we should meet sooner or later, as we lived on different floors of the same house."

"It was a coincidence that you should have taken that room."

"Why?"

Ashe felt damped. Logically, no doubt, she was right; but surely she might have helped him out a little in this difficult situation. Surely her woman's intuition should have told her that a man who has been speaking in a loud and cheerful voice does not lower it to a husky whisper without some reason. The hopelessness of his task began to weigh on him.

Ever since that evening at Market Blandings Station, when he realized that he loved her, he had been trying to find an opportunity to tell her so; and every time they had met, the talk had seemed to be drawn irresistibly into practical and unsentimental channels. And now, when he was doing his best to reason it out that they were twin souls who had been brought together by a destiny it would be foolish to struggle against; when he was trying to convey the impression that fate had designed them for each other—she said, "Why?" It was hard.

He was about to go deeper into the matter when, from the direction of the castle, he perceived the Honorable Freddie's valet—Mr. Judson—approaching. That it was this repellent young man's object to break in on them and rob him of his one small chance of inducing Joan to appreciate, as he did, the mysterious workings of Providence as they affected herself and him, was obvious. There was no mistaking the valet's desire for conversation. He had the air of one brimming over with speech. His wonted indolence was cast aside; and as he drew nearer he positively ran. He was talking before he reached them.

"Miss Simpson, Mr. Marson, it's true—what I said that night. It's a fact!"

Ashe regarded the intruder with a malevolent eye. Never fond of Mr. Judson, he looked on him now with positive loathing. It had not been easy for him to work himself up to the point where he could discuss with Joan the mysterious ways of Providence, for there was that about her which made it hard to achieve sentiment. That indefinable something in Joan Valentine which made for nocturnal raids on other people's museums also rendered her a somewhat difficult person to talk to about twin souls and destiny. The qualities that Ashe loved in her—her strength, her capability, her valiant self-sufficingness—were the very qualities which seemed to check him when he tried to tell her that he loved them.

Mr. Judson was still babbling.

"It's true. There ain't a doubt of it now. It's been and happened just as I said that night."

"What did you say? Which night?" inquired Ashe.

"That night at dinner—the first night you two came here. Don't you remember me talking about Freddie and the girl he used to write letters to in London—the girl I said was so like you, Miss Simpson? What was her name again? Joan Valentine. That was it. The girl at the theater that Freddie used to send me with letters to pretty nearly every evening. Well, she's been and done it, same as I told you all that night she was jolly likely to go and do. She's sticking young Freddie up for his letters, just as he ought to have known she would do if he hadn't been a young fathead. They're all alike, these girls—every one of them."

Mr. Judson paused, subjected the surrounding scenery to a cautious scrutiny and resumed.

"I took a suit of Freddie's clothes away to brush just now; and happening"—Mr. Judson paused and gave a little cough—"happening to glance at the contents of his pockets I come across a letter. I took a sort of look at it before setting it aside, and it was from a fellow named Jones; and it said that this girl, Valentine, was sticking onto young Freddie's letters what he'd written her, and would see him blowed if she parted with them under another thousand. And, as I made it out, Freddie had already given her five hundred.

"Where he got it is more than I can understand; but that's what the letter said. This fellow Jones said he had passed it to her with his own hands; but she wasn't satisfied, and if she didn't get the other thousand she was going to bring an action for breach. And now Freddie has given me a note to take to this Jones, who is stopping in Market Blandings."

Joan had listened to this remarkable speech with a stunned amazement. At this point she made her first comment:

"But that can't be true."

"Saw the letter with my own eyes, Miss Simpson."

"But—"

She looked at Ashe helplessly. Their eyes met—hers wide with perplexity, his bright with the light of comprehension.

"It shows," said Ashe slowly, "that he was in immediate and urgent need of money."

"You bet it does," said Mr. Judson with relish. "It looks to me as though young Freddie had about reached the end of his tether this time. My word! There won't half be a kick-up if she does sue him for breach! I'm off to tell Mr. Beach and the rest. They'll jump out of their skins." His face fell. "Oh, Lord, I was forgetting this note. He told me to take it at once."

"I'll take it for you," said Ashe. "I'm not doing anything."

Mr. Judson's gratitude was effusive.

"You're a good fellow, Marson," he said. "I'll do as much for you another time. I couldn't hardly bear not to tell a bit of news like this right away. I should burst or something."

And Mr. Judson, with shining face, hurried off to the housekeeper's room.

"I simply can't understand it," said Joan at length. "My head is going round."

"Can't understand it? Why, it's perfectly clear. This is the coincidence for which, in my capacity of Gridley Quayle, I was waiting. I can now resume inductive reasoning. Weighing the evidence, what do we find? That young sweep, Freddie, is the man. He has the scarab."

"But it's all such a muddle. I'm not holding his letters."

"For Jones' purposes you are. Let's get this Jones element in the affair straightened out. What do you know of him?"

"He was an enormously fat man who came to see me one night and said he had been sent to get back some letters. I told him I had destroyed them ages ago and he went away."

"Well, that part of it is clear, then. He is working a simple but ingenious game on Freddie. It wouldn't succeed with everybody, I suppose; but from what I have seen and heard of him Freddie isn't strong on intellect. He seems to have accepted the story without a murmur. What does he do? He has to raise a thousand pounds immediately, and the raising of the first five hundred has exhausted his credit. He gets the idea of stealing the scarab!"

"But why? Why should he have thought of the scarab at all? That is what I can't understand. He couldn't have meant to give it to Mr. Peters and claim the reward. He couldn't have known that Mr. Peters was offering a reward. He couldn't have known that Lord Emsworth had not got the scarab quite properly. He couldn't have known—he couldn't have known anything!"

Ashe's enthusiasm was a trifle damped.

"There's something in that. But—I have it! Jones must have known about the scarab and told him."

"But how could he have known?"

"Yes; there's something in that, too. How could Jones have known?"

"He couldn't. He had gone by the time Aline came that night."

"I don't quite understand. Which night?"

"It was the night of the day I first met you. I was wondering for a moment whether he could by any chance have overheard Aline telling me about the scarab and the reward Mr. Peters was offering for it."

"Overheard! That word is like a bugle blast to me. Nine out of ten of Gridley Quayle's triumphs were due to his having overheard something. I think we are now on the right track."

"I don't. How could he have overheard us? The door was closed and he was in the street by that time."

"How do you know he was in the street? Did you see him out?"

"No; but he went."

"He might have waited on the stairs—you remember how dark they are at Number Seven—and listened."

"Why?"

Ashe reflected.

"Why? Why? What a beast of a word that is—the detective's bugbear. I thought I had it, until you said—Great Scott! I'll tell you why. I see it all. I have him with the goods. His object in coming to see you about the letters was because Freddie wanted them back owing to his approaching marriage with Miss Peters—wasn't it?"

"Yes."

"You tell him you have destroyed the letters. He goes off. Am I right?"

"Yes."

"Before he is out of the house Miss Peters is giving her name at the front door. Put yourself in Jones' place. What does he think? He is suspicious. He thinks there is some game on. He skips upstairs again, waits until Miss Peters has gone into your room, then stands outside and listens. How about that?"

"I do believe you are right. He might quite easily have done that."

"He did do exactly that. I know it as though I had been there; in fact, it is highly probable I was there. You say all this happened on the night we first met? I remember coming downstairs that night—I was going out to a vaudeville show—and hearing voices in your room. I remember it distinctly. In all probability I nearly ran into Jones."

"It does all seem to fit in, doesn't it?"

"It's a clear case. There isn't a flaw in it. The only question is, can I, on the evidence, go to young Freddie and choke the scarab out of him? On the whole, I think I had better take this note to Jones, as I promised Judson, and see whether I can't work something through him. Yes; that's the best plan. I'll be starting at once."

Perhaps the greatest hardship in being an invalid is the fact that people come and see you and keep your spirits up. The Honorable Freddie Threepwood suffered extremely from this. His was not a gregarious nature and it fatigued his limited brain powers to have to find conversation for his numerous visitors. All he wanted was to be left alone to read the adventures of Gridley Quayle, and when tired of doing that to lie on his back and look at the ceiling and think of nothing.

It is your dynamic person, your energetic world's worker, who chafes at being laid up with a sprained ankle. The Honorable Freddie enjoyed it. From boyhood up he had loved lying in bed; and now that fate had allowed him to do this without incurring rebuke he objected to having his reveries broken up by officious relations.

He spent his rare intervals of solitude in trying to decide in his mind which of his cousins, uncles and aunts was, all things considered, the greatest nuisance. Sometimes he would give the palm to Colonel Horace Mant, who struck the soldierly note—"I recollect in a hill campaign in the winter of the year '93 giving my ankle the deuce of a twist." Anon the more spiritual attitude of the Bishop of Godalming seemed to annoy him more keenly.

Sometimes he would head the list with the name of his Cousin Percy—Lord Stockheath—who refused to talk of anything except his late breach-of-promise case and the effect the verdict had had on his old governor. Freddie was in no mood just now to be sympathetic with others on their breach-of-promise cases.

As he lay in bed reading on Monday morning, the only flaw in his enjoyment of this unaccustomed solitude was the thought that presently the door was bound to open and some kind inquirer insinuate himself into the room.

His apprehensions proved well founded. Scarcely had he got well into the details of an ingenious plot on the part of a secret society to eliminate Gridley Quayle by bribing his cook—a bad lot—to sprinkle chopped-up horsehair in his chicken fricassee, when the door-knob turned and Ashe Marson came in.

Freddie was not the only person who had found the influx of visitors into the sick room a source of irritation. The fact that the invalid seemed unable to get a moment to himself had annoyed Ashe considerably. For some little time he had hung about the passage in which Freddie's room was situated, full of enterprise, but unable to make a forward move owing to the throng of sympathizers. What he had to say to the sufferer could not be said in the presence of a third party.

Freddie's sensation, on perceiving him, was one of relief. He had been half afraid it was the bishop. He recognized Ashe as the valet chappie who had helped him to bed on the occasion of his accident. It might be that he had come in a respectful way to make inquiries, but he was not likely to stop long. He nodded and went on reading. And then, glancing up, he perceived Ashe standing beside the bed, fixing him with a piercing stare.

The Honorable Freddie hated piercing stares. One of the reasons why he objected to being left alone with his future father-in-law, Mr. J. Preston Peters, was that Nature had given the millionaire a penetrating pair of eyes, and the stress of business life in New York had developed in him a habit of boring holes in people with them. A young man had to have a stronger nerve and a clearer conscience than the Honorable Freddie to enjoy a tete-a-tete with Mr. Peters.

Though he accepted Aline's father as a necessary evil and recognized that his position entitled him to look at people as sharply as he liked, whatever their feelings, he would be hanged if he was going to extend this privilege to Mr. Peters' valet. This man standing beside him was giving him a look that seemed to his sensitive imagination to have been fired red-hot from a gun; and this annoyed and exasperated Freddie.

"What do you want?" he said querulously. "What are you staring at me like that for?"

Ashe sat down, leaned his elbows on the bed, and applied the look again from a lower elevation.

"Ah!" he said.

Whatever may have been Ashe's defects, so far as the handling of the inductive-reasoning side of Gridley Quayle's character was concerned, there was one scene in each of his stories in which he never failed. That was the scene in the last chapter where Quayle, confronting his quarry, unmasked him. Quayle might have floundered in the earlier part of the story, but in his big scene he was exactly right. He was curt, crisp and mercilessly compelling.

Ashe, rehearsing this interview in the passage before his entry, had decided that he could hardly do better than model himself on the detective. So he began to be curt, crisp and mercilessly compelling to Freddie; and after the first few sentences he had that youth gasping for air.

"I will tell you," he said. "If you can spare me a few moments of your valuable time I will put the facts before you. Yes; press that bell if you wish—and I will put them before witnesses. Lord Emsworth will no doubt be pleased to learn that his son, whom he trusted, is a thief!"

Freddie's hand fell limply. The bell remained un-touched. His mouth opened to its fullest extent. In the midst of his panic he had a curious feeling that he had heard or read that last sentence somewhere before. Then he remembered. Those very words occurred in Gridley Quayle, Investigator—The Adventure of the Blue Ruby.

"What—what do you mean?" he stammered.

"I will tell you what I mean. On Saturday night a valuable scarab was stolen from Lord Emsworth's private museum. The case was put into my hands—"

"Great Scott! Are you a detective?"

"Ah!" said Ashe.

Life, as many a worthy writer has pointed out, is full of ironies. It seemed to Freddie that here was a supreme example of this fact. All these years he had wanted to meet a detective; and now that his wish had been gratified the detective was detecting him!

"The case," continued Ashe severely, "was placed in my hands. I investigated it. I discovered that you were in urgent and immediate need of money."

"How on earth did you do that?"

"Ah!" said Ashe. "I further discovered that you were in communication with an individual named Jones."

"Good Lord! How?"

Ashe smiled quietly.

"Yesterday I had a talk with this man Jones, who is staying in Market Blandings. Why is he staying in Market Blandings? Because he had a reason for keeping in touch with you; because you were about to transfer to his care something you could get possession of, but which only he could dispose of—the scarab."

The Honorable Freddie was beyond speech. He made no comment on this statement. Ashe continued:

"I interviewed this man Jones. I said to him: 'I am in the Honorable Frederick Threepwood's confidence. I know everything. Have you any instructions for me?' He replied: 'What do you know?' I answered: 'I know that the Honorable Frederick Threepwood has something he wishes to hand to you, but which he has been unable to hand to you owing to having had an accident and being confined to his room.' He then told me to tell you to let him have the scarab by messenger."

Freddie pulled himself together with an effort. He was in sore straits, but he saw one last chance. His researches in detective fiction had given him the knowledge that detectives occasionally relaxed their austerity when dealing with a deserving case. Even Gridley Quayle could sometimes be softened by a hard-luck story. Freddie could recall half a dozen times when a detected criminal had been spared by him because he had done it all from the best motives. He determined to throw himself on Ashe's mercy.

"I say, you know," he said ingratiatingly, "I think it's bally marvelous the way you've deduced everything, and so on."

"Well?"

"But I believe you would chuck it if you heard my side of the case."

"I know your side of the case. You think you are being blackmailed by a Miss Valentine for some letters you once wrote her. You are not. Miss Valentine has destroyed the letters. She told the man Jones so when he went to see her in London. He kept your five hundred pounds and is trying to get another thousand out of you under false pretenses."

"What? You can't be right."

"I am always right."

"You must be mistaken."

"I am never mistaken."

"But how do you know?"

"I have my sources of information."

"She isn't going to sue me for breach of promise?"

"She never had any intention of doing so."

The Honorable Freddie sank back on the pillows.

"Good egg!" he said with fervor. He beamed happily. "This," he observed, "is a bit of all right."

For a space relief held him dumb. Then another aspect of the matter struck him, and he sat up again with a jerk.

"I say, you don't mean to say that that rotter Jones was such a rotter as to do a rotten thing like that?"

"I do."

Freddie grew plaintive.

"I trusted that man," he said. "I jolly well trusted him absolutely."

"I know," said Ashe. "There is one born every minute."

"But"—the thing seemed to be filtering slowly into Freddie's intelligence "what I mean to say is, I—I—thought he was such a good chap."

"My short acquaintance with Mr. Jones," said Ashe "leads me to think that he probably is—to himself."

"I won't have anything more to do with him."

"I shouldn't."

"Dash it, I'll tell you what I'll do. The very next time I meet the blighter, I'll cut him dead. I will! The rotter! Five hundred quid he's had off me for nothing! And, if it hadn't been for you, he'd have had another thousand! I'm beginning to think that my old governor wasn't so far wrong when he used to curse me for going around with Jones and the rest of that crowd. He knew a bit, by Gad! Well, I'm through with them. If the governor ever lets me go to London again, I won't have anything to do with them. I'll jolly well cut the whole bunch! And to think that, if it hadn't been for you . . ."

"Never mind that," said Ashe. "Give me the scarab. Where is it?"

"What are you going to do with it?"

"Restore it to its rightful owner."

"Are you going to give me away to the governor?"

"I am not."

"It strikes me," said Freddie gratefully, "that you are a dashed good sort. You seem to me to have the making of an absolute topper! It's under the mattress. I had it on me when I fell downstairs and I had to shove it in there."

Ashe drew it out. He stood looking at it, absorbed. He could hardly believe his quest was at an end and that a small fortune lay in the palm of his hand. Freddie was eyeing him admiringly.

"You know," he said, "I've always wanted to meet a detective. What beats me is how you chappies find out things."

"We have our methods."

"I believe you. You're a blooming marvel! What first put you on my track?"

"That," said Ashe, "would take too long to explain. Of course I had to do some tense inductive reasoning; but I cannot trace every link in the chain for you. It would be tedious."

"Not to me."

"Some other time."

"I say, I wonder whether you've ever read any of these things—these Gridley Quayle stories? I know them by heart."

With the scarab safely in his pocket, Ashe could contemplate the brightly-colored volume the other extended toward him without active repulsion. Already he was beginning to feel a sort of sentiment for the depressing Quayle, as something that had once formed part of his life.

"Do you read these things?"

"I should say not. I write them."

There are certain supreme moments that cannot be adequately described. Freddie's appreciation of the fact that such a moment had occurred in his life expressed itself in a startled cry and a convulsive movement of all his limbs. He shot up from the pillows and gaped at Ashe.

"You write them? You don't mean, write them!"

"Yes."

"Great Scott!"

He would have gone on, doubtless, to say more; but at this moment voices made themselves heard outside the door. There was a movement of feet. Then the door opened and a small procession entered.

It was headed by the Earl of Emsworth. Following him came Mr. Peters. And in the wake of the millionaire were Colonel Horace Mant and the Efficient Baxter. They filed into the room and stood by the bedside. Ashe seized the opportunity to slip out.

Freddie glanced at the deputation without interest. His mind was occupied with other matters. He supposed they had come to inquire after his ankle and he was mildly thankful that they had come in a body instead of one by one. The deputation grouped itself about the bed and shuffled its feet. There was an atmosphere of awkwardness.

"Er—Frederick!" said Lord Emsworth. "Freddie, my boy!"

Mr. Peters fiddled dumbly with the coverlet. Colonel Mant cleared his throat. The Efficient Baxter scowled. "Er—Freddie, my dear boy, I fear we have a painful—er—task to perform."

The words struck straight home at the Honorable Freddie's guilty conscience. Had they, too, tracked him down? And was he now to be accused of having stolen that infernal scarab? A wave of relief swept over him as he realized that he had got rid of the thing. A decent chappie like that detective would not give him away. All he had to do was to keep his head and stick to stout denial. That was the game—stout denial.

"I don't know what you mean," he said defensively.

"Of course you don't—dash it!" said Colonel Mant. "We're coming to that. And I should like to begin by saying that, though in a sense it was my fault, I fail to see how I could have acted—"

"Horace!"

"Oh, very well! I was only trying to explain."

Lord Emsworth adjusted his pince-nez and sought inspiration from the wall paper.

"Freddie, my boy," he began, "we have a somewhat unpleasant—a somewhat er—disturbing—We are compelled to break it to you. We are all most pained and astounded; and—"

The Efficient Baxter spoke. It was plain he was in a bad temper.

"Miss Peters," he snapped, "has eloped with your friend Emerson."

Lord Emsworth breathed a sigh of relief.

"Exactly, Baxter. Precisely! You have put the thing in a nutshell. Really, my dear fellow, you are invaluable."

All eyes searched Freddie's face for signs of uncontrollable emotion. The deputation waited anxiously for his first grief-stricken cry.

"Eh? What?" said Freddie.

"It is quite true, Freddie, my dear boy. She went to London with him on the ten-fifty."

"And if I had not been forcibly restrained," said Baxter acidly, casting a vindictive look at Colonel Mant, "I could have prevented it."

Colonel Mant cleared his throat again and put a hand to his mustache.

"I'm afraid that is true, Freddie. It was a most unfortunate misunderstanding. I'll tell you how it happened: I chanced to be at the station bookstall when the train came in. Mr. Baxter was also in the station. The train pulled up and this young fellow Emerson got in—said good-by to us, don't you know, and got in. Just as the train was about to start, Miss Peters exclaiming, 'George dear, I'm going with you—, dash it,' or some such speech—proceeded to go—hell for leather—to the door of young Emerson's compartment. On which—"

"On which," interrupted Baxter, "I made a spring to try and catch her. Apart from any other consideration, the train was already moving and Miss Peters ran considerable risk of injury. I had hardly moved when I felt a violent jerk at my ankle and fell to the ground. After I had recovered from the shock, which was not immediately, I found—"

"The fact is, Freddie, my boy," the colonel went on, "I acted under a misapprehension. Nobody can be sorrier for the mistake than I; but recent events in this house had left me with the impression that Mr. Baxter here was not quite responsible for his actions—overwork or something, I imagined. I have seen it happen so often in India, don't you know, where fellows run amuck and kick up the deuce's own delight. I am bound to admit that I have been watching Mr. Baxter rather closely lately in the expectation that something of this very kind might happen.

"Of course I now realize my mistake; and I have apologized— apologized humbly—dash it! But at the moment I was firmly under the impression that our friend here had an attack of some kind and was about to inflict injuries on Miss Peters. If I've seen it happen once in India, I've seen it happen a dozen times.

"I recollect, in the hot weather of the year '99—or was it '93?—I think '93—one of my native bearers— However, I sprang forward and caught the crook of my walking stick on Mr. Baxter's ankle and brought him down. And by the time explanations were made it was too late. The train had gone, with Miss Peters in it."

"And a telegram has just arrived," said Lord Emsworth, "to say that they are being married this afternoon at a registrar's. The whole occurrence is most disturbing."

"Bear it like a man, my boy!" urged Colonel Mant.

To all appearances Freddie was bearing it magnificently. Not a single exclamation, either of wrath or pain, had escaped his lips. One would have said the shock had stunned him or that he had not heard, for his face expressed no emotion whatever.

The fact was, the story had made very little impression on the Honorable Freddie of any sort. His relief at Ashe's news about Joan Valentine; the stunning joy of having met in the flesh the author of the adventures of Gridley Quayle; the general feeling that all was now right with the world—these things deprived him of the ability to be greatly distressed.

And there was a distinct feeling of relief—actual relief—that now it would not be necessary for him to get married. He had liked Aline; but whenever he really thought of it the prospect of getting married rather appalled him. A chappie looked such an ass getting married! It appeared, however, that some verbal comment on the state of affairs was required of him. He searched his mind for something adequate.

"You mean to say Aline has bolted with Emerson?"

The deputation nodded pained nods. Freddie searched in his mind again. The deputation held its breath.

"Well, I'm blowed!" said Freddie. "Fancy that!"

Mr. Peters walked heavily into his room. Ashe Marson was waiting for him there. He eyed Ashe dully.

"Pack!" he said.

"Pack?"

"Pack! We're getting out of here by the afternoon train."

"Has anything happened?"

"My daughter has eloped with Emerson."

"What!"

"Don't stand there saying, 'What!' Pack."

Ashe put his hand in his pocket.

"Where shall I put this?" he asked.

For a moment Mr. Peters looked without comprehension at what Ashe was holding out; then his whole demeanor altered. His eyes lit up. He uttered a howl of pure rapture:

"You got it!"

"I got it."

"Where was it? Who took it? How did you choke it out of them? How did you find it? Who had it?"

"I don't know whether I ought to say. I don't want to start anything. You won't tell anyone?"

"Tell anyone! What do you take me for? Do you think I am going about advertising this? If I can sneak out without that fellow Baxter jumping on my back I shall be satisfied. You can take it from me that there won't be any sensational exposures if I can help it. Who had it?"

"Young Threepwood."

"Threepwood? Why did he want it?"

"He needed money and he was going to raise it on—"

Mr. Peters exploded.

"And I have been kicking because Aline can't marry him and has gone off with a regular fellow like young Emerson! He's a good boy—young Emerson. I knew his folks. He'll make a name for himself one of these days. He's got get-up in him. And I have been waiting to shoot him because he has taken Aline away from that goggle-eyed chump up in bed there!

"Why, if she had married Threepwood I should have had grandchildren who would have sneaked my watch while I was dancing them on my knee! There is a taint of some sort in the whole family. Father sneaks my Cheops and sonny sneaks it from father. What a gang! And the best blood in England! If that's England's idea of good blood give me Hoboken! This settles it. I was a chump ever to come to a country like this. Property isn't safe here. I'm going back to America on the next boat.

"Where's my check book? I'm going to write you that check right away. You've earned it. Listen, young man; I don't know what your ideas are, but if you aren't chained to this country I'll make it worth your while to stay on with me. They say no one's indispensable, but you come mighty near it. If I had you at my elbow for a few years I'd get right back into shape. I'm feeling better now than I have felt in years—and you've only just started in on me.

"How about it? You can call yourself what you like—secretary or trainer, or whatever suits you best. What you will be is the fellow who makes me take exercise and stop smoking cigars, and generally looks after me. How do you feel about it?"

It was a proposition that appealed both to Ashe's commercial and to his missionary instincts. His only regret had been that, the scarab recovered, he and Mr. Peters would now, he supposed, part company. He had not liked the idea of sending the millionaire back to the world a half-cured man. Already he had begun to look on him in the light of a piece of creative work to which he had just set his hand.

But the thought of Joan gave him pause. If this meant separation from Joan it was not to be considered.

"Let me think it over," he said.

"Well, think quick!" said Mr. Peters.

It has been said by those who have been through fires, earthquakes and shipwrecks that in such times of stress the social barriers are temporarily broken down, and the spectacle may be seen of persons of the highest social standing speaking quite freely to persons who are not in society at all; and of quite nice people addressing others to whom they have never been introduced. The news of Aline Peters' elopement with George Emerson, carried beyond the green-baize door by Slingsby, the chauffeur, produced very much the same state of affairs in the servants' quarters at Blandings Castle.

It was not only that Slingsby was permitted to penetrate into the housekeeper's room and tell his story to his social superiors there, though that was an absolutely unprecedented occurrence; what was really extraordinary was that mere menials discussed the affair with the personal ladies and gentlemen of the castle guests, and were allowed to do so uncrushed. James, the footman—that pushing individual—

actually shoved his way into the room, and was heard by witnesses to remark to no less a person than Mr. Beach that it was a bit thick.

And it is on record that his fellow footman, Alfred, meeting the groom of the chambers in the passage outside, positively prodded him in the lower ribs, winked, and said: "What a day we're having!" One has to go back to the worst excesses of the French Revolution to parallel these outrages. It was held by Mr. Beach and Mrs. Twemlow afterward that the social fabric of the castle never fully recovered from this upheaval. It may be they took an extreme view of the matter, but it cannot be denied that it wrought changes. The rise of Slingsby is a case in point. Until this affair took place the chauffeur's standing had never been satisfactorily settled. Mr. Beach and Mrs. Twemlow led the party which considered that he was merely a species of coachman; but there was a smaller group which, dazzled by Slingsby's personality, openly declared it was not right that he should take his meals in the servants' hall with such admitted plebeians as the odd man and the steward's-room footman.

The Aline-George elopement settled the point once and for all. Slingsby had carried George's bag to the train. Slingsby had been standing a few yards from the spot where Aline began her dash for the carriage door. Slingsby was able to exhibit the actual half sovereign with which George had tipped him only five minutes before the great event. To send such a public man back to the servants' hall was impossible. By unspoken consent the chauffeur dined that night in the steward's room, from which he was never dislodged.

Mr. Judson alone stood apart from the throng that clustered about the chauffeur. He was suffering the bitterness of the supplanted. A brief while before and he had been the central figure, with his story of the letter he had found in the Honorable Freddie's coat pocket. Now the importance of his story had been engulfed in that of this later and greater sensation, Mr. Judson was learning, for the first time, on what unstable foundations popularity stands.

Joan was nowhere to be seen. In none of the spots where she might have been expected to be at such a time was she to be found. Ashe had almost given up the search when, going to the back door and looking out as a last chance, he perceived her walking slowly on the gravel drive.

She greeted Ashe with a smile, but something was plainly troubling her. She did not speak for a moment and they walked side by side.

"What is it?" said Ashe at length. "What is the matter?"

She looked at him gravely.

"Gloom," she said. "Despondency, Mr. Marson—A sort of flat feeling. Don't you hate things happening?"

"I don't quite understand."

"Well, this affair of Aline, for instance. It's so big it makes one feel as though the whole world had altered. I should like nothing to happen ever, and life just to jog peacefully along. That's not the gospel I preached to you in Arundell Street, is it! I thought I was an advanced apostle of action; but I seem to have changed. I'm afraid I shall never be able to make clear what I do mean. I only know I feel as though I have suddenly grown old. These things are such milestones. Already I am beginning to look on the time before Aline behaved so sensationally as terribly remote. To-morrow it will be worse, and the day after that worse still. I can see that you don't in the least understand what I mean."

"Yes; I do—or I think I do. What it comes to, in a few words, is that somebody you were fond of has gone out of your life. Is that it?"

Joan nodded.

"Yes—at least, that is partly it. I didn't really know Aline particularly well, beyond having been at school with her, but you're right. It's not so much what has happened as what it represents that matters. This elopement has marked the end of a phase of my life. I think I have it now. My life has been such a series of jerks. I dash along—then something happens which stops that bit of my life with a jerk; and then I have to start over again—a new bit. I think I'm getting tired of jerks. I want something stodgy and continuous.

"I'm like one of the old bus horses that could go on forever if people got off without making them stop. It's the having to get the bus moving again that wears one out. This little section of my life since we came here is over, and it is finished for good. I've got to start the bus going again on a new road and with a new set of passengers. I wonder whether the old horses used to be sorry when they dropped one lot of passengers and took on a lot of strangers?"

A sudden dryness invaded Ashe's throat. He tried to speak, but found no words. Joan went on:

"Do you ever get moods when life seems absolutely meaningless? It's like a badly-constructed story, with all sorts of characters moving in and out who have nothing to do with the plot. And when somebody comes along that you think really has something to do with the plot, he suddenly drops out. After a while you begin to wonder what the story is about, and you feel that it's about nothing—just a jumble."

"There is one thing," said Ashe, "that knits it together."

"What is that?"

"The love interest."

Their eyes met and suddenly there descended on Ashe confidence. He felt cool and alert, sure of himself, as in the old days he had felt when he ran races and, the nerve-racking hours of waiting past, he listened for the starter's gun. Subconsciously he was aware he had always been a little afraid of Joan, and that now he was no longer afraid.

"Joan, will you marry me?"

Her eyes wandered from his face. He waited.

"I wonder!" she said softly. "You think that is the solution?"

"Yes."

"How can you tell?" she broke out. "We scarcely know each other. I shan't always be in this mood. I may get restless again. I may find it is the jerks that I really like."

"You won't!"

"You're very confident."

"I am absolutely confident."

"'She travels fastest who travels alone,'" misquoted Joan.

"What is the good," said Ashe, "of traveling fast if you're going round in a circle? I know how you feel. I've felt the same myself. You are an individualist. You think there is something tremendous just round the corner and that you can get it if you try hard enough. There isn't—or if there is it isn't worth getting. Life is nothing but a mutual aid association. I am going to help old Peters—you are going to help me—I am going to help you."

"Help me to do what?"

"Make life coherent instead of a jumble."

"Mr. Marson—"

"Don't call me Mr. Marson."

"Ashe, you don't know what you are doing. You don't know me. I've been knocking about the world for five years and I'm hard—hard right through. I should make you wretched."

"You are not in the least hard—and you know it. Listen to me, Joan. Where's your sense of fairness? You crash into my life, turn it upside down, dig me out of my quiet groove, revolutionize my whole existence; and now you propose to drop me and pay no further attention to me. Is it fair?"

"But I don't. We shall always be the best of friends."

"We shall—but we will get married first."

"You are determined?"

"I am!"

Joan laughed happily.

"How perfectly splendid! I was terrified lest I might have made you change your mind. I had to say all I did to preserve my self-respect after proposing to you. Yes; I did. How strange it is that men never seem to understand a woman, however plainly she talks! You don't think I was really worrying because I had lost Aline, do you? I thought I was going to lose you, and it made me miserable. You couldn't expect me to say it in so many words; but I thought—I was hoping—you guessed. I practically said it. Ashe! What are you doing?"

Ashe paused for a moment to reply.

"I am kissing you," he said.

"But you mustn't! There's a scullery maid or somebody looking through the kitchen window. She will see us."

Ashe drew her to him.

"Scullery maids have few pleasures," he said. "Theirs is a dull life. Let her see us."

CHAPTER XII

The Earl of Emsworth sat by the sick bed and regarded the Honorable Freddie almost tenderly.

"I fear, Freddie, my dear boy, this has been a great shock to you."

"Eh? What? Yes—rather! Deuce of a shock, gov'nor."

"I have been thinking it over, my boy, and perhaps I have been a little hard on you. When your ankle is better I have decided to renew your allowance; and you may return to London, as you do not seem happy in the country. Though how any reasonable being can prefer—"

The Honorable Freddie started, pop-eyed, to a sitting posture.

"My word! Not really?"

His father nodded.

"I say, gov'nor, you really are a topper! You really are, you know! I know just how you feel about the country and the jolly old birds and trees and chasing the bally slugs off the young geraniums and all that sort of thing, but somehow it's never quite hit me the same way. It's the way I'm built, I suppose. I like asphalt streets and crowds and dodging taxis and meeting chappies at the club and popping in at the Empire for half an hour and so forth. And there's something about having an allowance—I don't know . . . sort of makes you chuck your chest out and feel you're someone. I don't know how to thank you, gov'nor! You're—you're an absolute sportsman! This is the most priceless bit of work you've ever done. I feel like a two-year-old. I don't know when I've felt so braced. I—I—really, you know, gov'nor, I'm most awfully grateful."

"Exactly," said Lord Emsworth. "Ah—precisely. But, Freddie, my boy," he added, not without pathos, "there is just one thing more. Do you think that—with an effort—for my sake—you could endeavor this time not to make a—a damned fool of yourself?"

He eyed his offspring wistfully.

"Gov'nor," said the Honorable Freddie firmly, "I'll have a jolly good stab at it!"

P G Wodehouse – A Short Biography

Sir Pelham Grenville Wodehouse KBE was born in Guildford, Surrey on the 15th October 1881, the third son of Henry Ernest Wodehouse, a magistrate resident in British Hong Kong, and his wife, Eleanor, daughter of the Rev John Bathurst Deane.

Eleanor was visiting her sister in Guildford when Wodehouse was born there prematurely. He was baptised at the Church of St Nicolas, Guildford, and was named after his godfather, Pelham von Donop. 'Pelham' was quickly reduced to the more manageable 'Plum' by friends and family.

Wodehouse and his mother left for Hong Kong and for two years he was raised by a Chinese amah (nurse), alongside his elder brothers Peveril and Armine. He and his brothers were then sent back to England to be raised by an English nanny, which was then entirely normal for parents who worked in the Colonies. Unfortunately, this lack of parental love and the clinical regime of this rearing left the boys with permanent and indelible emotional scars.

Despite this Wodehouse recollected that his childhood was generally happy; "it went like a breeze from start to finish, with everybody I met understanding me perfectly".

In 1886 the brothers were sent for three years to a dame-school in Croydon. When Peveril was diagnosed with a weak chest sea air was prescribed, and the three sent to Elizabeth College in Guernsey. In 1891 Wodehouse moved to Malvern House Preparatory School in Kent, which prepared pupils for entry to the Royal Navy. However, Wodehouse's eyesight was poor which meant he would never be accepted. He also found the curriculum too narrow and the discipline too harsh. One benefit of the experience though was its later use in his novels, with Bertie Wooster stating that his early years as a pupil were in a 'penitentiary ... with the outward guise of a prep school called Malvern House'.

During school holidays the boys were dispatched to various aunts and uncles. They had fifteen uncles of which four were clergymen. Again, the experiences later turned up in his characters; pious but fallible curates, vicars, and bishops.

At age twelve in 1894, Wodehouse was thrilled to follow Armine to Dulwich College. He was entirely at home there. He loved the camaraderie, was distinguished in cricket, rugby and boxing, and was a good, if not always diligent, student during his six years there. His literary leanings found an outlet in editing the school magazine, The Alleynian. During his entire life he remained devoted to the school.

Wodehouse's next step should have been Oxford, but his father had retired in 1895 with a pension paid in rupees that had fallen badly against the pound. Instead of university Wodehouse, in September 1900, was now working as a junior in the London office of the Hongkong and Shanghai Bank. He was a bad fit and although he wrote a humorous account of his experiences, he longed for the end of the day in order to return to his lodgings in Chelsea and write. At first, he concentrated, with some success, on serious sports articles for Public School Magazine. In November 1900 his first comic piece, 'Men Who Missed Their Own Weddings', was accepted by Tit-Bits. The Captain, a new magazine for boys, provided further well-paid opportunities, and during his two years at the bank, Wodehouse had eighty pieces published across nine magazines.

In 1901, Wodehouse worked writing for The Globe's popular 'By the Way' column. He held the post until 1909. In 1902 'The Pothunters', was published, first as a serial and then as a hardback. He now resigned from the bank to devote himself full-time to a literary career. In the next 6 years Wodehouse wrote eight novels and co-wrote another two. It was a prolific start.

In 1904 he fulfilled his wish to have saved enough to visit America and sailed to New York, which he found greatly to his liking; "In New York gathering experience. Worth many guineas in the future but none for the moment". This prediction proved correct.

Wodehouse's other new venture in 1904 was writing for the stage. The librettist Owen Hall invited him to contribute an additional lyric for a musical comedy 'Sergeant Brue'. His lyric, 'Put Me in My Little Cell', was a 'Gilbertian number' for a trio of comic crooks, with music by Frederick Rosse. It was well received and put him on a parallel career as a theatre writer that would span three decades.

His 1906 novel 'Love Among the Chickens' contained his first original comic creation: Stanley Featherstonehaugh Ukridge, an amoral, bungling opportunist that was based partly on his Globe colleague Herbert Westbrook. The two collaborated between 1907 and 1913 on two books, two music hall sketches, and a play, 'Brother Alfred'.

In early 1906 Wodehouse became the resident lyricist at the Aldwych Theatre with a remit to add topical verses to their shows. Jerome Kern was already there to write the music for such songs. The first Kern-Wodehouse collaboration, a comic number for 'The Beauty of Bath' titled 'Mr [Joseph] Chamberlain', was a show-stopper and briefly the most popular song in London.

In 1908 Wodehouse introduced in his novel 'Mike' a new and strikingly original character, Psmith. Wodehouse had based him on the hotelier and impresario of Gilbert & Sullivan fame, Rupert D'Oyly Carte—"the only thing in my literary career which was handed to me on a silver plate with watercress around it". Psmith featured in three further works: 'Psmith in the City' (1910), 'Psmith, Journalist' (1915) and 'Leave It to Psmith' (1923).

In May 1909 Wodehouse again visited New York and sold two short stories to Cosmopolitan and Collier's for a total of $500, a much higher fee than previously. He now resigned from The Globe to work in New York for a year selling many more stories on a freelance basis, but he was unable to obtain a permanent position and the ensuing regular income.

Wodehouse returned to England in late 1910, rejoined The Globe and also became a regular contributor to The Strand Magazine. He continued regular visits to America and was there when the Great War erupted in Europe. As he was ineligible for service due to his poor eyesight he decided to remain in America concentrating on his theatrical and literary concerns.

In September 1914 he married Ethel May Wayman, an English widow. The marriage proved happy and was lifelong. Ethel's personality was the opposite of the shy and impractical Wodehouse. By contrast she was gregarious, decisive and organised. Ethel took charge of his life ensuring he had the peace and quiet he needed to write. Although there were no children Wodehouse later adopted Ethel's daughter Leonora.

In 1915 the first story of Bertie and Jeeves appeared; 'Extricating Young Gussie'. Wodehouse would continue writing about them for the rest of his life. Towards the end of 1915 Jerome Kern introduced him to the writer Guy Bolton, who became Wodehouse's closest friend and collaborator. Bolton and Kern had a successful show, 'Very Good Eddie', running in New York but they thought the song lyrics weak and invited Wodehouse to join them on its successor 'Miss Springtime' which ran for 227 performances in 1916. Other hits by the team followed 'Leave It to Jane' (1917), 'Oh, Boy!' (1917-18) and 'Oh, Lady! Lady!!' (1918).

With the Great War now over Wodehouse was even more popular as his new characters and new works found eager readers. Although they now returned to their London house for some years Wodehouse continued to cross the Atlantic frequently, spending substantial periods working on Broadway. During the 1920s he collaborated on nine musical comedies either for Broadway or the West End, including 'Sally' (1920, New York), 'The Cabaret Girl' (1922, London) and 'Rosalie' (1928, New York). He also wrote non-musical plays, including 'The Play's the Thing' (1926), adapted from Ferenc Molnár, and 'A Damsel in Distress' (1928), from his own 1919 novel.

Although several of his works had been adapted into films it was not until 1929 that Hollywood summoned him there. Bolton was already there working as a highly paid writer for Metro-Goldwyn-Mayer (MGM). Ethel was taken with the financial and the social aspects of Hollywood life, and she negotiated a contract with MGM for Wodehouse that paid out $2,000 a week. Having lost a large amount in the Wall Street crash of 1929 this was very welcome news. He began work in May, 1930.

For Wodehouse, who was used to a prolific and demanding schedule, this new arrangement was somewhat baffling; "The actual work is negligible. ... So far, I have had eight collaborators. The system is that A. gets the original idea, B. comes in to work with him on it, C. makes a scenario, D. does preliminary dialogue, and then they send for me to insert Class and what-not. Then E. and F., scenario writers, alter the plot and off we go again".

With little actual work for him to do at the studio he had spare time to write one novel and nine short stories. Even when MGM found a project for him the committees and constant rewriting by numerous contract authors meant that his ideas were used infrequently. After a year the contract expired and was not renewed.

In the 1930s Wodehouse's theatrical ventures declined. Of the four plays he wrote or adapted for the West End only one 'Leave it to Psmith' (1930) had a decent run. In 1934 he worked with Bolton on the book for Cole Porter's Anything Goes (Porter wrote his own lyrics), but at the last minute their version was rewritten by others at the instigation of the producer, who disliked their script.

However, his novels and short stories were bringing Wodehouse an annual income of £100,000. This, of course, proved problematic as Wodehouse was spending time in both Britain and America with the relevant tax authorities both wanting to tax him as their resident. After lengthy negotiations the matter was resolved and the Wodehouse's decided to place their residential status beyond doubt by moving to Le Touquet in France.

In 1935 Wodehouse created Lord Ickenham, otherwise known as Uncle Fred, his last truly original character who was then paraded through four novels and a short story. The 30s produced perhaps his most widely admired and lauded works; 'Right Ho, Jeeves', 'Uncle Fred in the Springtime', and 'Blandings Castle'.

In June 1939 Oxford University presented him with an honorary doctorate of letters. His visit to receive it was the last time he set foot in England.

At the start of the Second World War Wodehouse and Ethel remained at their Le Touquet house. With the German advance the nearby RAF base withdrew. Wodehouse was offered the last seat on one of the aircraft, but he turned it down as it would have meant leaving behind Ethel and their dog.

The Germans occupied Le Touquet on 22nd May 1940 and Wodehouse had to report daily to the authorities. In July the Germans interned all male enemy nationals under 60, and Wodehouse was sent to a former prison in a suburb of Lille with Ethel remaining in Le Touquet. The internees were four to a cell, each of which had been designed for one. They were soon transported in cattle trucks to a former barracks, now prison, in Liège, Belgium, run by the SS. A week later they were moved on to Huy in Liège. In September 1940 they were transported to Tost in Upper Silesia.

No word on Wodehouse had been received by anyone since the fall of France but an article from an Associated Press reporter who had visited Tost in December 1940 revealed his presence and led to pressure on the German authorities to release the novelist, including a petition from influential people in the US. The Germans refused but provided him with a typewriter and, to pass the time, he wrote 'Money in the Bank'. Throughout his time in Tost, he sent postcards to his US agent asking for $5 to be sent to various families in Canada, mentioning his name. The postcards from Wodehouse was confirmation that their sons were alive. Despite the risk of severe punishment for this he managed to evade the German censor.

On 21st June 1941, while he was in the middle of a game of cricket, Wodehouse was visited by two members of the Gestapo. He was taken to the Hotel Adlon, a luxury hotel in Berlin. He stayed there at his own expense with royalties released from his frozen German book sales bank account. It seemed the Nazis had plans in mind for Wodehouse. He was now involved in perhaps the blackest part of his career. Whilst he was certainly naïve, he was, back in England vilified for making five broadcasts to the US via German radio. The broadcasts, aired on 28th June, 9th, 23rd and 30th July and 6th August, entitled 'How to be an Internee Without Previous Training', were largely humorous anecdotes about Wodehouse's experiences as a prisoner, including some gentle mocking of his captors. The German propaganda ministry, sensing their value, arranged for the recordings to be broadcast to Britain that August. The reaction in Britain was instantaneous and hostile; he was a traitor, a collaborator, a Nazi propagandist, and a coward. In Parliament Anthony Eden, the Foreign Secretary, regretted Wodehouse's actions. Libraries removed his novels from their shelves.

When Wodehouse heard the criticism he contacted the Foreign Office via the Swiss embassy to explain his actions, and attempted to return home via neutral countries, but again, as could be expected, the Germans refused to let him leave. He later wrote, "Of course I ought to have had the sense to see that it was a loony thing to do to use the German radio for even the most harmless stuff, but I didn't. I suppose prison life saps the intellect".

Ethel had sold all of her jewellery to afford a train fare to Berlin to join Wodehouse. Together they remained in Germany until September 1943, when, because of the Allied bombings, they were allowed to move back to Paris. Wodehouse reported to the American authorities the day after Paris was liberated and asked them to inform the British of his whereabouts. He was subsequently visited by Malcolm Muggeridge, then an intelligence officer with MI6. The young officer quickly came to like Wodehouse and considered the question of treasonable behaviour 'ludicrous'. On 9th September Wodehouse was visited by an MI5 officer and formally investigated over four days. On 28th September a report was filed that in regard to the broadcasts, Wodehouse's behaviour 'has been unwise', but advised no further action.

However, they were subsequently arrested by French police and placed under preventive detention, despite no charges being offered. When Muggeridge tracked them down, he had Ethel released straight away and, four days later, ensured had the French authorities declared Wodehouse unwell and put him in a nearby hospital, which was more comfortable than where they had been detained.

In December 1944 questions in the House of Commons wondered if the French authorities could repatriate him to stand trial. Eden stated that the 'matter has been gone into, and, according to the advice given, there are no grounds upon which we could take action'.

On 15th January 1945 the French authorities released Wodehouse, but waited until June 1946, to tell him he would not face any official charges and was free to leave.

In April 1947 they sailed to New York, where Wodehouse was relieved at the friendly reception he received from the waiting press contingent. The New York that he had known before the war was much changed. The magazines that had paid lavishly for his works were in decline, and those that remained were not much interested in him. Broadway was but he was not at home in the post-war theatre. He also had money problems, with large sums tied up in Britain, and, most worryingly, he had no ideas for a new novel. It would take another four years before he produced one.

Still unsettled he and Ethel left New York City for suburban Long Island where Bolton and his wife lived in the hamlet of Remsenburg, part of the Southampton resort area. In 1952 he and Ethel bought a house nearby. They lived there for the rest of their lives.

Between 1952 and 1975 he published more than twenty novels, as well as two collections of short stories, a heavily edited collection of his letters, a volume of memoirs, and a selection of his magazine articles. He continued to hanker after a revival of his theatrical career. A 1959 off-Broadway revival of the 1917 Bolton-Wodehouse-Kern 'Leave It to Jane' was a surprise hit, running for 928 performances, but other post-war stage works made little impression.

In 1955 Wodehouse became an American citizen, though he remained a British subject, and was therefore still eligible for UK state honours. In 1965 the British government indicated privately that he could return without fear of prosecution but by then he felt too old to make the journey. From 1967 he was considered for a knighthood but the honour was blocked by British officials. In 1974 the British prime minister, Harold Wilson, intervened to secure a knighthood (KBE) for Wodehouse.

The following month Wodehouse entered Southampton Hospital, Long Island, for treatment of a skin complaint. While there, he suffered a heart attack and died on 14th February 1975 at the age of 93. He was buried at Remsenburg Presbyterian Church four days later.

- The Pothunters (1902)
- A Prefect's Uncle (1903)
- The Gold Bat (1904)
- William Tell Told Again (1904)
- The Head of Kay's (1905)
- Love Among the Chickens (1906)
- The White Feather (1907)
- Not George Washington (1909) (with Herbert Westbrook)
- The Swoop! (1909)
- Mike (1909)
- A Gentleman of Leisure (1910)
- Psmith in the City (1910)
- The Prince and Betty (1912)
- The Little Nugget (1913)
- Psmith, Journalist (1915)
- Something Fresh (1915)
- Uneasy Money (1917)
- Piccadilly Jim (1918)
- A Damsel in Distress (1919)
- The Coming of Bill (1920)
- Jill the Reckless (1921)
- The Girl on the Boat (1922)
- The Adventures of Sally (1922)
- Leave It to Psmith (1923)
- Bill the Conqueror (1924)
- Sam the Sudden (1925)
- The Small Bachelor (1927)
- Money for Nothing (1928)
- Summer Lightning (1929)
- Big Money (1931)
- If I Were You (1931)
- Doctor Sally (1932)
- Hot Water (1932)
- Heavy Weather (1933)
- Thank You, Jeeves (1934)
- Right Ho, Jeeves (1934)
- The Luck of the Bodkins (1935)
- Laughing Gas (1936)
- Summer Moonshine (1938)
- The Code of the Woosters (1938)
- Uncle Fred in the Springtime (1939)
- Quick Service (1940)
- Money in the Bank (1946)
- Joy in the Morning (1947)
- Full Moon (1947)
- Spring Fever (1948)
- Uncle Dynamite (1948)

The Mating Season (1949)
The Old Reliable (1950)
Barmy in Wonderland (1952)
Pigs Have Wings (1952)
Ring for Jeeves (1953)
Jeeves and the Feudal Spirit (1954)
French Leave (1956)
Something Fishy (1957)
Cocktail Time (1958)
Jeeves in the Offing (1960)
Ice in the Bedroom (1961)
Service with a Smile (1962)
Stiff Upper Lip, Jeeves (1963)
Frozen Assets (1964)
Galahad at Blandings (1965)
Company for Henry (1967)
Do Butlers Burgle Banks? (1968)
A Pelican at Blandings (1969)
The Girl in Blue (1970)
Much Obliged, Jeeves (1971)
Pearls, Girls and Monty Bodkin (1972)
Bachelors Anonymous (1973)
Aunts Aren't Gentlemen (1974)
Sunset at Blandings (1977
The Luck Stone (1997)

Short Story Collections

Tales of St. Austin's (1903)
The Man Upstairs (1914)
The Man with Two Left Feet (1917)
My Man Jeeves (1919)
Indiscretions of Archie (1921)
The Clicking of Cuthbert (1922)
The Inimitable Jeeves (1923)
Ukridge (1924)
Carry On, Jeeves (1925)
The Heart of a Goof (1926)
Meet Mr Mulliner (1927)
Mr Mulliner Speaking (1929)
Very Good, Jeeves (1930)
Mulliner Nights (1933)
Blandings Castle and Elsewhere (1935)
Young Men in Spats (1936)
Lord Emsworth and Others (1937)
Eggs, Beans and Crumpets (1940)
Nothing Serious (1950)

A Few Quick Ones (1959)
Plum Pie (1966)
Jenkins Plum Pie (1967)

Plays by Wodehouse

After the Show Unknown (1911) (with Herbert Westbrook)
A Gentleman of Leisure (1911) (with John Stapleton; adaptation of the novel A Gentleman of Leisure)
A Thief for the Night (1913) (with John Stapleton; revival of A Gentleman of Leisure)
Brother Alfred (1913) (with Herbert Westbrook; adaptation of short story "Rallying Round Old George"
Nuts and Wine (1914) (with C.H. Bovill)
Have a Heart (1917) (with Guy Bolton; music by Jerome Kern)
Oh Boy! (February 1917) (with Guy Bolton; revised for the UK as Oh Joy!)
Leave It to Jane (1917) (with Guy Bolton; music by Jerome Kern)
Kitty Darlin' (1917) (with Guy Bolton)
The Riviera Girl (1917) (with Guy Bolton)
Miss 1917 (1917) (with Guy Bolton)
Oh, Lady! Lady!! (1918) (with Guy Bolton; music by Jerome Kern)
See You Later (1918) (with Guy Bolton)
The Girl Behind the Gun (1918) (with Guy Bolton; revised for the UK as Kissing Time)
The Canary (1918) (with Guy Bolton)
Oh, My Dear! (1918) (with Guy Bolton)
The Rose of China (1919) (with Guy Bolton)
Sally (1920) (with Guy Bolton, Clifford Grey, Buddy De Sylva and Anne Caldwell; music by Jerome Kern)
The Golden Moth (1921) (with Fred Thompson)
The Cabaret Girl (1922) (with George Grossmith; music by Jerome Kern)
The Beauty Prize (1923) (with George Grossmith; music by Jerome Kern)
Sitting Pretty (1924) (with Guy Bolton; music by Jerome Kern)
Hearts and Diamonds (1926) (with Laurie Wylie; adapted from The Orlov by Biuno Granichstaedten and Ernst Marischka)
The Play's the Thing (1926) (Adaptation of a play by Ferenc Molnár)
Oh, Kay! (1926) (with Guy Bolton; music by George Gershwin, lyrics by Ira Gershwin)
Her Cardboard Lover (1927) (with Valerie Wyngate; music by George Gershwin, lyrics by Ira Gershwin; based on Dans sa candeur naïve by Jacques Deval)
Good Morning, Bill (1927) (Adapted from a play by Ladislaus Fodor)
The Three Musketeers (1928) (with Clifford Grey; adapted from the book by Alexandre Dumas)
A Damsel in Distress (1928) (with Ian Hay; adaptation of the novel A Damsel in Distress)
Baa, Baa, Black Sheep (1929) (with Ian Hay)
Candle-light (1929) (Adapted from a play by Siegfried Geyer)
Leave It to Psmith (1930) (with Ian Hay; adaptation of Wodehouse's novel Leave It to Psmith)
Who's Who (1934) (with Guy Bolton; adaptation of Wodehouse's novel If I Were You)
Anything Goes (1934) (with Guy Bolton, Howard Lindsay & Russel Crouse; lyrics & music by Cole Porter)
The Inside Stand (1935) (with Guy Bolton; adaptation of Wodehouse's novel Hot Water)
Arthur (Adapted in 1947 from Jemand by Ferenc Molnár; not produced)
Game of Hearts (Adapted in 1947 from a play by Ferenc Molnár; not produced)
Don't Listen, Ladies (1948) (as Stephen Powys with Guy Bolton; adapted from a play by Sacha Guitry)
Nothing Serious (1950) (No major productions, but produced in the provinces by touring companies

Phipps (with Guy Bolton in 1951; not produced)
Come On, Jeeves (1956) (no major productions, but produced in the provinces by touring companies
Oh, Clarence! (1968) (Manchester, London and on tour. Apapted by John Chapman from Blandings Castle stories)

Films

A Gentleman of Leisure (1915) Jesse L. Lasky Feature Play Co. Based on the play A Gentleman of Leisure by John Stapleton and Wodehouse.
A Damsel in Distress (1919) Albert Capellani Productions. Based on the 1919 novel A Damsel in Distress.
Piccadilly Jim (1919) Selznick Pictures. Based on the 1917 novel Piccadilly Jim
The Prince and Betty (1919) Jesse D. Hampton Productions. Based on the 1912 novel The Prince and Betty.
Oh, Lady, Lady (1920) Realart Pictures. Based on the play Oh, Lady! Lady!! by Guy Bolton, Jerome Kern and Wodehouse.
A Gentleman of Leisure (1923) Paramount Pictures. Based on the play A Gentleman of Leisure by John Stapleton and Wodehouse.
The Golden Butterfly (1926) Sascha-Film/Phoebus Film. Based on the short story 'The Making of Mac's'.
Oh, Kay! (1928) First National Pictures. Based on Wodehouse's 1926 play Oh, Kay!
Those Three French Girls (1930) Cosmopolitan Productions. Dialogue by Wodehouse
The Man in Possession (1931) Metro-Goldwyn-Mayer. Additional dialogue by Wodehouse
Brother Alfred (1932) British International Pictures. Based on the play Brother Alfred by Herbert Westbrook and Wodehouse.
Leave It to Me (1933) British International Pictures. Based on the 1923 novel Leave It to Psmith.
Summer Lightning (1933) British and Dominions Film Corporation. Based on the 1929 novel Summer Lightning.
Anything Goes (1936) Paramount Pictures. Based on the play Anything Goes by Guy Bolton, Cole Porter and Wodehouse.
Piccadilly Jim (1936) Metro-Goldwyn-Mayer. Based on the 1917 novel Piccadilly Jim.
Thank You, Jeeves! (1936) 20th Century Fox. Based on the 1934 novel Thank You, Jeeves.
Step Lively, Jeeves (1937) 20th Century Fox. Based the characters created by Wodehouse.
A Damsel in Distress (1937) RKO Pictures. Screenwriter; Based on his 1919 novel A Damsel in Distress.
Rosalie (1937) Metro-Goldwyn-Mayer. Based on the 1928 musical play Rosalie by George Gershwin, Sigmund Romberg, Ira Gershwin and Wodehouse.
Thunder and Lightning (1938) Svensk Filmindustri. Based on the 1929 novel Summer Lightning
Anything Goes (1956) Paramount Pictures. Based on the play Anything Goes by Guy Bolton, Cole Porter and Wodehouse.
The Girl on the Boat (1961) Knightsbridge Films. Based on the 1921 novel The Girl on the Boat

Autobiographies & Miscellany

The Globe By the Way (1908) (with Herbert Westbrook; collected journalism)
Louder and Funnier (1932) (Articles written for Vanity Fair)
Bring on the Girls! (1954) (Semi-autobiographical stories, in collaboration with Guy Bolton)
Performing Flea (1953) (A collection of letters, with notes)
Over Seventy (1957)

The Parrot and Other Poems (1990)
Yours, Plum: the letters of P.G. Wodehouse (1988)
A Life in Letters (2011)

CPSIA information can be obtained
at www.ICGtesting.com
Printed in the USA
BVHW041459281122
652941BV00003B/346